the ballad of ami miles

the ballad of

ami miles

KRISTY DALLAS ALLEY

Swoon READS

NEW YORK

A SWOON READS BOOK

An Imprint of Feiwel and Friends and Macmillan Publishing Group, LLC
120 Broadway, New York, NY 10271

Our books may be purchased in bulk for promotional, educational, or business use.
Please contact your local bookseller or the Macmillan Corporate and Premium
Sales Department at (800) 221-7945 ext. 5442 or by email at
MacmillanSpecialMarkets@macmillan.com.

Library of Congress Cataloging-in-Publication Data

Names: Alley, Kristy Dallas, author.
Title: The ballad of Ami Miles / Kristy Dallas Alley.
Description: First edition. | New York : Swoon Reads, 2020. | Audience: Ages 13-18. |
    Audience: Grades 10-12. | Summary: Raised in isolation in a post-apocalyptic
    world, Ami Miles escapes to seek her long-lost mother after her grandfather,
    knowing she is one of the few surviving women capable of child-bearing,
    arranges her marriage to a stranger.
Identifiers: LCCN 2019036442 | ISBN 9781250222138 (hardcover)
Subjects: CYAC: Survival—Fiction. | Mothers and daughters—Fiction. |
    Cults—Fiction. | Love—Fiction. | Science fiction.
Classification: LCC PZ7.1.A4398 Bal 2020 | DDC [Fic]—dc23
LC record available at https://lccn.loc.gov/2019036442

Book design by Liz Dresner

First edition, 2020

10 9 8 7 6 5 4 3 2 1

swoonreads.com

FOR RICHARD

One

I'd like to think that if I'd been home, they would have told me he was coming. Or that they didn't know he was coming and that's why I didn't know either. I'd like to believe that my family wouldn't ambush me like that, but after everything that's happened, believing such things is just about impossible. I'm sure now that they did know, and whether I had been home or not, whether he surprised them or not, it doesn't matter. Wouldn't have mattered. I still would have run, and nothing would be different.

I walked up into the yard of the compound that late afternoon without the slightest idea that anything had changed. It was early summer, and I had a bucket brimming with the first ripe blackberries and sweet dewberries, an old cloth sack full of odds and ends I'd found, plus my blanket roll, which I always took now that I was allowed to sleep out in the woods. I could go farther that way, find new things to see and maybe bring back. It wasn't like there were too many people around to do me harm, and those woods were my home—I knew them better than any stranger ever could. It was too early in the season to be real hot yet, and I was singing and galloping along like a silly little girl, and then I looked up and everyone was standing real still watching me. I take that back; the man was watching me, and Ruth was, but Papa was watching the man.

He was not as old as either of them but a lot older than me. I guessed he was about the age my mama would be now. My mother got me in sin, with one of the last of the travelers to ever come down the hi-way, but since almost no one could have babies anymore, the ways of thinking on that had changed. Now, Papa argued, it would be a bigger sin not to try to plant more children on God's still-green earth, and if there was not a suitable husband for a woman who was able, then he guessed the Lord would send her a chance some other way. "The Lord works in mysterious ways," he would say, "that is not always for us to understand." Papa Solomon had a lot of ideas about the ways things have changed and the messages God is sending to us by way of those changes. He said since Jesus has not come back and the Rapture has not occurred, that is how we know that God means for us to keep on struggling in His name. He will let us know when it's time to lay down our weary load, and until then ours is not to wonder why. Our job is to read the signs He *is* sending and try to do His will. I wonder now if Papa wasn't confusing God's will with his own, but back then it didn't occur to me that he might not be right about everything. I was raised to question the world but never Papa.

Anyway, this man was about the age my father might have been, but I knew he was not my father the second I laid eyes on him. I didn't know who he was, but as soon as I saw him, the understanding of why he was there flew all over me like an awful swarm of gnats. I closed my eyes and mouth and held my breath against the knowledge, hoping I could make that swarm move on if I didn't let them in, but I knew I couldn't. In the best case, he was there to marry me, and failing that, if we didn't spark to each other in that way, he was there to put his seed in me while everyone prayed it would find fertile ground. Because I was the last hope, and if I could not have a baby, the bloodline would die out. According to Papa, we were some of the last living people in the former state of Alabama and probably some of the last godly people on earth. Since my mama was able to have me, there was a chance I was also immune to the sickness that had left most women barren. It was down to me to bring new life into the world, and instead of facing up to it like the godly woman I was raised to be, all I wanted to do was run away like a little girl.

I guess deep down, I had known this was coming, or something like it. In a way, I had spent my whole life being made ready for it. This was my purpose, they told me. Even my name came from the Hebrew word for *mother*. But I wasn't ready. Not for that! It's one thing to be talked to about such things, but it is something else altogether to just come home one day and find your possible husband standing in the yard like he has every right to be there.

"Ami," Ruth said, her voice kind and quiet like always, but also sounding a little bit strange. "There you are, child. We was about to send out the search parties." This was a little joke, since we scarcely had enough people to scrape together a single search party, much less part*ies*. I didn't say anything, since I knew as well as she did that she had not been expecting me back any sooner. Also, I did not want to open my mouth at all. It felt real important to hold all of myself in, even my voice.

"Cat got 'er tongue?" the man asked Papa with a little laugh. I saw right then how it was. He did not ask *me* if the cat had my tongue, and he did not address Ruth although she stood closer to him. This was men's business. It didn't matter if the cat had my tongue, because I would have no say in the things about to happen.

"Well now," Papa said, "she is prolly just surprised is all. We don't get too much company out here these days. She ain't used to strangers." Papa said everything real slow and deliberate, no matter who he was talking to or what the subject was. He knew that he was the final authority at Heavenly Shepherd, and that meant he did not have to bother with raising his voice or explaining himself any more than he ever felt like. As he spoke these words to the stranger in his same patient way, he looked at me and the message was clear. I had better get my tongue back real fast. I'd been taught manners, and I'd better act like it.

"Hey," I said stupidly. It was all I could think of. I cast my eyes to the ground but saw the full berry bucket and cloth sack still in my hands, so I held them out to Ruth and stepped forward. "Berries are just comin' ripe, but I still found plenty. Queen's lace was bloomin', so I dug some of the carrots for you too." I handed it all to Ruth without looking up.

"Our Ami is a real good little forager," Papa said. It was rare praise, and it should have made me feel good, but it didn't. "Been raised to know what is safe and good to eat and what ain't since she was a babe. Can hunt too." This last was stretching the truth—I wasn't much of a hunter at all, and Papa knew it.

"That right?" The stranger looked at me then, letting his eyes move from the top of my head to the tips of my toes like he was sizing me up and maybe didn't like what he saw. But when those eyes met mine, he made his face blank. Now, I had never seen more of myself than could fit in my little round mirror with a lid that closed, which I kept hidden in a secret place in my room. So I knew only a little bit about how I looked, but I knew even less about what a man likes to see. My hair was coppery red and crazy curly, and pieces of it tended to pull loose from any braid or tie I could contrive. I wished I could cut it off, but Papa preached that it was ungodly for women to wear their hair short like a man's. I was not allowed to wear pants for this same reason. I had on a long shift dress made of the same speckled muslin as all our clothes, but I had dyed it blue with spiderwort. My feet were bare as usual and dirty from the long walk. I thought of the way the little circle of my face looked in that pocket mirror, tanned by the sun and freckled all over, with goldy-green eyes set wide apart. I had no idea if any of that was good or bad, so I decided to try to focus on what I saw instead.

"Yessir, that is right," Papa replied. "Knows how to set snares and fish too. Knows how to garden and put up what she grows. Her grandmother there has taught her all the ways of a godly woman in these strange times." Ruth looked pleased at this, but I still could not feel good about anything Papa was saying.

"Who shall find a good woman?" the man replied, and I knew he was not asking a question. He was quoting the Proverbs, trying to get on Papa's good side. For some reason, this made me mad enough to really look at him. I noticed right off that he was tall and bony. His hair and eyes were both real light, and he had a beard the same whitish-yellow as his hair. Maybe it was those light blue eyes, almost clear like ice, but it seemed to me that there was a coldness about him that I did not like. His pants and shirt were both a dusty gray, and he looked hungry. Ruth must have thought so too, or else she read my mind, because the next thing she did was ask him to come inside and eat.

"We was just about to eat supper, Mr. Johnson," she said. "Won't you join us?"

"It's Ezekiel, ma'am, but please, call me Zeke," he said. "I have not ate much since I left our property yesterday morning, if you're sure there's enough." I could tell what it cost him to add that last politeness, and it softened me to him, just a little. I was lucky enough not to know what real hunger was. Ruth said the way we lived at Heavenly Shepherd was primitive compared to the way things once were, but that we had luxuries that plenty would kill for now. That was because my great-great-grandfather, Jedidiah Miles, went overboard on the planning and laying in supplies, and also because there ended up being nowhere near as many people on the compound as he planned.

One of the people who should have been there with us, enjoying all of Jed's foresight and supplies, was my mama, forced to run away and leave me for her parents to raise. I thought of her as I stood there in the yard, looking up at that strange man, not of my choosing, who had been brought to make a baby with me. What would she think of that, I wondered, after all she had given up to keep me safe? She had to leave her home and her family to avoid being picked up and taken to a C-PAF—Center for the Preservation of the American Family—and bred to strangers. Was this really all that different? But no sooner had these thoughts flashed into my mind than I shooed them away. Of course it was, I told myself. This was God's will, and I figured my mama would tell me that herself if she could. This man was not a monster; I just didn't know him yet. We would have time, wouldn't we, to talk and learn about each other? *Please Lord*, I prayed as I followed the three of them into the main house, *just give me some time.*

TWO

R uth had gone all out for supper, so I knew then that she had been expecting company. She'd killed a chicken and stewed it in salty broth with the soft dumplings that were my favorite. I couldn't decide if this was by way of apology or her sign to me that something special was about to happen. There was a big pot of young poke leaves, boiled in three changes of water and then scrambled with eggs from the henhouse. The first muskmelons were in, and she had cut one into neat cubes and put them with new blueberries in a clear glass bowl to show off their pretty colors. There were warm rolls of soft white bread and fresh-churned butter. That meal was a message to the man, and I read it loud and clear. This was my dowry, meant to sweeten the pot. Looking over the table spread with food like this man had probably never seen, a worried thought crossed my mind: *How ugly am I, if it takes all this to entice a starving man?*

I didn't know where that thought came from, and I tried to

send it away. I tore my eyes from the table and looked where everyone else was looking: at the man. His eyes were welling up with tears that did not quite spill over, and his hands shook. I knew he had probably never had white bread in his life, for starters. Most people hadn't had the foresight to stockpile things like flour, salt, and sugar, at least not like Jed had. From the looks of him, this man, Zeke Johnson, had not seen food of any kind for more than just the day and a half he claimed it took him to get to our place. I tried to feel compassion for him, a hungry stranger who, after all, had not done me any wrong or harm. I was being selfish and mean-spirited, and I knew that if Ruth could read my thoughts, she would be ashamed of me.

We all sat down, and Papa asked Zeke if he would like to say grace. He looked up then, almost guilty looking, like he had been caught at something sneaky. "No sir," he said shakily, "this is your table." Papa's eyes stayed on the man's face in a long, shrewd gaze before he closed them and began to pray in that formal preacherly way he had.

"Heavenly Father, we thank you for this food and for the fellowship at this table. We thank you for your many gifts to us, for the chances you give to your sinful creations again and again even though we are not worthy. We pray that you will bless this food to the nourishment of our bodies, that we might be strong enough to do your work. Make our bodies the vessel for your will, Lord, and make our minds and hearts clear, that we may receive your signs and messages when you send them. For Thine is the power, and the kingdom, and the glory, forever and ever. In Jesus's name we pray, amen."

When I opened my eyes, Papa was looking right at me. Could he know my thoughts? Did he know that my heart and mind were not clear but were as dark and cloudy as a July thunderstorm? Ruth glanced from him to me to Zeke, then quickly picked up Papa's plate first and began heaping it with food. This was a message too. Papa was the man of the house, and this was his table. But was the message meant to put the stranger in his place, I wondered, or to reassure Papa? Next she filled Zeke's plate, and he watched it hungrily with his hands in his lap, like he had to fight hard to keep from reaching out and snatching it. I did feel a little sorry for him then. I knew how it felt to have to wait and control myself when I couldn't have what I wanted until it was given to me. Being the only child in a world of cranky adults had not always been easy.

Zeke looked at Papa and saw that he didn't wait for everyone to be served before he started eating, so he followed suit. Ruth chattered on while she filled the plates for my uncles, Jacob first and then David, then the plates of my aunts Rachel and Billie, then mine. She served herself last, as always. My aunt Amber was not at the table, which was true about half the time, but it surprised me that she would not come to see the rare guest. When all the plates were full, Ruth sat down, and for a while there was no sound except for forks clinking against plates and teeth. We never went hungry at Heavenly Shepherd, but we didn't have meals like this every day either. Gradually, though, the eating sounds faded away, and the lack of talk started to feel less natural. No one seemed to want to look up from their plates.

Zeke took a long swallow from his glass, and Ruth seized the opportunity. "I hope that sassafras is not too sweet for you, Mr. Johnson," she said. "Of course we can't get lemons anymore, but it reminds me of the lemonade my mama used to make when

I was little, so I like to make it a little sweet like she did." She looked at him expectantly.

"No, ma'am, not too sweet," he replied, "although I can't say when I last tasted sugar. And how did you get it to be so cold?"

"Well, I make it up by the jug and set it in the spring house," she said, smiling. "Do you have a spring house on your place?" She was digging a little now.

"We had one when I was a boy, but since I went out on my own, I haven't thought about such comforts." He seemed to be weighing his words carefully, and he looked straight at Papa before he spoke again. "My father was not such a strong man in the Lord like yourself, Reverend Miles, and I'm sorry to say that the state of things got to him and broke him down until he wasn't really no kind of man at all. My mama did the best she could, rest her soul, but she kinda just curled up and wasted away by the time I was the age of Ami here, and I knew I'd have to strike out if I was going to survive."

Papa was quiet a moment, his eyes never leaving the man's face, and then he nodded slightly in agreement. "Yes sir, sometimes we have to leave the beaten path if we want to survive. That's just what my grandfather Jedidiah Miles understood when he built this compound." I leaned back in my chair and tried to get comfortable because I had heard this story many times and knew what was coming next.

"Heavenly Shepherd started out as just one of a whole chain of dealerships owned by the Miles family—did you know that?" Zeke shook his head, but he needn't have bothered. Papa's storytelling did not require audience participation. I thought I saw Billie roll her eyes, and Jacob slid down a little in his chair. Rachel started to stand up and clear the table, but Papa gave her a look and she sat back down.

"My grandpa Jed was a godly man in a time of *true* evil. He stood fierce in his faith even as the wicked world tried to tear him down and paint him as the enemy of righteousness. They condemned him when he spoke God's truth about the mixing of the races and the tolerance of heathen religions and Christ deniers. The world told him to accept all kinds of abominations, but he stuck fast to the word of God even when it meant defying man's laws." Papa's eyes were shining, and his face was starting to turn red like it did every time he told this story. You could tell he wished he was preaching it in front of a church instead of just that supper table, but at least he had one new listener.

"Before the plague of barrenness became undeniable even to the faithless, Jed saw the signs and made his plan. He ordered in ten new trailers, ten! Then refused to sell a one of them, or any of the eight he already had either. He made sure they were all solar models, then converted all the bathrooms to these composting toilets we got. Not a one of the sinks ever ran a drop of water, but he had a deep well dug on the property while he could still pay for the men with them big machines to come and do it."

This was before his family finally made good on their threats and cut him off. By then, he had made his changes to all the trailers and locked them into concrete block foundations besides, so they left him with what he had. I noticed that as I got older, Papa left out this part of the story. Or maybe it was as *he* got older and the idea of rebellious offspring became less appealing to him.

"While he still had money and credit, he laid in supplies. Bought every kind of book on survival and homesteading and edible plants and herbal medicine that he could find." He pointed to the shelves that lined one side of the room, where those very books still sat, dog-eared and with covers half torn off. "What he knew would be hard to grow or find or make, he bought." Papa waved his hand in the vague direction of our storage barn as he went on. "You seen that big metal barn back on the rear of my property? The whole thing is insulated and refrigerated, runs on solar. Using the sun to keep food cold, think on *that*! Jed got it rigged up, then loaded it with fifty-pound bags of flour, sugar, cornmeal, coffee, and oats piled near about to the roof, all in them big plastic tubs to keep the critters out. We got cases and cases of candles and matches, tools and guns and ammunition. He bought seed enough for fifty years of crops." *On a farm ten times the size of our little garden*, I thought but didn't say.

"He bought hand-cranked grinding machines for peanuts because he had a weakness for peanut butter." Here Papa gave a fond little laugh, and for once I thought of him as a little boy with a grandpa who loved peanut butter. It was strange, and I couldn't quite picture Papa as a little boy. "*But* he drew the line at storing more than a few cases of his favorite kind. He knew that the Lord requires sacrifices of those he chooses, and he did not want to appear unworthy." Was it my imagination, or did he look pointedly at me then? I sat up a little straighter in my chair. "He built a henhouse and stocked it with laying hens and put a couple of roosters behind a fence so there could be generations, chickens in perpetuity! He even bought a few head of cattle and put them to pasture out back so there would be fresh milk, butter, and sometimes beef. I bet you never had beef before, have ya, boy?" Zeke looked like he might not like being called "boy," but he wisely held his peace. He might not know what to make of me yet, but I saw he was getting the measure of Papa pretty quick.

"Ol' Jed bought bolts and bolts of muslin and five working

antique foot-pedal sewing machines, which my grandmother had to learn how to use. Women was spoiled back then, you know, used to the easy life." He sneered at those lazy women and shook his head sorrowfully. Ruth nodded in agreement, but Rachel and Billie darted their eyes at each other and then away. Rachel smirked, but Billie looked mad. "He started his own church there in the dealership office and preached the hard truth of what was coming to the farm families that came around, until pretty soon there was eleven families besides his own living right here on this compound. They called him crazy, but ol' Jed got the last laugh." *Did he?* I wondered. They had cut themselves off from the world, I knew, but that didn't keep the sickness from touching their daughters.

Zeke looked around the table. There are only a few other people on the compound now besides Papa Solomon and Ruth, who are my grandparents. My mother's two sisters were still there: Rachel and Billie. They were not much older than her, but they had caught the invisible sickness that kept so many from being able to have babies, and Ruth said it had just dried them up and made them bitter and old before their time. There was Rachel's husband, David, though they had lived in separate trailers for as long as I could remember, and David's sister, Amber, who was strange and did not come out of her own little single-wide much. She told me that her and my mama were friends from the day David brought her to live with us, after their parents died. Their family owned one of those old farms about a day's walk from us, and when they died, Amber was the last one left there. I don't think the rest of my family was all that thrilled to have her, with her puffy yellow hair hanging loose just barely past her shoulders and her hand-me-down, store-bought clothes carried in two big sacks, but they were not going to leave her out there by herself to go crazy and waste away either. Plus, there was always the chance that she could bear a child by Jacob, just like Bilhah did for Rachel in the Bible (which is Billie's real name too).

But one way or another, that never did work out. Jacob was the only boy and the oldest child. He always seemed nearly as old as Papa to me, although I guess he cannot be. I know he had a wife once, named May, but no one would ever talk about her, and if I asked, they all got real stiff and mad-seeming, so I learned not to ask pretty quick. I thought maybe she died and they were still sad about it. I doubt she would have left. She couldn't have any babies, so there was no need for her to go off and hide like my mother had to after I came. There was nowhere to go and no one to go to, anyway, after all that had happened. No way to get there if there was. This was what I was taught from the time I could talk and understand words. I know different now, but I'm still not sure if it was all lies or if they believed it themselves and just didn't know any better.

I guess Papa saw the question in Zeke's face, because he went on before there was a need to ask it. "Out of those eleven families, only four had daughters who were blessed with children." He shook his head sorrowfully. I definitely saw Billie roll her eyes then, but luckily Papa didn't notice. "Of those four, three had only sons who lived past infancy. That shook the faith of the weak, and things got bad between Jed and some of the other men." I didn't know all the details, but I knew that one by one, then all in a flurry, the others went away. "Jed's son Micah was a grown man by then, and he had married one of those precious daughters, so her family stayed. Her name was Leah, and she bore Micah two sons. You're lookin' at one of 'em."

Leah's younger son was my grandfather, Solomon Miles, and

he stayed at Heavenly Shepherd to carry on with Jedidiah's plan. Micah died when I was just a baby, but I remembered my great-grandmother Leah as a cranky old woman whose bony face and hands terrified me. She died when I was about six.

By the time my grandfather was born, the world outside had gotten terrible. The government put out reports saying that only one in every ten thousand women could still produce a child. When I was around ten, I found some boxes full of old news clippings that told about scientists who worked day and night to figure out the problem and fix it. At first, Ruth just snatched the box away and refused to answer my questions, but I kept asking until she finally gave in. Those scientists had done studies—"more like experiments," Ruth would say with a shudder—that showed how it was a virus that caused the barrenness, and those rare women who didn't get it seemed to be immune. Over time, those "lucky" girls became nothing but the government's breeding stock, kept hidden and safe from any threat to their ability to reproduce. Later, the government heard rumors that a few babies were being born in secret, outside of their control. No one saw the C-PAFs as a safe haven anymore or went into them willingly. Then there were agents assigned to wide territories, making their rounds over the course of a year or so, checking in with folks in case any miracles had occurred. But that was a few years off yet.

Solomon and his bride, my grandma Ruth, were blessed with four healthy babies, three of them girls. Three children still safe at Heavenly Shepherd, but one of them lost. That was the youngest: my mother, Elisabeth, and when she was born in 2084, they didn't have to worry yet about the C-PAF men, as folks came to call them. But by the time Elisabeth had me in 2104, she *did* have to worry about the C-PAF men. My family knew this, and like Great-Great-Grandpa Jed, they made a plan. By the time that agent came around, they knew that spies might have told him I had been born. Somehow, they often seemed to know before they got to the families that a baby would be waiting for them. Just hiding me would be too dangerous, so they dug a tiny grave and filled it with the bones of some poor baby buried a hundred years before in the old church graveyard. They would say my mother had run off, crazy with grief, headed north to the C-PAF, where she could have more babies under the proper medical supervision. This story would be checked, of course, and he might be back again when she did not turn up.

It was easy enough to hide a little infant on a moment's notice, but my mother couldn't risk being found and dragged behind those walls to be bred like a dog to strange men. She *had* run away, and I liked to think that she *was* filled with grief for the daughter she left behind, but she surely was headed south, as far from the Centers as she could get. Soon after that, the president of the United States took his own life, as thousands of others did in those terrible days so empty of hope. Ruth used to say that despair is a sickness, and it spreads the same as any other. The new president announced a change of policy: We would cut our losses, she said, and focus all our resources only on those who wanted to be helped. Lines were drawn, and those who chose to remain outside them were cut loose. We thought then that my mother would come back, but she never did.

"So now here we are," Papa said, looking around the table at all of us and letting his eyes come to rest on me. "These is hard, strange times, no doubt. A man has got to make his own way if he wants to find what the Lord has in store for him. But there comes a time when every wanderer must find his home. It just might not be where he left it." This was an invitation, and everyone knew it. I saw Jacob shift a little in his seat and look down, hiding his expression. Rachel and Billie both had their lips pressed tight in a line, their faces so alike in disapproval, but they took care not to meet their father's eyes. David was sopping up the juices on his plate with a roll and seemed to be the only one not interested in the conversation.

"Well, sir, I believe that you are right," Zeke said. "A man is not truly a man until he has a home and a family, is he?" Now, slowly, all eyes turned to me, not just Papa's. I felt my cheeks burn with shame, and then Jacob knocked his glass right off the table and it landed on the linoleum with a dull thunk, sloshing out cloudy sassafras tea as it rolled. Ruth jumped up to mop up the mess while Jacob made apologetic noises.

Papa focused his gaze on his son now in a way that made me squirm. "That's the truth," he replied to Zeke's question. "Sometimes I fear that the lack of children will keep a man from fully reaching his potential, no matter what he comes from." Poor Uncle Jacob. He had always been sweet to me, whittling me little animals from pine branches and telling me silly stories he made up as he went along, singing me songs that Ruth claimed she never taught him. It wasn't his fault if May couldn't have a baby. And I didn't think he was such a poor example of a man. He was not like Papa, but maybe that wasn't such a terrible thing. Surely there was room in this big empty world for more than one kind of man?

Jacob didn't seem to feel as sorry for himself as I did for him, though. If Papa's hurtful words had found their target in his heart, he didn't let on. Instead he looked at David and said,

"Speaking of a man's family, David, I hate for your sister to miss out on this fine meal." David jumped a little, like he'd just remembered something his belly had made him forget all about.

"Well, Amber is feeling a little poorly today. Women troubles, I suspect. Why don't you take her a plate of this delicious supper, Ami? I think it would do her good, don't you?" His voice was light and even, but his eyes were steady on mine in a way that felt serious. I jumped up before Ruth could protest. I knew she would want me to help clear up, show off my woman skills for Zeke. And then Rachel and Billie surprised me by jumping in.

"Bless her heart," Rachel said. "Lord knows we've all been there. That is sweet of you to think of your sister, too, David! Billie and me can take care of all this, can't we, B?" Rachel was already up and stacking plates with her quick, strong hands, so Billie gave a little grunt of agreement and followed suit. I moved quickly then, grabbing a clean plate and filling it with dainty portions of each food. Amber did not eat much, and I had my doubts about whether she would want this dinner at all. I wasn't sure what my aunts and uncle were up to, but wasting food was still a sin, so I went easy.

All this time, Papa sat still, a king on his throne while the women buzzed around him. David was swapping hunting stories with Zeke now, keeping him talking, while Papa listened and interjected the occasional comment or his gruff bark of a laugh. If Zeke was concerned about my leaving, he didn't show it. In fact, he seemed more relaxed than he'd been all afternoon. As I swung toward the door with the full plate, Rachel put a hand on my shoulder to stop me. "Don't forget the bread," she said, just an ordinary reminder, but her eyes seemed to search my face. Everyone was behaving so strangely. Suddenly I needed to get out of that room. I wished I could drop the plate and run across the road and into the woods until the house and everyone in it disappeared. Maybe I could have gotten away with that as a little girl, but those days were over for me now, and I knew it.

"Thanks," I said to Rachel, grabbing a roll and adding it to the plate. Then as quick as I could go and still be walking, I was out the door and headed toward Amber's trailer.

Three

mber called for me to come in as soon as I knocked, as if she had been expecting me. Her trailer was the farthest one from the main house and the closest to the road. I had always wondered how she filled her time, sitting alone in there day in and day out. She liked her privacy, I guess. I could count the number of times I'd been inside on one hand. My eyes took a minute to adjust to the darkness in her trailer after the still-bright sunlight outside. Before I could even see her clearly, she was pulling me by my wrist back to her bedroom and closing the door behind us. And then she was talking, her face very close to mine.

"There's not a lot of time, Ami, and I'm sorry that I didn't do this sooner, but now we just have to make the best of a bad situation, so I'm sorry for what I'm about to say. Do you understand why that man is here?" I felt embarrassed and could only stare at the floor. "He is here to try to make you have a baby. Has Ruth ever . . . do you know how that happens?" I nodded, still studying the ratty brown carpet at my feet. "I know what your papa says, and I know you've been taught that this is the right thing to do, but I don't think so. And neither does David or Jacob or your aunts. And Ami"—she put her hand under my chin and pulled my face up to look at her—"neither did your mama."

Now my heart started pounding and my stomach felt like every fluttering thing on earth was in there flying around. My mama? My mama hadn't seen me since I was a week old. What did she know about it? Amber must have seen the confusion in my eyes, because she answered as if she had heard me.

"I know it's hard that your mama never came back for you. I know it's hard for her too. If your grandfather wasn't such a . . ." She stopped and took a deep breath. "It just wasn't like you think, Ami. It was complicated, and I wish I had time to explain it all to you now, but I don't. I think they'll give you tonight to yourself, but tomorrow they're going to expect you to get cozy with that man, and tomorrow night I don't think you're gonna have much choice in the matter. So I'm askin' you now: Is this what you want? Because if it's not, I'm gonna help you."

I didn't know what to say. What did my wants have to do with anything? This was my duty. It was my place in God's plan, according to Papa and Ruth. I had to try, didn't I? I had to make myself *a vessel for His will*. How could Amber help me? Could she make me not a sixteen-year-old girl with a good chance of being one of the last fertile mothers on earth? Could she rewind time and keep my mama here to protect me? Could she make me be born somewhere else, in the time before the sickness? All those thoughts raced through my mind in the space of a few breaths, but all I could say to her was "How?"

She turned around and took something out of a dresser

drawer. "When you were little, maybe nine or ten, a . . . a traveler came through. You probably don't remember. He knew your mama. He knew where she was. He only told that to me on your mama's instructions, but I told David, and pretty soon your aunts and Jacob knew too. He gave this to me, and over the years, we all agreed that when this time came, when they tried to *breed* you to some stranger, we would give it to you and let you choose." She put the thing she held into my hand.

It was a thickly folded rectangle of glossy paper covered with words and a photograph of a big building by a lake. Across the top it said *Lake Point Resort*. I looked down at it, confused, and then understanding began to dawn on me. Could it be possible? Amber must have seen the question on my face, because all she said was "Yes." My hands were shaking so hard I almost dropped that paper, but I held on to it like it was the only thing keeping me standing. *Mama*, I thought, over and over like it was the only word I knew. *Mama, Mama, Mama.* And just like that, I knew that I would go. I would run away from Zeke Johnson and Papa Solomon, from Heavenly Shepherd and everyone I had ever known, and run toward the person I had never known but always needed—my mother.

"What do I do?" I managed to choke out while the tears spilled over and my breath felt trapped in my chest. But Amber was focused and determined, and she started moving around the room, collecting things and piling them in one place, talking all the while.

"All right now, Ami girl, it's all gonna be okay. I know you wasn't expecting none of this, least not *like* this, not *today*. I'm just sorry we didn't never tell you or do more to get you ready. I tried to tell your aunts we was running out of time, but what do I know? They don't never listen to a word I say. But what's done is done, and we'll just have to make the best of it now. You'll take your bedroll and a change of clothes. The one good thing about the way you've been raised is that you know how to take care of yourself in the woods. Eufaula, where this place is, is not really *that* far from here, I think. I went there once with my parents, when I was a little girl, and it seems like it was just two or three days' ride on horseback. I don't know; it was a long time ago . . ." I wondered if she was really talking to me anymore, or to herself, as she paced around the small trailer picking things up and sometimes putting them back down, sometimes adding them to the growing pile on the couch.

"If you follow the hi-way, it should lead you straight there. But they'll be looking for you, so I don't want you out on the road in plain sight, understand? We'll try to throw them off, send them a different way if we can. That damn Solomon, though, can't nobody tell him nothing. Maybe I should tell him to look exactly where you're going, that way he'll be sure not to do it. Ha!" I barely registered the shock of hearing her cuss on top of insulting Papa, who was the man of the house and the spiritual leader of this family. My mind was already spinning. Was my mother alive all this time? A few days' ride, maybe a week's walk from me, in Eufaula, at this Lake Point place? If that were true, why hadn't she ever come back for me? I didn't want to believe that she would do that, abandon me like that, but at the same time, I wanted more than anything to believe that she was there. I didn't have the strength to do what I was about to do without telling myself that it was her I ran to.

Amber still talked and paced. "Might be four days' walk, maybe five. I know you can forage, but you'll need food and drinking water. And do you even own a pair of shoes? I don't think I've ever seen you wear them."

"What?" I asked, dazed. "What do I need shoes for? I can walk all day just fine without them, and it's not like it's cold outside."

"Well, this is walking for *days*, Ami, and then who knows after that. And you won't just be in your regular stomping grounds. This is uncharted territory you're heading into. Here, try these on." She dug around in the back of a closet and pulled out a pair of bright blue-and-green shoes that laced up across the top of the foot. They looked foreign to me.

"Lord, girl, you're lookin' at them shoes like they was made of snakes! They're just runnin' shoes. My mama said that everybody used to wear them. Fast and light and already broken in for you. I used to be like lightnin' in these old shoes of hers. Not that it did me much good . . ." She trailed off and I had the feeling again that she was talking to herself more than to me, but she still held the shoes out, so I took them. She dug around in a drawer and then handed me a pair of small white socks. She watched me expectantly and then motioned impatiently toward the couch.

"Go on! Try them on." I wore socks and boots sometimes in the winter, but even then they sometimes felt like an unnecessary and bothersome addition to my own trusty feet. But these were different than anything I'd ever worn, and there was something exciting about putting them on. I could almost imagine I was someone else, another girl from another time and place. I stood up and took a few experimental steps. They felt springy and cushiony under my feet. *I could get used to them*, I thought.

"Okay, this is way too much stuff," she said, and we both looked at the pile of things that covered half of the couch. We looked at each other and started laughing, and then we couldn't stop. We laughed until we were bent double, imagining me in the woods with a pack twice my size strapped to my back. I laughed until tears streamed from my eyes, and at the feeling of those tears, I started to cry again.

"I feel like I'm going crazy," I said. Amber stopped laughing then, and she looked at me with a mixture of pity and something that might have been envy.

"Ami girl, you're goin' somewhere, but crazy ain't it. You are gettin' out of this place! You might find out crazy is where you been all along." I was about to ask her what she meant by that, but there was a knock at the door.

"It's me." I recognized David's voice. Amber opened the door for her brother, and he stepped inside. He looked big and out of place inside the tiny trailer, but he didn't seem to notice. He looked at me, then at the pile on the couch, then raised his eyebrows and turned to Amber.

"I know, I know!" she said. "I already know. I'll get it down to a reasonable-sized pack before tonight. How does it look at the house?"

"I told them I'd send Ami back over there. The girls are fussing and cooing over him, and I think Solomon's too busy playing king of the castle to think anything, but Ruth is getting antsy."

Back to the house, I thought. Zeke Johnson and Papa and Ruth were still there, probably talking about me and what a fine wife I would make. I'd managed to block all that out for these few minutes, and now it came down on me like a load of rocks on my head. How could I go anywhere? What was I thinking? I was a wicked, selfish girl to even think of running! This might be my only chance to fulfill the role that God had planned for me. But even as the thought entered my mind, my heart pushed it away. There had to be another way. This couldn't be my only choice, could it? For just a second, I tried to imagine Zeke Johnson's arms holding me, his face coming close to kiss me. I felt like I was going to be sick.

"Ami, are you hearing me? Are you okay? You look a little green. Here, sit down." I saw a worried look pass between the two of them as Amber went to pour me a glass of water from the pitcher she kept on the counter. I sat, and David knelt in front of me.

"I know this is a shock to you, Ami. And I know that Amber and me, we're outsiders in this family. But the two of us, and Billie and Rachel and Jacob, too, we've always thought of you like our own little girl. The only daughter any of us would ever be able to have. We've tried not to lay that on you too heavy because we figured you had enough on your shoulders without having to carry all of us, too, but I want you to know it now. And we've all talked about it so many times, that we didn't think it was right what they did. We wondered if we should tell you, but it never seemed like the right time. And then when we heard Solomon and Ruth talking about this Johnson fella, we knew we'd waited too late. But we all agreed that we wouldn't let them do it to you. We couldn't, not like this."

I didn't understand what he meant, but just then Amber shot him a look and started hustling me out the door.

"Okay, Ami, this is real important and it won't be easy, but you have got to go in there and act normal. Whatever that means when your own people are trying to breed you like you're a Jersey cow. Just . . . just go in there and act like you have been. I don't imagine you were the life of the party in there, were you?" I shook my head and looked at the floor.

"You were doing just fine," said David. "A proper girl *shouldn't* know how to act anything but shy in a situation like this! Just keep right on like you were, acting bashful, speaking when spoken to or asked a question. Then as soon as you're able, ask to be excused. Go to your room just like you was going to bed. Gather up what you can't stand to leave behind, but you can't take much."

I nodded my head. "Just some clothes, I guess. My knife. And my crank flashlight." *And my little mirror*, I thought but didn't say. And the one picture I had of my mother. But Amber was shaking her head.

"No clothes. You just leave them god-awful gunny sacks right in the drawer. I've got what you'll need. You go on, now. Back up to the house before they come looking for you. Lord knows the last thing we need is for them to come pokin' around in here!" And before I could argue, she had hustled me out the door and shut it behind me. It felt strange to be alone so suddenly after the confusion of things and talk inside that tiny trailer. The sun was just starting to set, and I looked up at the ribbons of pink clouds that seemed to glow all across the sky. It helped me calm down, looking up like that. *Lord help me*, I said inside my head. I didn't know if it was a prayer or just habit that made me say it.

Four

I can't really tell you how I got through the rest of that night before I excused myself and pretended to go to bed. It's all just a blur of feeling scared and ashamed. I was scared of being stopped and ashamed of wanting to go. I was afraid of going and ashamed of my own fear. I didn't know what to think or what to say, so I just followed David's advice and put on the bashful act. It wasn't much of an act, really. Who wouldn't feel bashful in the face of a stranger your family has brought in to see if he can make you pregnant as soon as possible? I kept my eyes on the floor and mumbled answers when I had to. I avoided the warning looks from Papa and the worried ones from Ruth. I let my aunts and uncles steer the conversation away from me again and again and wondered how Papa couldn't see what they were doing. And finally, thankfully, there was a general movement toward bed, and I escaped to my safe little room.

As soon as I was inside, I leaned back against the door and looked around. This room had been mine since I was born, and now I had to choose just a handful of things to take with me. What if I never slept in my bed again? What if everything I had to leave behind was left forever? *No*, I told myself. No. I wasn't leaving forever. I was going to find my mother, and she would help me. She would know what to do. I had to believe that. Maybe she would even come back with me. I could tell her that the C-PAF men had never come looking for her, that it was safe to come home now. Didn't she miss her family? Didn't she miss *me*?

So I told myself I would be back, and I looked around for what I could not leave behind. I saw the rows of pretty stones lined up across the windowsills, my treasures found on walks in the woods. I saw my shelf of Little House on the Prairie books— the only books I had ever been allowed to read besides the Bible and a raggedy old set of encyclopedias. I grabbed my favorite, *On the Banks of Plum Creek*, and laid it on my bed. It was a comfort to think of Laura and the rest of the Ingallses, that traveling family, traveling with me. They would keep me company.

Before I could think of what else I needed, there was a soft knock on the door. I panicked, thinking it was one of my aunts come to get me so soon. I wasn't ready! But then I heard Ruth's voice, real quiet and low, saying my name as she turned the knob and came in. She closed the door behind her, then just stood and looked at me for a minute. I felt her eyes searching my face, and I had to look away for fear that she would find my plans there, plain as day.

"Ami," she said. "Look at me, child." It was so hard to drag my eyes up to meet hers. Here was Ruth, my own grandma who had done nothing but love me and take care of me all my life. She'd been the only mother I'd ever known. She taught me to read and write, to say my prayers and sew, to make bread that would rise every time. How could I look her in the eye, knowing that I was about to take everything she'd ever given me and throw it back in her face? If I couldn't say goodbye, if I couldn't tell her where I was going and why or promise that I would come back and make it all right again, the least I could do was look at her when she asked me to. I made myself do it.

She gave me a sad little smile before she spoke. "Well, I guess you know what this is about." It wasn't a question, but I gave a little nod anyway. "I know you must be scared. But he seems like a nice man, don't you think?" I was surprised to hear a little tremor in her voice. I couldn't answer this time, even with a nod or shake of my head. I didn't know if he seemed like a nice man or not, but I knew I wasn't sticking around to find out.

"The Lord moves in mysterious ways, and we have to trust in His will, Ami. Isn't that what your papa and I have always taught you? Just *think*, Ami. A baby! You might have a sweet little baby all your own; can you imagine?" Her eyes were shining now, and I saw the hope all over her face. But the truth was, I couldn't imagine. I'd never seen a real, live baby in all my life. I didn't know how to hold or feed or take care of a baby. I tried to picture myself holding a tiny baby, but all I could see was the puppies I'd played with over the years.

"Now, you know I've told you about how babies are made, the good Lord willing . . ." I felt myself blushing, and I saw that Ruth felt as embarrassed as I did. In my mind, I begged her to stop, but I couldn't be disrespectful enough to ask her out loud. "You remember how it works?" she asked. I could hear the determination in her voice. This conversation was happening, no matter what.

"Yes, ma'am," I mumbled. *Please Lord, don't let her tell me again*, I thought. It had been bad enough the first time.

"It's not so bad, really. You don't need to be afraid. Just . . . think about something else and it will be over before you know it."

I felt like my eyes were going to burn a hole in the floor, I was looking down so hard. Think about something else and it will be over before I know it? That's the best I could hope for? I might not know a whole lot about husbands and wives and love, but I had certainly thought, hoped, for more than just *grin and bear it*. I was starting to understand why Rachel and Billie and Amber didn't want this for me. As for my uncles, well, just the thought of *them* knowing that I was going to have to do *that* made me wish the ground would open up and swallow me right that very instant. Ruth kind of patted me on the arm, then drew me into a stiff-feeling hug.

"All right, then. I'm glad we had this little talk. Because tomorrow you are going to have to do better, Ami. Me and your papa, we want what's best for you. And we know this visitor has caught you by surprise. But you're not a little girl anymore, are you? Your Heavenly Father built your body to be ready for babies at this age, and I reckon He knew what He was about. We just have to trust and pray and accept His will. Now isn't that right?" Her voice struck me right in my heart. I could hear her pleading with me, asking me to be the good and godly woman she'd trained me to be. But also asking, maybe, that I wouldn't be angry. That I wouldn't hate her for giving me away like this. That I would understand why.

"Yes, ma'am," I said. I couldn't look up. I couldn't give her the answer she wanted.

As soon as Ruth was gone, I started packing. If I had doubts before, they were long gone now. I could not do what they wanted. I was scared and ashamed but also sure that I could make it right. I would go to Eufaula and find my mother. She would help me. But Amber had said the traveler brought her that brochure for Lake Point years ago. My mama could be anywhere by now. Then again, how many places were there left to go in this world? Why would she send word if she didn't mean to wait for me there? Even if she was gone, maybe someone there would know where she was.

All of these thoughts ran wild through my mind as I unstrapped and unrolled my blankets. I threw in my book, my little round mirror, my knife, and the only picture of my mother I'd ever seen. In the encyclopedias, there were photographs of people, but Jedidiah hadn't believed in such vanity as keeping cameras about. The picture I had was a drawing, but everyone said it looked just like her. She smiled for the artist in a way that made my heart ache. No one seemed to know who had drawn it, but it was left among her things when she ran. I liked to think that she left it for me, just as I had always pretended her smile was for me. I held the picture for a moment, trying to imagine how she would look now. Would I know her if I saw her, all these years after the drawing was made?

Maybe I had her eyes or her smile. I knew I didn't have her hair because in the picture it hung long and straight. The drawing was only done with a regular pencil, but her hair was left with a lot of the paper showing through faint pencil strokes, so I guessed it was a lighter color. Billie's hair was light brown, but Rachel's was honey with streaks of lighter blond running through it. None of them had ringlets like mine. Their eyes were both grayish blue. Would my mother's eyes be that color or hazel like mine? I didn't see any freckles in the drawing either. What if she didn't believe that I was her daughter?

There was no time for such thoughts, and I pushed them aside. I had days of walking ahead of me, and there would be plenty of time to worry and dream. But now it was time for me to go. I looked at my open bedroll. A book, a knife, a drawing, a pocket mirror. I added my little windup flashlight, then looked around for what else to take. In all the world, were these the only things I really needed? Amber had said she'd give me different clothes, and I wondered what they would be. Strange things to go with the strange "running shoes" she wanted me to wear. Did they make shoes just for running away? Surely not, but I couldn't understand why else you would run in them.

I let my mind wander like that for another hour, until I had heard the doors all close and the voices fade away. Then I opened my window, grabbed my roll, and slipped out. Without making a sound, I ran to Amber's trailer. The moon was almost full, and I could see the hi-way shining like water in its silvery light. It would be my path, but I couldn't really imagine where it would take me.

Amber opened the door and pulled me inside. "What are you doing, standing out there? Wake up, girl! You got to get moving!" She left me standing just inside the door while she buzzed around, talking the whole time.

"Okay, I've got you four water bottles. Any more would be too heavy. That's one a day if it takes four whole days, but maybe try to save a little in case it's longer. And I know you can find water if you have to, right? There's some food, but it ain't nothing fancy. Bread and some jerky, some of that soft cheese Billie makes. A little sack of peanuts. I know there's peaches and such you'll find along the way. Smart girl like you, you'll manage just fine."

Amber thought I was smart? I wasn't sure anyone had ever called me that before. I remembered the way Papa had praised me to Zeke when I first came up into the yard and saw them all standing there, watching me. The memory made my stomach twist up. But Amber saying I was smart felt different. She thought I could do this. She believed that I could strike out into the woods on my own, walk for four or five days, and find my mama. For some reason, thinking about that made my eyes tear up. I must have sniffled a little, because Amber's head snapped up and her rambling talk stopped in the middle of a thought.

"Well, shit," she said.

"Amber!" I had heard the men cuss a little here and there, when they broke something or just thought no one was around to hear. But never my grandma or my aunts! But Amber just ignored my shock.

"Here I am rushin' around and runnin' my mouth, not giving a thought in the world to how *you* are taking all this. Shit, shit, shit." My eyes must have been huge by then because she took one look at my face and busted out laughing.

"You should see yourself! What, ain't you never heard a woman cuss before? Lord, child, they have kept you in a little glass box all your life, haven't they? Well, all the better, then. It's time for you to get out there in the world a little bit. See some things! Lord knows one of us should. I wish I knew half the things you know how to do. I'da been long gone from here before you was old enough to remember you met me. My mama didn't know too much herself, and my daddy . . ." She made a soft grunting sound, almost like the wind had been knocked out of her. But then she waved her hand, like she was brushing something aside. "Well, my daddy wasn't shit. And when David married Rachel, it was just me and him left. He took care of me the best he knew how. He brought me here, and I guess I can't complain too much. Things sure could have been a whole lot worse for me. But not you. Ami girl, you're about to have you a little adventure!"

Five

Before I knew it, I had my bedroll and Amber's pack strapped to my back. Strangest of all, I was wearing pants! Amber gave them to me and told me to put them on, and she wouldn't listen to any arguments. They were made of some kind of thin material that she said would keep me cool without leaving too much skin out for the bugs and would dry real quick if it got wet. She said she'd packed me an extra pair plus some shorts, but I couldn't wear those after sundown if I didn't want the mosquitoes to eat me alive. Same went for sleeves on the shirts she'd packed. It felt strange wearing those pants after a lifetime of nothing but loose dresses, and I wasn't sure I liked the feeling of having my legs all closed up in material. And the shoes! It seemed crazy to be walking around in the heat of June with those springy, spongy shoes tied onto my feet.

After a rushed goodbye, Amber all but shoved me out the door and told me to be careful. She said the others had wanted to be there to see me off, Rachel and Billie and David and Jacob, but they couldn't risk rousing Papa's suspicion. That made sense, but I still wished they could've been there to tell me good-bye. That first moment after Amber shut the door behind me, I think that was the loneliest I've ever felt in my life. And for a motherless girl, that is saying something.

I felt sure that everyone was asleep, but I avoided the hi-way just the same. All it would take was for Papa or Ruth or *that man*, as I still thought of him, to look out the window and see me in the bright moonlight, and my little adventure would be over before it ever got started. I sprinted across the wide, shining road and down the slope into the woods. From there I followed alongside it without too much trouble. When the sun came up, I'd have to move deeper into the woods.

It wasn't that long ago, my grandma Ruth used to tell me, that cars came down that hi-way all day and most of the night, heading down to the Gulf from places like Mississippi and Tennessee. We had an old truck that could go a little ways on a sun charge, and I had seen Tennessee and Mississippi as shapes on a map and been made to learn the spellings of their names, but those places seemed so far away to me, not just in place but in time, that I could never really imagine them. I would look at the old junk heaps of cars and trucks that rusted on the hand-ful of abandoned farms around us and try to picture it in my mind, a whole river of them moving down that hi-way, full of people going somewhere. Their destination, the Gulf, was even harder to imagine than Tennessee or Mississippi, since both Ruth and Papa told me those places weren't really too much dif-ferent from Alabama, where we were. I knew they had cities, just like Alabama once did, but they also had the country, which was where the compound was and always had been, according to them. But the Gulf was told to me as a place of wide, sparkling blue-and-green water as far as the eye could see, bordered by sand that was white like sugar, which I had both seen and tasted, thanks to Great-Great-Grandpa Jedidiah. Having no real way to imagine it, I would confuse things in my mind, thinking of that soft white sand as a taste of sweetness on my tongue, bordered by endless salty water.

I had seen a picture of the ocean, which the Gulf was a special part of, in those old 1992 encyclopedias Ruth used to teach me out of when I was little, but she said pictures didn't do it justice. I had also seen pictures of children in those same books, some even with light brown or almost black skin, wearing every kind of thing you can imagine, alone and in groups and with their parents. There were little babies in those pictures, held so sweetly by their mamas or tied to their backs in bright strips of colored cloth. But they were still the hardest thing for me to picture when I tried to imagine that stream of cars passing in front of Heavenly Shepherd Trailer Sales, which is the name on the sign that still stands, somehow, in front of the compound. I mean the children. Families with little boys and girls, yellow-haired or dark-headed or reddish like me, smiling out from back seats on their way to swim in all that big water. I had never seen a real, actual, flesh-and-blood child, and like the Gulf or China, I found them hard to imagine. Until I ran, I was always the smallest person in my world, and what I knew about the outside of myself was no more than could fit in the palm of my hand.

It was late when I set out, and I should have been tired, but I was too wound up. I thought back to that afternoon, when I'd walked into the yard after my foraging trip. Could that have really been that same day? It felt so long ago, like years had passed since I'd been that silly girl swinging a bucket of berries and singing while I walked. I hadn't been worried about a thing in the world. The last thing I ever expected was to find a stranger waiting to give me worries aplenty. For the first time, I thought to wonder where he'd come from. How had Papa and Ruth planned the whole thing? I had definitely never seen the man on the compound before that day, and no one really left for more than a day or two of hunting, fishing, or hauling. I guess it could have been then. I never really gave much thought to the comings and goings of Papa or my uncles. The women mostly stayed on the place, cooking and cleaning, sewing and growing the garden, tending to the chickens, churning butter. The men handled the cattle and the big peanut field, hunted deer and rabbits. A couple of times a year, they'd make a longer trip to the river, about a day's walk from the road, to fish and go duck hunting.

Maybe it had been on one of those trips that Papa had met Ezekiel Johnson. It made sense, I guessed. A man with no home, or not much of one, might drift along the riverbanks living off the land. I felt a little surprised as I realized how good that sounded to me. I started to imagine myself in a little cabin some fisherman had left behind, close enough to hear the sound of the water through my windows when I lay down to sleep at night. I could fry up a fish fresh-caught from the river for my breakfast. I could set snares and traps in the woods, forage for wild carrots and poke and strawberries. It was easy enough to find peach trees and even plums in summer. It could be my own Banks of Plum Creek.

I walked along for hours, my mind wandering. I was thankful for the bright moon that saved me from needing my flashlight. It felt funny to think that same moon was shining over the compound, that it was still there the same as always, with my whole family asleep in their beds. I wondered how long they would be awake before they knew I was gone. Well, before Papa and Ruth knew. My aunts and uncles had known even before I did, hadn't they? As soon as they heard about Zeke Johnson, they must have started planning. Maybe even before that, I guessed. They all knew this day would come.

Eventually the day started catching up to me, and then all at once I felt so tired I could barely stand. I went a little deeper into the woods, farther from the road, and found a good spot to make camp. There was a small tarp and some lengths of cording in the pack Amber had given me, and I strung up a little shelter from a low branch. Then I unrolled my blankets and was gone as soon as my head hit the pillow. You'd think I'd be too scared or worried to fall so quick into such a black, heavy sleep, but I guess those hours of walking had given my mind time to run itself out. I slept for hours and woke up when the sun was already high in the sky. I figured they'd be up and looking for me now around the compound.

I wondered how long it would take for the thought to settle in that I might have gone farther than just across the woods to my usual stomping grounds. My clothes were all still there, I'd barely taken anything from my room, and no one knew what Amber had in that little trailer to recognize that things were missing. Oh, Ruth and Papa would be hopping mad that I wasn't right there at breakfast, showing off my woman skills to *that man*. But I was pretty sure it would be tomorrow before they really started to think I was gone. They didn't think I had it in me. It gave me a little bit of satisfaction to know that they were wrong, but the thought of them coming after me still made my heart pound.

It was hot and muggy enough to make me wish I'd gotten up sooner, so I decided to change into a pair of the shorts and a short-sleeve shirt Amber had packed for me. Now, I slept out in the woods all the time, but I'd never felt the need to change clothes out there before. I felt silly looking around and worrying that someone might see me when I knew good and well it was just me, the birds, and a family of squirrels watching from their nest in the fork of the big oak I'd camped under, but I couldn't help it. Then I found out that taking pants *off* didn't work exactly the same way as putting them *on*, which I had only ever done the one time, and I got my feet tangled up and fell over trying to get out of the blame things. Since I was down there I figured it might be safer to stay that way, so I scooted myself over to where I was sitting on my bedroll and peeled them the rest of the way off.

Putting on the shorts was a lot easier, but I had to laugh when my feet came right back out the leg holes almost as soon as I'd stuck them through the waistband. It felt more like putting on underpants than pants! The short-sleeve shirt wasn't so bad, and I tied the shoes back on even though I still wasn't sure they were strictly necessary. I got up and walked around in a little circle, trying to get used to having so much skin out in the open. It felt strange, but these clothes were admittedly cooler and easier to move around in than my old dresses. By the time I ate a little bread and goat cheese from the pack and rolled and tied up my blankets, my hair had fought its way almost completely out of the braid I'd started out with the night before. It stuck to the sweat on my face and neck, and on impulse, I picked up my knife to hack the whole mess off. I knew I was just bluffing, though. I could never go back home with short hair. Clothes were easy to take off and put back on, but I'd been growing that hair since I was twelve and Papa made Ruth stop cutting it off at the shoulders to keep the tangles at bay. I dropped the knife into my pack and twisted the whole mop into a big knot as high up on my head as I could get it.

The undergrowth got too thick for me to venture very far from the road, but I pushed in as far as I could for fear of being seen. The sun was too hot out on the road anyway, but the mosquitoes were worse in the shade. I walked for a few hours in a sweaty daze before I came across the exit to what was left of a town. It curved off the hi-way so part of it hung in the air, held up by big round concrete pillars, and the pavement had broken off in big chunks and fallen to the ground underneath.

I knew I should keep moving, but curiosity got the best of me and I picked my way down the embankment to the low road. It was all abandoned gas stations and restaurants up above, but down there was just houses. It looked like they had been laid out in neat rows, with little square yards out front and a porch on each house, but now the yards were all grown up in tangles of weeds and vines, and a lot of the houses had either burned or caved in from weather. The brick ones had held up best, but only a few with metal roofs still looked anything like whole. There were old rusted-out cars and trucks in front of a lot of them.

It was spooky, walking along those abandoned streets. I was used to big empty spaces, but this was a place meant to hold people in. There used to be families living in those houses, and now there was nobody left. I guess I'd never really felt it before, what it meant that the world had emptied out. It looked like God had reached His mighty hand and turned the whole place upside down and just shook it until all the loose pieces fell away and were lost. All that was left either grew out of the ground or was nailed to it, and every bit of it looked broken and wrong. I could hear the sound of my own breathing all of a sudden, too loud and heavy. Even the silence was wrong in that place. Papa preached that vengeance was God's, and it sure looked like He had taken vengeance on the people who used to live in this town.

And all the towns like it, all the cities and countries of the world. It took my breath away to see even that little piece of it.

At first when the scientists and the government agents noticed the birth counts going down, they didn't think nothing of it. This was a story Ruth had told me many times and one I had heard all the grown people talking about since I was too little to really even understand it all. Things were different back then in the mid-2000s—people lived fast lives. Everything was lit up and electric and run by machines, everyone driving their cars around everywhere they went. This made the air and the water real dirty, even though most of the cars had changed over to run on electricity instead of gasoline, and it made the people tired and run-down and mad all the time. Papa said his grandpa Jed had often preached about things he heard growing up and how, back then, children were not always looked at as blessings from God, and sometimes people even did terrible things to them. This hurts me to try to think about, and Ruth would not explain what kind of terrible things, since she said it was in the past and gladly so. I'm not too sure she even knew the specifics, having been born and raised a girl on the compound, but I guess they'd both heard the grown-ups' whispers and stories the same way I did. I walked through that empty town and tried to imagine what terrible things might have gone on inside those houses, but I couldn't. The whole place felt empty and sad now, but it was hard to believe that the people who lived in those little houses and sat on the porches had been evil.

Ruth said that at first it seemed like people just didn't want to have so many babies anymore, which should have showed right off that something was wrong, because, to hear her tell, they *shouldn't* have had babies since they didn't want to take care of them and barely knew how anymore. That would have showed *sense*, she said, and Lord knows people didn't have too much good sense in those days. For one thing, young girls and unmarried ladies had been having babies on accident for as long as anyone could remember, which was a whole possibility that I couldn't really get clear on, but then all of a sudden, that wasn't happening so much. And then by the time Jed married my great-great-grandmother Anna, it was hardly happening at all.

People were glad about that at first, since this had always been a real big problem as far as they were concerned. But then they added that up with the fact that ladies were also not having babies when they *did* mean to, and suddenly they had much bigger problems than all those accident babies put together. People panicked. Then came the parts that Ruth would not tell me much about, but I have heard bits and pieces when they thought I wasn't listening or forgot I was around. I know that some that could still have babies were not godly women, and they didn't waste any time turning a profit on what they could do. Other people who were lucky enough to have babies and little children had them stolen away, or one parent would sell them without the other one knowing. It was terrible times, when the right hand could not trust the left, and the whole world just started to fall apart. That's when the government stepped in.

At first, they didn't take the babies away. They opened Centers for the Preservation of the American Family in every state in the nation. Couples with children under twelve were invited to come and live there, where the kids would be safe and the husbands and wives could trust each other again (and make more babies), since it would not be possible to sell a child off on the sly the way they had been doing. Unmarried mothers and their kids could come too. I'm not sure when the invitation became a requirement, or how, but Ruth had told me many times that when people are scared, they will agree to almost anything. And they *were* scared. I guess no one really understood until it was too late that if there are no children to pass things on to, well, what is the point of anything? Their whole society was based on the idea that your parents sent you to school so you could grow up and get a good job making lots of money, then you could get married (or not!) and have kids and start the whole thing over again with them. Even the ones who didn't want to have kids of their own knew that *somebody's* kids would be around to keep everything going. I heard Papa preach on this many times. He said this was the folly of modern life and the reason the Lord brought about the downfall. He had to break the cycle.

Pretty soon, the children and babies living in the Centers got old enough to start trying to have babies of their own. And here is where I think things started to get sticky. I guess some of those boys and girls did like any young people would have done before in their towns or at school and found sweethearts in the C-PAF where they lived. But some didn't. States would organize party weekends and things with the teenagers from three or four C-PAFs so those who were unattached could try to meet a partner. Sometimes this worked, but other times it didn't. I used to ask Ruth why this should be so hard and didn't they want to get married and have babies so they could carry out God and the government's plan, but she would just look at me darkly and say I should never confuse God and the government. Also, she said that not all people want to do God's will and follow the natural way, but when I pushed, she wouldn't say any more on the subject.

But as it turned out, even those who wanted to follow the plan were mostly out of luck. That is where the sticky part comes in. Because once those girls got old enough to start trying and once it was shown that the trying wasn't going to work for some of them any more than it had for all the women still living on the outside, those girls and their families had to go. They had been sheltered and given everything they could need or want in the C-PAF, and then all of a sudden, they were out in the real world, where things were considerably worse than they had been when they went in ten or fifteen years before. It also did not take too long for the government to figure out that all those boys were a whole lot of trouble and that it didn't take that many to do what needed to be done, so they weeded out all but the cream of the crop. Only the smartest, healthiest boys were kept to father the last hope of the dying human race.

But it was maybe worst of all for the girls who *could* have babies, because by then, things were so desperate that the government said they could no longer leave the future of America to chance. Those babies were taken to be raised in nurseries so the mothers would be freed up to make more. At first, this wasn't full-time, but pretty soon the "visits" were said to upset everyone too much, and the people in charge put a stop to them. This started happening in some other countries first, and back then there was TV and the internet so everybody knew what was happening everywhere every minute. Of course our government said this was just awful and not the American way, right up until they started doing it themselves. I had heard Papa preach on this too. *The Evils of the Government* is one of his favorite subjects. It runs in the family, since hatred of the government was what drove his grandpa to create the compound in the first place.

But for all that talk about the *natural way* and how people had defied it and how the government had twisted it for their own purpose, I still didn't have a real clear understanding of what that meant. I knew the mechanics from that embarrassing talk I'd had with Ruth around the time of my first moon cycle, but that was just a small part of it all, wasn't it? I thought the natural way meant courting and falling in love with the person God had chosen for you. But then if there were so few people left in the world, how could that happen? Was that why Ruth and Papa Solomon had brought that man into our home, even though it didn't feel too *natural* to me at all? Weren't they interfering the same way the government had done? I knew they probably didn't think so, but that was how it felt to me. *There has to be a better way*, I thought. I just needed to find my mama so she could help me figure it out.

I wandered the streets of that empty town, trying to imagine the people who'd lived there and understand how it all went so wrong, until I was too spooked to stand it anymore. My shoulders were just about up around my ears, and then a loud crashing noise sent me running back toward the hi-way. It came from far away, at least a few streets over. Maybe that same sound in the woods would've just put me on alert for some kind of animal, but this was unfamiliar territory and I didn't wait around to find out who or what could have made it. I'd been so sure the whole place was empty, but how did I know that? If my family could survive at Heavenly Shepherd all this time, maybe there were survivors here too. And they might not take too kindly to strangers. Besides, the sun was getting ready to set, and I didn't want to be caught in that haunted place after dark. I scrambled back up the embankment and across the hi-way into the familiar shelter of the woods before I finally slowed down and caught my breath. I gave myself a few minutes to drink some water and get my bearings, then set off walking again.

I tripped over a tangle of ground vine just after dark and cut my legs up pretty good, but none of the cuts was deep and

I made myself keep moving even though I felt like sitting down to pout about it. I'd wasted time in the town when I should've been moving forward, and I wanted to put as much distance between me and Heavenly Shepherd as I could before the next morning, when they would surely start looking, even though part of me still wanted to turn right around and go home. At times, I almost convinced myself that I should do it, turn around and beg Papa and Ruth for forgiveness, but then I thought about Zeke Johnson's hands on me and kept going. Sometimes I sang songs and sometimes I talked to myself. I cried hot tears full of shame, then cold, angry tears full of resentment. I said a prayer for the lost men and women and children of that town, and I prayed that I would find something different at Lake Point. *Let there be hope, please God*, I prayed, and I didn't just mean hope for me. It felt like I had been walking through the empty world for a hundred years, though it had only been a night and a day. I guess I didn't know how much I needed to believe there were more people, good people, at Lake Point until I saw what it might be like if there weren't.

Six

Even after sleeping so late that first day, all the walking got me ready to sleep a little earlier each night, so I gradually worked my way back to a more normal wake-up time. I was surprised how good it felt to get up early out in the woods, with the air still a little cool and the sounds of birds in the trees all around me. The outdoors had always been my place. Whenever I couldn't stand another minute of being cooped up with all those grown-ups hovering and fussing around me, I'd run outside, where I could breathe. By the time I was five years old, I was allowed to help take care of the chickens and collect their eggs. I could weed and water the garden and collect the ripe strawberries and tomatoes and cucumbers in a little basket I had. I liked how keeping my hands busy with those simple tasks gave my mind time to wander.

It was my uncle Jacob who taught me the woods. Ruth fussed a little about it being no place for a girl, but by the time I was eight years old, I knew how to set a snare for rabbits and how to skin and gut what I caught. Jacob showed me how to spot the tender shoots of greenbrier and snap off the ends for a snack, and he taught me which plants would give me an itchy rash so I could keep away from them. When I was ten, he showed me how to load and shoot the hunting rifles we had, but I didn't take to it. I told him it was the noise and kick that bothered me, but truth was, I couldn't bear the thought of shooting a deer or anything else. Snaring rabbits wasn't so bad because they were dead when I found them, curled up like they were just sleeping. I didn't love dressing them once they were caught, but I knew it would be wasteful not to. And I knew that a deer gave us meat, and we never killed more than we needed to eat, but I still didn't want to be the one to bring it down.

As I walked, hidden in the trees but always keeping the south-bound path of the road to my left, I started to notice a sound coming from deeper in the woods, to my right. It sounded like a low roar. The longer I walked, the closer it got. I wondered if I should be afraid, but it didn't sound like an animal or person; it was too steady. Finally, my curiosity got the best of me and I decided to find out what it was. Carefully I made my way through the trees and undergrowth. All along the road, mimosa trees were bloomed out with their little feathery pink fans. They crowded together, almost like they wanted anyone coming down that hi-way to see their show. But farther in were all kinds of trees. Some stretches along the road, all you saw were tall, skinny pines. But here the trees were all shapes and sizes, growing wild and leafy and lush. The light shining down through all those leaves glowed green like jewels, and the air underneath them felt cool and soft, even in the heat of the day.

The sound got closer and closer, and then suddenly I stepped out of the trees and saw that it was water I heard. This was the

Chattahoochee that made the border between Alabama and Georgia on the old maps I had seen. It rushed along over rocks like another road, but wide and muddy and alive. Of course! There was a small creek not far from the compound where I liked to go sometimes, but it just bubbled up from the ground and ran on a ways before it made a little pool surrounded by rocks and ferns and moss. The sound it made was like the tiny echo of this river. Jacob had even taken me out to our fish camp a couple of times, but then he said he couldn't anymore, and I got the feeling that Papa had made him quit. But that was years ago, and I'd forgotten the rushing sound of the water. I realized this must be the same river, only closer to the road down here where I was. For a minute, I felt afraid. They kept some little fishing boats at the river camp. How much faster could those boats move than I could walk? They could be here in a flash, couldn't they?

Picturing Papa tearing down that river to get me was terrifying, and I had to stop myself from running back into the trees to hide. Amber said she and the others would try to steer Papa to believing I'd gone north toward the cities, and they might not know the river came close to the road here even if they did follow me southward. It made more sense that they would travel the way I traveled if they wanted to catch my trail. I told myself that over and over, but part of me stayed scared. I sat down on the grassy riverbank and let the rushing sound and the sparkle of sun on water calm my mind. *They wouldn't follow me down the river*, I thought. They would stick to the road. I wished he wouldn't follow me at all, but I knew he would never let me go that easily. He would hunt me down and punish me, and I would be even worse off than before I left.

The water looked cool and inviting, and I wanted nothing more than to jump in and rinse off, hot and dirty and scratched up as I was. But the banks were rocky and steep, and the current was swift. I decided it was safer to stay put on the wide, flat shelf of rocks that overlooked it. I could see a long way upstream, too, so I knew I'd have time to run and hide at the first sign of a boat. I noticed a long, thin branch on the ground not far from where I sat, so I dug around in Amber's pack, and sure enough, I found a roll of fishing line with a couple of hooks wrapped in a little square of paper. My food was already running thin, and I thought if I could catch a fish or two, I'd be in better shape to keep going. I tied some of the line to the end of the branch and tied a hook onto the loose end, then walked around a little until I found a flat rock near the tree line that was small and loose enough for me to pry it up and see the beetles and crickets scrambling away from the light. I caught a cricket and threaded it onto the hook, and I was ready to fish.

I knew I should keep moving. I had to be getting close to Eufaula now, maybe a day's walk or so to go. I should have been in a rush to get there, but here I was, hanging back. What did I know about this place or what I would find there? If my mama really was at Lake Point, then she wouldn't be alone. How many people were there, and why? What kind of life had she been living all these years without me? Was she happy? And how did I feel about that if she was?

I needed to believe that if there were people surviving and building a life together at Lake Point, that was a sign that God was ready to let the world heal. It might not matter so much then that I had run away from my place in the family. If everything was God's plan, did it even matter what I did? Wouldn't that mean my running away was also His plan? I had heard Papa Solomon talk again and again about free will, but it was still confusing. What if the virus hadn't happened and the world was still full to bursting with people and babies and children? Would I matter less? Was I more important to God now that there were so few of us left? Did I matter more than others because I might be able to have a baby? Did God care less about Billie and Rachel and Amber than he did about my mother because they couldn't have children? I didn't like to think so. But how could I know the mind of God?

It wasn't too late, I knew. I'd been gone for four days, long enough that they'd be angry but short enough that things could still go back to normal. I could always turn around and go home. But even as I thought so, I knew that I couldn't really. Or wouldn't. All my life, I'd been taught to submit to His will, but I couldn't submit to this. I could not give myself over to that man to be touched in that way, no matter what the rewards might be. There had to be another way. And then I had a thought that made me jump up and laugh. Of course! I might be one of the only fertile females left in the world, but Zeke Johnson wasn't the only fertile man. And if there were other people at Lake Point with my mother, surely some of them were men, maybe even boys my own age. I could go there and make my own choice. This was the answer, I just knew it.

Didn't Papa always say that the Lord moves in mysterious ways? Surely when I came home with a real husband, he and Ruth would see that this was all God's plan the whole time. They would take me back with open arms, and I would have a whole passel of babies, and everything would be right again.

Just then I felt a tug on my line. I'd forgotten I was even holding my makeshift fishing pole. The tug turned into serious pulling pretty fast, and it was hard to lift up and bring in my catch without a reel. I did it, though, and it was a big one! I saw this as a sign that I was on the right path with my new idea. God knew my heart, after all. He could hear my thoughts. He was showing me that He approved by sending me this fish. Wasn't He? *Maybe the fish wouldn't agree*, I thought as it struggled and flopped in my grip. I needed to keep him in the water while I built a cook fire, so I cut the line to just a few feet and tied it to a little sapling right on the bank. Poor little fish. He was back in the river, but he was still caught.

I pulled the knife from my pack and found a flat rock to use as a table. I never did like cleaning fish, but I loved eating them. As I scaled and then gutted my catch, I realized I didn't have any kind of skillet. There was a folded square of foil in the pack that I opened to find was really several sheets stacked together. *Thank you, Amber*, I thought. She had thought of everything I would need. When I saw her again, I would tell her that she was a blessing. I used one of the sheets to make a little envelope around the cleaned fish, then laid it right at the edge of the fire, where it would cook without burning to a crisp. It only took a few minutes. Before I opened the foil, I bowed my head to pray. For some reason, I felt like I wanted to speak out loud, even though I usually didn't.

"Dear Heavenly Father, I thank you for this food. Thank you for sending me this fish, and please let me be right that it was a sign from You. I'm sorry I ran away, Lord. I know that You know my heart and You know my fears. Please help me to trust You and carry out Your plan. I believe that You have someone for me. Please help me to know him when I meet him. Help me to feel the way I'm supposed to feel so I can do Your will. In Jesus's name I pray, amen."

I wolfed down my delicious catch and felt full of new energy and purpose. I wouldn't delay any longer; it was time to get where I was going. Whatever awaited in Eufaula and whatever was happening at Lake Point, I knew it was time to find out.

Seven

Since the river seemed to run mostly parallel to the road now, I stayed by its side as I walked. The sound and sight of the water was a comfort to me. I daydreamed about building myself a little raft out of branches and letting the current carry me all the way to the Gulf. For some reason, being by myself on a raft didn't sound as lonely as you would think. I could see little tree-covered islands here and there out in the middle of the river, and I imagined pulling up to one or another of them and making camp for a night or two. It seemed like time would stop for me if I could make that journey. No one would miss me or want anything from me as long as I stayed off the mainland. I would never get any older either.

I guessed that eventually I would wish for someone else to talk to, though. I'd start to miss my family. Maybe if I had someone with me, that wouldn't happen. It was hard for me to imagine spending that much time with one person, always together, with no end in sight. How would I know if I had chosen the right person until it was maybe too late? In the Little House books, Laura fell in love with Almanzo Wilder when she was only fifteen, but it took time for her to grow up and for him to take her seriously. Later on, when Laura finished school, she moved to a nearby town and became a teacher. That was when Almanzo started courting her. He would pick her up in his sleigh and wrap her with furs to keep her warm. I tried to think what would be the equal of that in my world, but nothing came to mind except my imaginary raft. Maybe my Almanzo would be a river man, and he would take me for boat rides to court me. I tried to picture his face, but I couldn't. Then I imagined Zeke Johnson coming for me, riding swift down the river like he knew right where I would be, and my heart started pounding. I knew I would have to learn to separate the idea of love from the fear that I felt.

I decided to change the subject with myself, so I pulled out the Lake Point brochure that Amber had given me. On the back was a map that showed the Chattahoochee flowing right into Lake Eufaula and then back out the other end. Lake Point was right on the lake, but it was up and over on the other side from where I'd end up if I kept following the river. I decided it was time to get back to the road, where there might still be signs that would tell me where to turn off. I had never seen a lake, so it was hard for me to imagine how it would be. I thought again of my little stream near the compound and how it pooled up among the rocks at its end. Although the stream flowed in a way that I could see, the pool seemed still and quiet. Just like the river was really only a bigger version of that stream, would the lake be a bigger version of the little pool? I still couldn't picture it.

For four days I'd heard nothing but birds, water, and the sound of my own voice singing and thinking out loud, but when

I heard the new sound, it barely registered at first. It was far off, just barely a hum, but then I realized it was getting louder and closer every second—a boat. I had been walking along between the riverbank and the tree line, right out in the open, so I scrambled back into the trees and jumped behind a huge live oak that was deep enough in the woods not to stand out but close enough to the bank for me to have a clear view of the river. I wished I could look back in the direction they were coming from, but the trees were so thick I could only see the section of the water that was right in front of me. Who was on that boat? Was it Papa Solomon? Had he seen me?

My heart was pounding so hard I thought I might faint. *Please, God*, I thought, but then I stopped. How could I ask God to hide me from Papa when I was being so disobedient? How could God be on my side when I was breaking every rule and commandment I'd ever been taught? I might still belong to God, but right then I felt like He did not belong to me. Not anymore. I had to lean against the tree to hold myself up. Was this how it felt to be godless, cut off and alone? I felt terrified, but then I felt something else creeping in—anger. How could God belong to Papa and not me when I was trying so hard to find my way? Well, if I couldn't talk to Him, I could still talk to myself.

Ami, I whispered, *quit trying to read God's mind and pay attention! What do you hear? What do you see?* I tried to figure how far upriver the boat had been when I saw it. I was a lot smaller than a boat, too small to be seen from so far off, wasn't I? The sound got closer and seemed to be building up to a high-pitched whine until it sounded like it was right on top of me, but I still couldn't see it. Then the sound cut off so suddenly it felt like I had gone deaf, and something floated into my line of sight.

It was more of a raft than a boat, long and flat, much bigger than I'd thought when I first saw it. There was a cabin like an upside-down box toward the back of it, big enough for a few people to sleep in, I guessed. There were men standing at its railing, three of them, one at the front and one on each side. Another man stood up from a crouch at the back, where they'd rigged up some kind of huge motor that must have made the buzzing sound. He'd turned it off so the raft drifted now, slow and quiet, and then I could hear them talking. They sounded closer than they were, and I guessed it was a trick of sound bouncing off the rocky bank.

"Aw, what'd you stop for?" the man facing me called out. He wore a dirty old floppy hat and had a big bushy beard that hid most of his face, and nothing on except a pair of old pants cut off above the knees. The skin of his chest and arms was tanned so dark I thought he must never wear a shirt, but the little bit of his face I could see looked pale beneath the brim of his hat.

"I told you I seen somethin' movin' right along here," said the one at the front. He looked a lot like the first man, but he was taller and heavier. They all looked alike from where I hid, just hats and beards and skin turned to leather by the sun. "They was over on your side, why ain't you watchin' out?" The first man rolled his head back on his neck and looked up at the sky before he answered.

"You always thinkin' you seen somethin' when ain't nothin' there. Waste of time. We already gotta go the long way around the far edge of the damn lake to skirt them crazy hippies, and I'm ready to get home."

"Just look," the man in the back said. His voice stayed low and even, and something about it reminded me of Papa. *He must be the one in charge*, I thought. The first man dropped his head back down to level and made a show of shielding his eyes with his hand while he scanned the riverbank, first one way and then back the other. I ducked back behind the tree so I couldn't see, and my skin prickled even though I knew he couldn't see me either. Could he? I got the feeling he wasn't looking that hard.

"I don't see nothin'," he said in a stubborn voice. I peeked out around the side of my tree, but they had already drifted past the edge of what I could see. In a minute, I heard the motor crank up again, but I waited until it faded away to nothing before I bolted back toward the road.

Stupid, I thought as I ran. *Stupid stupid stupid*. Did I really think I was the last person alive between the compound and Lake Point? I pictured Zeke Johnson, dirty and underfed, and imagined the woods crawling with men just like him. What were the men on that raft out looking for? What would they do if they caught me? Could Papa have hired them to track me down? Surely not—I couldn't imagine how he would have met up with rough men like that. Then again, I had no idea how he'd met up with Zeke Johnson either. The thought sent chills over my body. Then I remembered my own thought: *I might be one of the only fertile females left in the world, but Zeke Johnson isn't the only fertile man.* I'd been so happy to realize that, but now it knocked the wind out of me. There were plenty more men like Zeke out there, only they weren't buttering up my papa for a place at his table. "You're not in your own woods anymore, Ami," I muttered to myself. "You're out here alone, you've cut yourself off from your family, even cut yourself off from God. You got to pay attention now, girl. No more strolling along out in the open! Amber said you were smart, so act like it!"

I'd reached the road again, but I didn't step out onto it. People travel down rivers and roads, and I knew I had to be more careful. All I'd thought about before was Papa catching up to me, but now I understood that even worse things could happen. I trudged along, following the road but staying hidden in the tree line. It was slow going at first, but after a while, the walking calmed me down some and I realized I was naming the trees I passed, touching the trunks and softly chanting *tulip poplar, maple, pin oak, pine*. I'd never had much cause to feel scared tromping through the woods back home, and my mind wasn't used to it. I couldn't seem to hold on to the scared feeling for long. *The trees are hiding me*, I thought. *They'll keep me safe.* My heart slowed back down to normal, and the soft green light filtering down through all those leaves felt like a comfort. I figured I could be careful and smart without having to feel scared the whole time. I just had to pay attention.

I got into a good rhythm of weaving through the trees and checking the road. After a while, I noticed I was seeing a lot more signs than I had before. They were big rectangles set up on tall poles, I guess so people in cars would see them as they came by. It seemed funny to me that people would need to see a sign that was a message from a dentist, reminding them to brush their teeth, or another one telling them where they could buy some fancy-looking "genuine leather cowboy boots." Other signs made me feel sad and strange, like the one for the C-PAF that showed a happy mother smiling down at her newborn baby. The sign was old and faded by the weather, but the message was plain as day: BABIES ARE HAPPINESS. The baby's face barely peeked out of its wrappings, but I guess people back then didn't need to see a baby clearly to know what it was. Maybe what they needed to see was the mother's face and how it should look as she held that precious cargo in her arms. I tried to put myself into that picture, with my own face smiling down at my own little baby, but it was hard to do when I barely even knew what my own face looked like. I realized that the woman in the picture had been a real person, and I wondered how it was for her, if she knew her picture was up there so huge and that everyone who passed was looking at her in such a private kind of moment. I wondered if anything about her life was ever really hers after that.

But it was the next sign, a much smaller and simpler one, that made my heart thump: EUFAULA, 5 MILES, it said. And underneath that: LAKE POINT RESORT, NEXT EXIT. A big part of me wanted to turn around and run, all the way back to Heavenly Shepherd and all that was familiar and safe. But the other part of me knew that wasn't possible, that everything had changed and I could not go home until I could make right what I had done. I couldn't stop and think about it too much or I would never go. I took a deep breath and headed toward the exit ramp.

Eight

I guess I had this idea that I would walk up to some kind of big fancy gate, and my mama would be standing right there on the other side, just waiting for me like she somehow knew I was coming. And even though she hadn't seen me since I was a baby, she would recognize me right off as her daughter. The reality was a little bit different. For one thing, Lake Point didn't have any kind of gate. Instead it had a wide, crumbling parking lot, faded ashy gray in the Alabama sun, that seemed to go on and on until it finally narrowed and split into three little roads. The first led to the big lodge. The other two went in opposite directions around two sides of the lake and were lined with little cottages and cabins. I didn't know which one to take, but I figured if there was any kind of main office or person in charge, they would be in the lodge, so that's where I headed.

The big double doors to the lodge were the closest thing I'd seen to my daydream of the gate, and I felt my heart speed up as I pulled one open and stepped inside. But then I forgot to feel scared for a minute because I could never have imagined a room like the one I was in. For one thing, it was huge, with a ceiling high overhead supported by long, polished wooden beams going up into a point. In the far back of the room, most of the wall was made of glass that showed the lake behind, all silver and sparkling with ripples of light. A few sections of glass had broken and been covered over with boards, but they didn't block the view enough to matter. It almost felt more like being outside than inside a building. Between me and the wall of glass was a long room filled with tables and chairs and couches but almost no people, and nearest to me, a kind of counter where a woman stood watching me.

She was tall and thin with mousy grayish-brown hair that lay lank and oily on her head. The sleeves had been cut off her shirt to show wiry, muscular arms. I couldn't have looked too dangerous, but her face was suspicious. I figured they saw more strangers here than we did at Heavenly Shepherd, but this woman still didn't know who I was or why I was there. I looked down at the floor for a minute, embarrassed and terrified. In my whole life, I'd never met more strangers than I could count on one hand and probably without needing all the fingers. Now here I was, alone and far from home, about to probably sound like a crazy person searching for a ghost. But when I looked up again, the woman's face seemed to soften a little, and she raised her eyebrows in question. I took a deep breath and walked over to her.

"My name is Ami Miles, and I'm looking for my mother. I mean, I think she might be here or might have been here, at least, about six years ago. Do you know her?"

"Well now, that's hard to say without just a little bit more information," she said in a flat kind of voice. "What's her name?"

"I . . . sorry. Um, her name is Elisabeth? Miles. Elisabeth Miles." The woman kept her face blank, and she looked up at the ceiling like she might find my mother there.

"*Elisabeth* is a fairly common name, but *Miles* don't ring a bell. Could she have another last name now, like a married name? Can you tell me what she looks like?"

"Married name? She's not—" *Married*, I started to say. But what did I know about her, really? Not even her name. Would she even want me to find her? I hoped so. I had to keep believing that she would. And then there was the other thing of what she looked like. How could I tell this woman that I had never laid eyes on my own mother? She might think I was lying. I was scared she'd throw me out before I even got a chance to look around.

I stood there looking at her for about a minute and then dropped to my knees, shrugging off my bedroll as I knelt. She could probably just see the top of my head over the edge of the counter, and I should have known better than to make any sudden moves. I heard a click and looked up to see a pistol cocked and aimed at me. Instinctively I held my hands up to show they were empty and said, "Sorry! I have a picture. Can I get it?"

"Nice and slow," she said. I still don't think she was all that worried about me, but she wanted to make sure I knew who was boss. She watched as I unrolled the blankets with my cheeks burning in embarrassment, then reached in and grabbed the drawing of my mother. I stood and handed it to the woman. I was more terrified than I had ever been in my life—that she wouldn't recognize her, that she would say she had been here but left years ago for no-one-knows-where, that she would refuse to give the picture back and tell me to leave. Any one of those things scared me more than the gun pointed at me. It felt like anything could happen. I knew that I should say something, but I couldn't make my mouth open, and I was too afraid to come up with words.

"This her?" the woman asked, holding the drawing out from her face a ways. I guessed she was farsighted like Ruth. There was something so familiar about the way she held the paper out to see it that I almost broke down. *Don't*, I told myself. Instead I just nodded yes. She studied the drawing thoughtfully.

"I guess this ain't too recent, unless your mama had you when she was about eight." She gave a little laugh like she found her own self funny, but I could tell she was also stalling for time. She didn't recognize her. Or she did and she didn't think she should tell me. My eyes started to well up then, and a tear made it over the edge, but I refused to break down all the way.

"No, ma'am," I managed to squeak out. "I don't . . . I haven't seen her recently. Since I was a baby." I saw understanding dawn in the woman's eyes. Could she guess my age, that I was sixteen and so I'd been born during the last years of the C-PAF agents? That my mother had me and then ran to avoid capture and forced breeding in one of the Centers? She didn't look quite as old as my grandma Ruth but not much younger either. She'd been around long enough to know the story. She looked at me another moment, then back down at the picture. I saw her make up her mind, and she let out a long sigh.

"Well," she said, "maybe . . . It's hard to say." After what seemed like a long time, she looked back up at me. "I think I know who this might be," she said, "but—what did you say your name was?"

"Ami, *a-m-i*. Ami Miles."

"Okay, Ami, I think I know who this might be. But I'll need to talk to her to make sure. Even if I did know for sure, I would need to ask her. If . . . if she wanted to see you. I feel pretty sure that she would, but you understand. We try to respect one another's privacy here." She waited for me to respond, so I nodded. I tried to stop them, but the tears welled up and slipped down my cheeks anyway. I made myself keep watching her face. I felt like if I looked down, I would turn and run, and then what? I had run away from home and disappointed my family, myself, and God. I needed my mother to help me figure things out. She had to be here, and she had to see me. I tried to have faith that this was God's plan. *Please*, I prayed. *Please*.

Something new entered the woman's face, and it was pity. My cheeks burned with shame. I felt about as miserable as I had ever been in my life.

"You must have walked a long way," the woman said now in a tired but kinder voice. "Let's get you into a room. It's a few hours till supper, so that'll give you time to get cleaned up and rest some." She was letting me stay! She came around from behind the counter and started walking, so I followed. We went down a short hallway and then up some stairs, then down another longer hall until she stopped at a door and opened it.

"This should do. The bathroom is right through there. We got running water 'cause of the tanks on the roof, and of course we're solar powered, but we do try to conserve." She looked at me then, from the rat's nest of my hair to the dusty shoes on my feet. "*If* you stay, we'll have to put you on the schedule for water use, but I think this counts as special circumstances. You look like you could use a good long soak. Get you a bath and then rest your eyes while I go talk to . . . uh . . . this person, and then I'll be back around supper time. I'm Helen. If anyone asks what you're doing here, tell them I put you in this room." And just like that, she was out the door and gone.

Back at Heavenly Shepherd, all the trailers had stand-up showers rigged to small roof tanks, so I hadn't soaked in a tub since I got too big to fit in the old metal washtub that Ruth used to bathe me in out in the yard when I was tiny. I couldn't really picture a tub that could hold all of me now at my size. Part of me was screaming, *Who cares about a stupid bathtub? Take me to my mother!* But the rest of me knew that there was nothing I could do but wait. I thought maybe a bath would help me calm down, not to mention the fact that four days of walking through the woods in summer doesn't do much for the way a person smells.

I sat down on the edge of the bed, which was almost twice as wide as my bed at home and also twice as lumpy. I wondered about all the people who'd slept in this room over time and about the years it must have sat empty before the last survivors started to make their way here, as I peeled off Amber's running shoes and the pants and shirt she'd given me. I had to admit, they had been more comfortable and practical than my muslin dresses and bare feet would have been, but after sweating in this particular set all day, it felt good to get out of them. I laid the clothes across the bed, wondering when and if I would get a chance to wash them, and also thinking maybe I would just lay my body down like those clothes and sleep for a while. But I was still curious about the bath, so I walked over to the doorway the lady had pointed to and turned on the light. Then I screamed.

There was someone already in the bathroom! At least, that was what I thought at first. But after I had scrambled backward through the door, it seemed strange that there wasn't any sound coming from in there. I peeked my head around the doorframe and got a look at the girl I'd seen. She was peeking around the doorframe, just like I was. Because she was me. Even after everything I'd been through, realizing I was about to see my whole self, *naked*, in the big bathroom mirror might have been more terrifying to me than when I thought there was someone else in there.

I saw a couple of towels folded on a shelf above the toilet and thought I might be able to at least wrap a towel around myself before I looked, but they were too far to reach without stepping into the room. The mirror was old and cloudy around the edges, but I could still see better than I wanted to. Finally, curiosity got the best of me, and I locked eyes with my own self in the mirror. They were just about the only part of myself I was used to seeing in my little round pocket mirror, so that part was kind of comforting and familiar. I thought that maybe if I could just keep looking myself in the eye, I could find the courage to step out and look at the rest of me. And sure enough, I started to feel calmer. Keeping my eyes on their reflection, I slowly stepped into the bathroom.

When I was a few steps away from the mirror, I stopped. The towels were within reach now, but I was feeling braver. I let my eyes focus on my whole face and then outward just a little more to take in my hair. I had pulled it back into a thick braid at some point, but it was escaping in wisps and curls like it always did. Like it wanted to be free. So I pulled the long tail of the braid over my shoulder and untied the end, then worked my fingers through it until it was loose and wild around my shoulders and down my back. I pulled it all around me like a cape, and then I let my eyes drop so that I was looking, finally, at all of myself.

I saw a girl whose face and neck were freckled and brownish from the sun but whose body was pale and blank in comparison. Now, I know I didn't need a mirror to look down at my undressed self, but I never really had. I was taught that vanity is a sin and the body is the devil's trap. The only time I wasn't covered from neck to ankle and wrist in a loose muslin dress was when I was bathing and changing clothes, and that was a quick, no-nonsense business. Even standing in that bathroom so far from Heavenly Shepherd, I felt like I was doing something shameful and wrong. I felt afraid. But another, newer feeling was also fighting its way out: I felt bold.

I was a girl who had left home on a quest, and I had done it alone, and I had made it. I felt, maybe for the first time, like I belonged to my own self and I could look at that self as much as I wanted to. That girl in the mirror was me, and her body was my body, and when I looked at her, I just could not see anything for her to be ashamed of. Feeling bolder by the minute, I pushed the tangled curtain of my hair back behind my shoulders so that it no longer hid me. I saw my breasts, rounded and high with nipples small and pinkish brown. Automatically I heard Ruth's voice telling me that my breasts could nurse babies if I was good enough for God to bless me with them, but I pushed her voice out of my head. I saw the line of my waist curving in and then back out to my hips. That was where the bottom of the mirror cut off, so I took a deep breath and looked down. I let my eyes skim over the nest of dark hair (*Babies*, Ruth whispered) to my legs, standing long and strong right here in the world. My legs had carried me far from home, and I felt love for them swelling up in my heart. I laughed out loud, and then I felt tears fill my eyes and spill over.

"Ami girl, you are acting crazy!" I said it out loud, used to talking to myself because wasn't I the only friend I had in the world? All of a sudden, I felt how lonely I was and had always been. The tears came harder, but I also felt happy because I knew that my loneliness was about to end. I was in a new place with new people, probably more than I had ever thought I would meet in my life, and maybe one of them was my mother. Maybe one or two of them would become my friend. And maybe, just maybe, one of them would be my match.

Those thoughts made me antsy all over again, so I turned and fiddled with the handles over the tub faucet until I figured out how to fill it with warm water; then I stepped in and laid my body down against the hard white walls of the tub. The loud rush of the water and the warmth of it rising up over my skin made me feel how tired I really was. I wanted to just close my eyes and sleep, but I figured that sleeping in a tub of water up to my neck was probably not the best idea. There was a chunk of some kind of soap sitting there, so I lathered it up and started to work on the matted mess of my hair. The soap was slippery and made it easier to work my fingers through like a comb, sliding them down through the tangles over and over again until they all came loose. I felt hypnotized and half asleep as I washed the rest of myself and then pulled the plug to let the soapy, dirty water drain out. Finally, I rinsed myself under the shower, dried off, and crawled under the covers of the big white bed. I was asleep before my head hit the pillow.

Nine

The sound of knocking woke me, and for a minute, I had no idea where I was. Some light was still coming in the window, but it looked like the light just before the sun goes down. I had been dreaming of the woods, and this added to my confusion at waking up inside a strange room. Then I heard someone calling me through the door, and the voice was familiar. It was Helen, the woman who had brought me to this room. It all came back to me then, and I struggled to sit up and answer her.

"Yes, ma'am, uh, I fell asleep," I called through the door. "Can you . . . hang on just a minute?" I was up and looking for clothes. The ones I'd been wearing were too dirty to put back on, but I had saved one clean pair of shorts and a shirt Amber had packed for me. I stumbled around pulling them out of my pack, tripping as I tried to get my legs into the shorts. I felt funny with so much of my bare legs sticking out now that I was back around people, but I didn't have time to worry about it. I put the shirt on backward and had to pull my arms back in and spin it around on my neck to get it right, but eventually I managed to get to the door and open it. Helen was standing there looking impatient, then I saw her eyes go straight to my hair and she laughed. I reached up self-consciously and tried to smooth it back away from my face a little.

"Fell asleep with my hair wet," I mumbled. I wondered what time it was and how long I'd slept. There was still daylight coming through the room's one window, but the sun set late this time of year. I hoped I hadn't slept through supper, and just as that thought crossed my mind, my stomach gave a loud, empty rumble.

"Well, it sounds like I'm right on time," Helen said with a smirk. "It's just about supper time. But I guess you'll want to hear about your mama first. Come on, let's sit down." She put a hand on my shoulder and steered me the few short steps to the edge of the bed. There was a new kindness in the way she looked at me then, and I panicked, thinking it was pity. *She hasn't found my mother*, I thought. I was on my own with no way to go back home.

"It turns out I was right about knowin' who it was in that picture of yours. Your mama is here." This was so much the opposite of what I'd expected to hear that it took me a minute to grasp what she had said. Helen seemed to understand this because she didn't say anything else for a minute, just nodded when I looked at her and started to laugh and cry at the same time. She waited for me to get myself together before she went on.

"But," she said, "she's not here *right now*. She left two days ago on a foraging trip with a few other people from the community. These trips usually only last a week or so, and then she'll be back." I tried to understand what she was saying. My mother was here but she wasn't? Helen was sure this person was my mother even though she couldn't talk to her or show her the picture?

"How . . . how do you know it's her if she's not here right now?" I asked. "How can you be sure she'll come back? Maybe she'll find someplace she likes better. She could just leave. She . . . she's done it before." I felt the tears well up, and I looked down at my hands in embarrassment. *What if it isn't really her?* I thought. *What if she never comes back?* Helen looked uncomfortable, like she wasn't sure what to tell me.

"Well damn," she said softly, more to herself than to me, then shook her head irritably. "I don't like gettin' into other folks' business like this. I'd rather wait and let her tell you, but there's no way to really explain how I know it's her without you knowing." She sighed again, and I looked up from my hands to her face. "I know it's her because her husband told me it was."

"Her husband?" I stared at Helen's face, trying to make sense of what she'd said. "My mother doesn't have a husband. She never married my father." But even as the words were coming out of my mouth, I knew they didn't mean anything. I didn't know my mother at all. I hadn't seen her or talked to her once in sixteen years. She didn't marry my father when she had me, but she could have married anyone since then. She could have done anything and I wouldn't know it.

"I figured that would be a surprise. I don't know your mama all that well, but when I saw the drawing you had, I was pretty sure it was her. She doesn't use the name you told me, though. So I went to her cabin and talked to her husband. He recognized the drawing right away, and as soon as I showed it to him, he said, 'Ami, she's finally here!' He seemed pretty happy about it."

I didn't know how to feel. Part of me felt happy that she

must talk about me, that she was expecting me and was maybe even hoping I would come. But another part of me felt like I was farther away from her than I had ever been. Somehow I had never thought about her life after the compound or what she was doing while I was growing up from the baby she left to the grown girl I had become. I guess in my mind, she was just frozen in time, waiting for me so her life could start again. But now time was thawed out all at once, and the flood was more than I could really handle.

"He said that he couldn't wait to meet you but that . . . your mother . . . would want him to wait for her. In fact, he said anytime she goes on a trip, she tells him what to do if you come. I wish there was a way to let her know you're here, but these trips don't follow any certain route. There's just no way to know where she is right now."

There was nothing I could really say right then, so I nodded and looked down at my lap. Helen seemed sure that my mother and her husband would be happy to see me, and I wanted to think she was right, but what I really wanted was to *know* it. I wanted to see my mother smile at me. I wanted to feel her wrap her arms around me and hear her say that she had missed me, that she wanted me, that she never meant to leave me for so long. I had always wanted those things, but now that I was so close to finding her, I needed them so bad it hurt like lightning in my chest.

"You'll stay here in the lodge till she gets back, and then y'all can figure out what's next. I'll put you on the work schedule, so you can earn your keep," Helen said. I must have looked surprised because she smirked and said, "Ain't no free lunch, missy. You stay here, you earn your keep." I nodded and tried to look agreeable. Helen was kind of scary, but I suspected her bark was worse than her bite. "Now, let's see about gettin' some food in you. You came on a good night—some of the boys got a deer today, and everyone is out back for a big cookout. This'll be a good chance for you to meet some of the people who live here, if you're up to it. I think it will be easiest if we just tell people you're a visitor for now. That way you and your mama will have some time to talk and decide things without getting anyone else mixed up in your business. That sound okay to you?" I nodded and made myself look up at her.

"Yes, ma'am. If you think that's best." I didn't want to have to explain to anyone why I had never met my own mother, but I was hungry and also, in spite of everything, curious. How many people lived at Lake Point, and how did that all work? Would there be any kids my own age? Were there *babies*? "I guess I'm as ready as I'm gonna get." I stood up from the bed where we'd been sitting, but Helen stayed put and looked up past my face to my hair. She looked like she was trying to think of a nice way to tell me that I looked a mess. I started laughing, and reached up to try to feel how bad it was, and she smiled. It was the friendliest smile she'd given me so far.

"Why don't you go on in the bathroom and get yourself fixed up a little bit. I'll wait right here." I was confused. Why did I need to go in the bathroom to pull my hair back? But I did need to pee after my nap, so I did as she said. Only after I flipped on the light and saw the mirror again did I understand what she meant. Other people looked in the mirror when they fixed their hair. I still wasn't used to having one.

The Ami in the mirror still looked unfamiliar to me. My hair looked clean, and it was still mostly untangled from my bath, but it puffed out wild on one side while the other was smooshed down flat where I had slept on it. I wet my hands and smoothed it back the best I could before braiding it into a long, thick tail. I stared into the mirror once it was done, trying to get back some of that boldness I'd felt the first time I saw myself there. I had met my own full reflection for the first time today, and now I was about to meet a whole lot of other new people. I wanted to give myself a little pep talk, but talking to myself felt funny with someone in the room who could hear me. Instead I heard Amber's voice in my head saying, *Ami girl, you're about to have you a little adventure.* I took a deep breath and smiled at myself.

Ten

The big room with the high ceiling and wall made of windows felt even bigger as I walked through it behind Helen. There were a few people there now, talking and laughing in small groups. I felt like they were looking at me and wondering who I was, but I didn't catch anyone staring. Helen had said it was best if we just said I was visiting, so I must have been right that company wasn't as rare at Lake Point as it was back at Heavenly Shepherd. The thought of home made my heart thunk in my chest like it was rolling over. Ruth and Papa Solomon had to be looking for me by now. I wondered what excuses they were making to Zeke Johnson about my disappearing act or if he was even waiting around. What could my aunts and uncles say that would throw them off my trail? What if one of them broke down and told the truth?

As soon as we stepped through the big double doors in the glass wall, I let out a breath I didn't even know I'd been holding. Being outside just felt right to me. I could see the lake stretching out far into the distance, and the sky was turning bright pink and orange as the sun dropped low over the water. But between me and the lake, there were people. More people than I had ever seen in my whole life, just standing and sitting, walking around and talking to one another like they didn't even know they were anything special. This was just a regular day to them, but I felt like I was witnessing a miracle. You might think that I was scared or nervous after spending my whole life seeing only a handful of other people, but right then I wasn't. Not at all.

A feeling like pure happiness bubbled up inside me, and I wanted to run and wrap my arms around every person I saw. *There you are*, my heart was saying. *Finally.* And I knew then that no matter what happened, I was going to be just fine. There were people here, and that meant there must be more people in more places than I had ever known about. I was not alone. It was not all on me. I don't think I really knew how that pressure was a part of me until I felt it lifted away. *Thank you, God*, I thought in silent prayer. Tears of relief slipped down my cheeks, and Helen asked me if I was okay. I guess she thought I was upset or overwhelmed, so I just nodded and smiled and wiped my cheeks.

There was a wide concrete-and-stone patio attached to the back of the building we'd just come from, with one part of it off to the side raised up higher by a few steps. Right in the center was a kind of round firepit, built about waist high and covered with a metal grate. A few people stood around it, tending to the hunks of meat that cooked over the flames. Other people were already eating, balancing plates of food on their knees. I wondered what else they were eating and where it all came from. Helen seemed to guess what I was thinking, because she answered my questions like I had said them out loud.

"This whole place used to be somewhere families came to get away for a few days, back when everyone worked at paid jobs and kids had to sit in school all week. They called it a 'vacation,' just a little time away from the hustle and bustle, I guess. But after the Break, when people gradually gathered here to start over, they turned it into a working farm. There's plenty of hunting around, so we don't bother with much livestock except chickens and some dairy cows and goats. We even get wild pigs out in the woods, descended from farm pigs that survived the Break and got free. But we grow wheat and oats and rye, corn, every kind of greens you can think of, tomatoes, peppers, okra, eggplant, melons, all kinds of squash, fruit, and herbs for seasoning and medicinal purposes. And of course, peanuts. You can't hardly keep peanuts from growing around here anyway. There's a grove of walnut and pecan trees too. It's a lot of work, but everybody pitches in. You ever done any farming?"

"Yes, ma'am, we grow some crops back at . . . where I'm from. Not much grains, though, because we have a lot of flour and oats and stuff stored up from before. Before *the Break*, you called it? I never heard it said like that before. But I been helping take care of cows and chickens and making butter and cheese and all that since I was little. I can forage and hunt a little bit too." I stopped there, feeling suddenly embarrassed. Pride is a sin, as I knew. "I don't mean to sound prideful," I mumbled at the ground. Helen snorted.

"Prideful? More like useful, I'd say! Half the folks that wander in here don't hardly know how to find their backsides with both hands! I'm glad to know somebody out there still has some sense. And manners to boot!" She looked at me appraisingly, and for once, I felt like I could keep my head up. Luckily I didn't have to respond because we reached the group of people around the grill and they turned to greet us.

"Everybody, this is Ami. She's come a long way to get here, and we gonna make her feel welcome." She said this with an authority that made me wonder what it would be like if she didn't issue those instructions. "Let's get her fixed up with some supper, alright?" It was mostly men around the grill, and I felt kind of nervous being that close to all of them at once, even though their faces seemed friendly when I managed to look. I felt my own face get hot, and I had a hard time speaking or looking any of them in the eye. Helen handed me a plate and waited just long enough for me to put some meat and an ear of corn on it, then hustled me over to the steps leading up to the raised part of the patio. There were a few people sitting on the steps, and there were several tables with chairs up on the round platform. I had noticed people sitting there when we first came out, but now that we were closer, I understood why she was taking me to them. They were young like me.

I was so shocked that I didn't know what to say. Just seeing them all sitting there together, three girls and two boys, like it was no big deal, made me want to cry. I wondered how long they had been there and whether they had all grown up together. What would it have been like to have other kids to play with? I couldn't even imagine. They were talking about something when we came up, but they stopped and turned toward us with curious faces when they saw us. My heart was pounding, but I tried to look calm.

"Hey, Miss Helen," one of the girls said. I immediately wondered if I should have been calling her *Miss Helen* instead of just *Helen* all this time. I guessed that if you were talking to a grown-up woman who wasn't in your own family, you had to call them something to show respect, like how Laura called her teachers *Miss* in my books. It had not even crossed my mind, but if it bothered Helen, she hadn't let on. "Who's this?"

"This is Ami Miles. She's gonna be visiting with us for a little while. Ami, this is Hanna, and I'll let y'all do the rest of the introductions yourself because I need to be gettin' on back." I felt kind of panicky watching her walk away and had to stop myself from running after her. I watched her go down the steps and disappear into the building. When I looked back at the table, I saw that the kids there were scooting their chairs around to make a space for me. One of the boys jumped up and pulled another chair over from an empty table nearby. The girl called Hanna spoke first.

"Hey, Ami! I'm Hanna, like Miss Helen said." Hanna had deeply tanned skin, dark eyes, and straight, shiny dark brown hair that ended in a sharp line even with her chin. I had never seen a girl with short hair before, but it was pretty on her. She gestured to the girl sitting next to her, whose hair was curly and long like mine, but blond, with bright blue eyes, pale skin, and a scattering of freckles across her nose. "This is Melissa." Melissa gave me a huge smile and a funny little wave and said, "Hi." Next to her was a boy with the same darker skin and shiny dark hair as Hanna. "This is my brother, Ben." Ben must have been a little shy because he just kind of nodded and mumbled hello. "I'm a year older than him."

"And I'm Will." There was another girl between Ben and Will, but he jumped in and introduced himself before Hanna could get to her. Everything about this boy looked like sunlight. His hair was goldy blond, and a fine scruff the same color covered his cheeks and chin. His eyes were clear golden brown with a dark ring around each iris, and they looked lighter than the tanned skin of his face. I imagined that if he smiled, light would shine out from his mouth, but he wasn't smiling at me then. He looked curious, like I was a kind of bird or plant he'd never seen before. His eyes were studying my face so hard that I blushed and could barely get out a hello.

"Will and Melissa are twins," Hanna said. She shot him a look and added, "And he's kind of bossy." I expected Will to rebuke Hanna for speaking to him like that, but he just laughed and winked at her. Were girls allowed to speak to men this way here? Papa Solomon had been very firm on the idea that God made men to lead and women to follow, but I was already getting the feeling that not everyone saw it that way. The closest I'd come to meeting someone who seemed to be in charge around the place was Helen, but I didn't know if she would call herself the boss. I was also amazed by the idea of twins, which I had only read about in the encyclopedia. Will and Melissa didn't look exactly alike the way the picture showed them in my book, though. I would have to ask about that later.

"And this is Nina," Hanna said, motioning to the girl that Will had skipped. Nina looked a little younger than the others, maybe thirteen or fourteen years old if I had to guess. But what made her stand out to me was the fact that she was brown. Her skin was a deep, smooth brown all over, and her hair stood out from her head in a fluff of dark corkscrew curls. I had seen brown-skinned people in my encyclopedias, and Papa had preached about the mixing of the races being against God's law, but I'd only ever seen a handful of people in real life, and all of them were white. She gave me a shy smile and said hello, and I realized that I was probably looking at her in the same curious way that Will had just done with me, so I made myself smile back.

Ruth had told me that when the first black people were brought to America on slave ships, white women fainted at the sight of them. Looking at an actual black person there in front of me, I thought that seemed awfully dramatic. I wondered if my lack of reaction was because she really wasn't all that shocking, or because everything else that was happening *was*. I didn't really know how I should react, but I had been taught that good manners are never wrong, so I fell back on politeness.

"So, Ami," Will said, drawing my attention back to him, "tell us about yourself. Where did you come from? Why are you here at Lake Point?"

"God, Will, give her a minute! You're so rude," Melissa said, and I felt grateful. I hadn't had much time to think about my story. I also was not used to talking to people I didn't know. Melissa turned to me and said, "Don't mind him, Ami. If you want to tell us about yourself, you can, but you take your time getting comfortable. *My brother*"—she threw him a look— "sometimes forgets that the way we grew up here isn't normal for most people. But you aren't the first person to come here from out there, and from what we've heard, you can go a long time without seeing other people. So we know you might not be used to . . . this." She waved her hand to include everyone at the table. They were all looking at me.

"Yeah, uh, I . . . I've only ever been around my family where I lived." Melissa nodded, satisfied that she had been right. But Hanna seemed to be the one who steered the conversation, and she changed the subject back to whatever they had been talking about before I showed up. I knew she was trying to give me room to breathe, and I was grateful, but I had trouble following the conversation. I still couldn't believe I was here, sitting at a table with other kids my age, and I was supposed to just eat my dinner and talk like it was the most normal thing in the world.

"Where was I?" Hanna asked. "Oh right, Teenie. What does your mom say, Nina?"

"Nina's mom is the midwife," Melissa directed at me. Nina looked pleased to have the conversation turn to her, and she sat up a little straighter.

"She put Teenie on bed rest." There were sympathetic noises from the group. "She's holding too much water. When Mama pressed a thumb into her ankle, the dent stayed for almost a minute."

"Pitting edema," muttered Will. I couldn't imagine what either of those words meant, but everyone else ignored him.

"She's not due for six weeks, but Mama's not sure she'll make it that long. She's gotta watch her pressure 'cause it might be the clamps." She looked around at all of us seriously, but I had no idea what that meant. Will sighed and rolled his eyes.

"Pre-UH-clamp-see-uh," he said in a smarty-pants voice. "I've been reading about it. It's very serious." He looked like he was about to give a big speech about this, but Melissa cut him off.

"How's Matthew handling all this, Nina? Is he taking care of her?"

"You know," Nina said, "he's . . . Matthew. He's trying, but he's not the best at remembering all those instructions, and Teenie's not exactly the easiest patient. Lurene is there, of course, but she's got that palsy pretty bad now, so there's only so much she can do. Mama tried to talk to Jessie about helping, but you know how she feels about this baby. She wasn't hearing it." Everyone nodded and looked worried. I was mostly lost, but I gathered that this Teenie person was pregnant and something was wrong, and Matthew must be the daddy. I didn't know who Jessie would be, but Hanna filled me in.

"Jessie and Teenie are best friends," she explained. "Or they were until . . . Jessie wasn't too happy about Teenie getting pregnant again."

"Again?" I said.

"She had a . . ." She stopped and looked down.

"She was pregnant before, but the baby came too soon and it died," Melissa said softly. "And Teenie almost died too. Margie, that's Nina's mama, she told Teenie it would be best if she didn't try again."

"She told Matthew, too, but I guess he didn't listen." This was Ben, who had been so quiet up till then, and I was surprised to see his face angry. Hanna looked at him sadly, then turned away.

"That's who Jessie's really mad at," Nina said. "When Mama tried to talk to her about helping Teenie, Jessie started hollering about how Matt needs to help her by leaving her alone and not trying to kill her with any more babies. Then she ran off."

I didn't know what to think. I knew that babies sometimes didn't survive their birth, but I'd never thought about it hurting the mother. All Ruth ever talked about was the baby. Wasn't it worth any risk to bring new life into the world? I wondered about this Jessie person.

The conversation moved on to lighter things and I lost track. I didn't know the people they talked about, and my head was still spinning from the newness of being in a strange place with so many people everywhere. I let their talk wash over me, and they didn't push me to join in any more than I wanted to. After a while, everyone went their separate ways, and I went back to my little room and to bed.

I opened the window in my room to catch the breeze and then lay down in the dark. It seemed so quiet after all that talk, and I wondered if I'd ever really noticed how quiet a room could be when I was the only one in it. All my life, being the *only one* had felt so normal to me, so permanent. The wonder of finding all these people was still washing over me in waves, and I felt tears leak out of the corners of my eyes and roll down into my hair as I lay there on my back replaying that first look at them when I came out onto the patio with Helen. And I hadn't even known then that I was about to meet a whole handful of kids my age, or close enough. And they'd mentioned a few others. It was like finding treasure, and I would have the chance to get to know them all. I drifted off to sleep, smiling up at the ceiling like a fool.

They were all there again at breakfast the next morning, like a miracle. They were sharing a table when I came down to eat, and Melissa motioned for me to come sit with them. They talked, and I tried my best to keep up. Just by listening and watching, I started to get to know their personalities. Melissa seemed thoughtful and sweet, never saying a bad word about anyone. Nina was funny and quick to pick up on any chance to make a joke. Ben was quiet, almost as quiet as I was, even though he'd been there all his life. Will seemed to think he knew more than anyone else about every subject, and Hanna would roll her eyes at him and shush him sometimes. I got the feeling she didn't really mind, though. I saw the way she watched him when he wasn't looking.

They let me get through breakfast without saying much of anything, and I stayed to help clean up when they all went off to their jobs for the day. I wasn't sure what to do with myself, but keeping busy seemed like a good idea, and the other people in the kitchen didn't seem to mind the extra hands. Then cleanup from breakfast turned into setup for lunch, and I hadn't even left by the time they all came back to eat. They saw me coming out of the kitchen and waved me over to sit with them again. I figured I was in for another hour of listening to them talk about people I didn't know, but I guess they'd decided I was settled in enough for them to start asking me questions about myself.

"So, Ami," Hanna began, "you said last night that you were only ever around your family back where you came from. You want to tell us about them? What was it like growing up with no other people around?" The way she said it and looked at me reminded me of the time I found a stray cat and tried to tame it, but I was thrown off guard.

"Well," I began slowly, "I was the only child."

"Oh," Melissa said, "you don't have any sisters or brothers?"

"No. I mean, I don't. But also, no one else did either. Have any kids. I was the only . . . person my age. I've never met anyone younger than my aunts and uncles, and they're . . . not young." My face felt like it was on fire, and I could only stare down at my food. Why was this so hard?

"So none of them could have babies?" Nina asked.

"No. They tried, but my mother was the only one who could." I had not meant to mention my mother!

"But just you?" Hanna asked. "She couldn't get pregnant again after you were born?" I tried not to look shocked at the words she had used. *Get pregnant* seemed like such a bold way to say it!

"I don't know. I don't think she did? I've never met her. She ran away after I was born to hide from the C-PAF men." Will let out a bark of a laugh, then no one said anything for a minute, and I dragged my eyes away from my plate to see why. They were looking at me with a mixture of confusion and something that seemed suspiciously like pity.

"That doesn't make sense!" Ben blurted out. Hanna said his name sharply, and he got quiet again. I figured he just meant it didn't make sense that she hadn't come back by now, since C-PAF kind of fell apart soon after I was born. But then Will spoke up.

"There were never any C-PAF agents, Ami. That's just a story they put out to scare women into turning themselves in. Everyone knows that!"

Eleven

W hat? No!" I said.

"What Will *means*," Hanna said, throwing him a look, "is that according to our records here, there's no evidence that the C-PAF men existed. There's no record of anyone ever meeting one or being taken in." I didn't understand.

"There's a woman here, her name is Miss Jean and she's the librarian, along with her sister, Evelyn," Melissa said. "They've lived here all their lives, and their family has been here since the Break. They've kept kind of a journal of everything that's happened since then."

"But that's just for here, right?" I asked. For reasons I didn't really understand, my heart was pounding and I felt like I might be sick. "Just because the last C-PAF men never came here, that doesn't mean they weren't anywhere else." Hanna was nodding and she started to agree with me, but Will cut her off.

"That's only partly true. The librarians since way before Miss Jean went out on scavenging trips, but instead of looking for supplies, they looked for information and news from all around. Now, it's true that they couldn't go out that far because they were on foot or horseback and they still had to get back here. But I'm guessing you don't live more than a few days' walk from here, do you? They found a lot of stories that kind of match up to older boogeyman stories from folklore, like the Night Doctor. But nothing firsthand. They would have known if a real agent came within a hundred miles of here." He leaned back in his chair and looked kind of satisfied after he stopped talking. I felt like I wanted to punch him in the mouth.

"Shut up, Will. You don't know everything." This was Nina. She was small, but she didn't seem afraid to speak up. I still wasn't used to the idea of girls talking to men or boys like that. "Even though the librarians went out all around here, that doesn't mean they hit every single house and place where people were still living. Some of those old farms and stuff are hard to find. I've read the journals, or at least a lot of them. They never said they were sure they knew every single thing that happened."

"That's right. Ami"—Melissa looked at me encouragingly— "did you come from one of those hidden farms? Or way back in the woods or something?" I was having a hard time looking at her or making the words come out, so I looked down at the table and shook my head. No one said anything for a minute. My mind was racing, and it felt like the only way I could start to sort out all the thoughts was to say them out loud.

"No," I said. "Our compound is right on the road. On the hi-way, you know? It used to be a dealership a long time ago, to sell house trailers? My great-great-grandfather saw the signs, so he took it off the grid. He stocked up on all kinds of food and supplies for the families, but they . . . anyway, it was for selling trailers, and it's right on the road where people could see it when they drove past." My voice trailed off to a whisper. "It's not . . . it wouldn't be hard to find."

"Ami," Hanna said softly, "just because we were taught that the C-PAF men were never real, that doesn't mean your family knew. You said you didn't leave your compound much, right? You never talked to many people outside your family, but you heard stories that were handed down from before. So it makes sense that they would still believe those stories too. They probably just didn't know."

I wanted to believe her. And she was right, it made sense that no one on the compound could have known the stories weren't true. But it *was* very likely that the librarians would have come by Heavenly Shepherd, since it was right there in plain sight along the main road, so if a C-PAF man had ever come to the compound, that would have gone into the journal. Probably. Maybe. But then I realized something that made me understand a bigger truth: If my mother came here when she left me, then she would have known what Hanna and her friends knew. She would have known the C-PAF men weren't real. But I hadn't mentioned that my mother was here, or had been here, and I didn't feel like talking about it right then either.

"Ami?" Hanna was looking at me like she was worried about me, even though we'd just met. And suddenly I felt really mad. Not at Hanna but at my mother. I was a stranger to Hanna; she'd just met me, but she already acted like she cared if I was okay or not. Where was my mother? Why didn't she care if I was okay or not? Why did she leave me and never come back even though she had to know there were never any C-PAF men? It seemed to me that there was only one answer to that question: She just didn't want me. Was there something so wrong with me that even as a tiny little baby, my own mother couldn't love me? And whatever it was, could Hanna and the rest of these kids see it too?

"I have to go," I mumbled, pushing myself away from the table and standing up. I could feel hot, bitter tears starting to spill over, and I didn't want them to see me crying on top of everything else. Just the day before, I had been so excited and happy to meet other kids my own age. Now all I wanted was to be alone again so they wouldn't see whatever was wrong with me. I heard them calling my name as I walked away, fighting the urge to break into a run and just keep going, but no one came after me. The tears were coming fast, and I somehow made it back to my room without making eye contact or talking to anyone in the big room. As soon as I was safely inside, I threw myself onto the bed and let it all out.

Angry, rough sobs tore themselves from my throat, but instead of draining away my anger, they seemed to feed it. My whole life, I had tried to be good, I had controlled myself like Ruth taught me, I didn't let myself dwell on what couldn't be changed. But there in that little room at Lake Point, I felt a different Ami being born. It had started when I saw myself in the bathroom mirror and grown stronger when I saw all those people and knew I wasn't alone, but those had been feelings of happiness. When Ruth talked to me about birthing babies, she sometimes called it "the crisis." Understanding that my mother could have come back for me but didn't was like that: a crisis that finished forming this new, stronger Ami and pushed her out into the world.

Suddenly my tears stopped and I felt real calm. I finally understood that my mother could not help me. If I wanted to find a way to make things right and go back to Heavenly Shepherd to stand in my rightful place, I would have to do it alone. This was not about my mother; it was about me, and I needed to concentrate on the other idea I'd had on the road: that I could find a husband and take him back home with me. I rolled away from the tear-soaked pillow and went to splash some water on my face in the bathroom. My face in the mirror was splotched red, and my eyes were puffy.

"You look like some kind of prize," I said to myself. I needed to think, and I did my best thinking outside. The little white bathroom felt too small to hold me, and I had to get out. I wasn't sure how I could get outside without seeing or talking to anyone, but there had to be a way. I opened the door a crack and peeked to make sure no one was in the hall, then slipped out and down the stairs. Then instead of going back toward the big room and the front desk where I'd first come in, I decided to go the other way, down a long hallway that matched the one upstairs toward the other end of the building. Sure enough, there was another, smaller door with a sign above it that said EXIT.

I wasn't sure where I'd be coming out, so I cracked open the door and looked around to make sure the coast was clear. It looked like I was at the far end of one wing of the building, and I only had to cross a small grassy area to get to a path leading into some woods. As soon as I walked into the shade of the trees, I felt my heartbeat slow down. I breathed in the smell of pine and felt at home the way I always did out in the woods. For a long time, I just walked. I let myself notice the lacy patterns the light and shadows made on the forest floor and the sounds the birds and other animals made. I felt the cool dirt and leaves and pine needles beneath my bare feet the way I always had. All that crying had left me feeling hollowed out, but now a peaceful feeling was seeping into the empty spaces like cool green light.

I walked for a long time before the path I was on ran out.

When I stepped out from the trees, I saw that I had been following the curve of the lake, and now I was at the edge of the
water. The lake looked even bigger from here, and the lodge and
cabins of Lake Point seemed far away and tiny. About halfway
between me and the buildings, I could see where the woods I'd
been in were pushed back farther from the lake, and the space
in between trees and water was filled with big garden beds. As
soon as I saw them, my body remembered the feeling of kneeling
between the rows of our garden back home, pushing my fingers
into the warm dirt to get at the roots of stubborn weeds. I felt
homesickness tear through my body so hard it hurt.

Finally, I let my mind go back to the question of home. How
could I make everything right again? What would I have to do
to get back there? I wasn't sure if Hanna and the others were the
only kids here, but what if they were? Did either of those boys
seem like maybe they could be right for me? I pictured each of
them, Ben so quiet with his cap of dark, shiny hair, and Will so
golden but so pushy. Neither of them made me feel anything
much, but I'd just barely met them. And there might be other
boys my age that I hadn't met yet and maybe some young men
not so much older than me. I reminded myself that I had only
been here a couple of days and that anything could happen.
When I thought about how I couldn't go home unless I found
someone to have a baby with, I felt panic filling up my chest and
making it hard to breathe. Even if I met a boy and we fell in love,
why would he want to leave a place like this and go with me to
Heavenly Shepherd, where there was just my little family and
Papa Solomon ruled the roost? Somehow I hadn't thought about
that on my long walk to this place. I guess I couldn't imagine
what Lake Point would be like, so I didn't understand why a
person might not want to leave it.

But when I thought about not going back at all, I felt home-sick and lost. Everything I knew about myself was tied up with my family and the idea that I could keep it going. But already Heavenly Shepherd seemed smaller now, and sadder. There was something about Lake Point that felt hopeful, like it was fill-ing up with life and people, while the compound was shrinking in on itself. I'd already stopped believing that my mother could help me, but maybe, over time, we could at least get to know each other. It was hard to imagine an explanation she could give that would make things right between us, but I still hoped she might have one. She was family, but not the family I knew and missed so hard it hurt. I'd thought I missed her all my life, but now I felt what it was to really miss the people you were used to seeing every day.

I thought maybe I could send word back to Amber and find a way to bring her here. Ruth and Papa Solomon would never leave the compound, but my aunts and uncles might. But then what would happen to my poor grandparents? Everything they'd worked for would be gone. Could we rebuild our family here and leave the isolation of the compound behind? Could I start a new life that might include friends and maybe even start my own little family? I looked at the shiny surface of the big lake, with the sun shining off it in little rippling waves. There were so many things in the world that I had never seen and so I never knew to ask if they were possible, but now I was asking.

Twelve

I realized the sun would be going down before too long, and I had walked pretty far, so I started back. This time instead of going back through the woods, I kept closer to the lake. I made my way along to where the gardens were and studied the way someone had set up an irrigation system to pull water from the lake to the crops. On one row, a strawberry winked at me so red and pretty that I had to pluck it and pop it into my mouth. On another, okra plants were as tall as I was, and snap peas climbed their way to the top of each stalk. Tomorrow I would ask Helen if I could get on the schedule to work in the gardens. It would help the time pass while I waited for my mother to come back, and it would make me feel useful.

By the time I made it back to the big patio behind the lodge, the sun was setting. From that angle it looked like a big fiery ball dropping right into the lake. I stood and watched it until the last burning edge disappeared into the water, then I turned around and noticed other, smaller fires burning here and there beyond the hard edge of the patio. It wasn't cool enough for big fires, but small ones helped keep the mosquitoes away from the groups of people that still sat talking and laughing around them. I felt a shy quietness come over me as I looked at all those people again. Was I welcome in any of those circles? Was there a place for me at one of those little fires?

Then I heard a sound that was not like anything I had ever heard before. There had been singing of hymns back home, so I knew that I was hearing music, but this music didn't come from human throats. I followed it to one group around a fire at the far end from where I had been standing, and I saw that it came from a sort of curvy wooden box with a hole and strings across it and a long handle sticking up with the strings going all the way to the top. And this musical box was being cradled in the lap of a girl whose hands seemed to play the strings at both ends. She was looking at her hand at the top of the handle, and her hair fell across her face in a long, smooth sheet, black as a crow's wing and shining in the light of the fire. Then she turned her face to look off into the darkness, and she started to sing.

> *Come all ye fair and tender ladies*
> *Take warning how you court your men*
> *They're like a star on a summer morning*
> *They first appear and then they're gone*

A murmur rippled through the group around her, and she flashed a smile that was as bright as her hair was dark. Then she went on.

> *They'll tell to you some loving story*
> *And they'll make you think that they love you well*

> *And away they'll go and court some other*
> *And leave you there in grief to dwell*

This was not a song like any I had ever heard before, but somehow I could feel that it was old, old. Much older than the girl singing it, the words too full of knowing for someone so young. Her bright smile faded, and her voice cracked with sorrow on the next part.

> *I wish I was on some tall mountain*
> *Where the ivy rocks were black as ink*
> *I'd write a letter to my false true lover*
> *Whose cheeks are like the morning pink*

She looked into the fire as she sang, and her eyes reflected its light. But my eyes could not look away from her face, and my heart was fluttering in my chest. I felt like she was singing right to me.

> *I wish I was a little sparrow*
> *And I had wings to fly so high*
> *I'd fly to the arms of my false true lover*
> *And when he'd ask, I would deny*
> *Oh love is handsome, love is charming*
> *And love is pretty while it's new*
> *But love grows cold as love grows older*
> *And fades away like morning dew*

She repeated the last line twice and let it fade away a little more each time. Her hands strummed the strings like an echo of the echo of her voice, and then the song was done. Her friends around her clapped and whooped, and she flashed that smile again and laughed. A few people called out words, maybe the names of other songs they wanted to hear, and she fiddled with the little pegs at the top of the long handle for a minute. Then she tossed her hair back from her face, and her eyes lit on me. I felt frozen to the spot; I could no more have moved or spoken than I could fly away, which I started wishing I could do, just like the girl in the song. I felt my face get hot and was thankful I was outside the ring of faint light cast by the fire so she couldn't see me turn red. Then someone beside her called out to me.

"Ami! There you are. Come and sit by me." It was Melissa, and she was smiling and waving me over. She scooted and made a place for me right between herself and the singing girl, and somehow this felt like the thing I wanted most in the world, and also the thing that would make me fall down dead right then and there. But I managed to walk over and sit, my face burning the whole time. I kept my eyes on the ground and hoped the darkness hid my crazy reaction to what was happening. I guessed it must have been the song, its words so sad and strange to me, but I knew that was only part of it.

"Hey, Ami." I looked up and saw Hanna sitting not far from me, and then Nina gave me a little wave from across the circle. I scanned the rest of the small group for Will and Ben but didn't see either of them. Seeing those familiar faces helped me calm down a little, and I hoped my own face was returning to a normal color. Melissa gave me a friendly pat on the knee as she turned to the singer.

"Jessie, this is Ami Miles. She's visiting, got here yesterday." The big smile changed then to a crooked grin as Jessie turned her body toward me a little. We were sitting so close that we couldn't really face each other, but she still managed to give me a good looking over.

"Ami Miles." It was just my name, but she said it like it meant something else and gave a little nod like whatever those words meant, she approved. "I'm Jessie," she said, then she turned her attention back to the pegs and strings. For some reason, I wanted that attention for myself, and before I knew what I was doing, I blurted out the first thing that popped into my head.

"What is that?" I asked. She looked back at me and made a face like she was confused, so I reached up and tapped the thing she held.

"This? Why, Ami Miles, this here is a guitar! Ain't you never seen a guitar before?" She sounded so surprised and amazed that I almost didn't feel embarrassed over my ignorance. *Almost.* Before I could answer, Hanna spoke for me.

"Ami's been *out there* her whole life, Jessie, but just in one place. They don't have guitars everywhere, looks like." She offered me a reassuring smile.

"Well, Ami, that makes me real sad. Did you have any kind of musical instruments at all?"

"Just our mouths," I said. I didn't mean it funny, but she laughed, and I couldn't help but smile and then laugh along with her.

"Well, all right then, let's hear you use it. That song was so sad I need cheerin' up, so we're gonna sing a fun one next. You'll catch on quick, I promise." Everyone in the circle seemed to know what song she would sing, because they all laughed and started to clap in time with each other before she even started to play. Jessie had the guitar propped on her knee, and her toe tapped out the rhythm.

Gonna buy me a sack of flour
Bake a hoecake ev'ry hour
Keep my skillet good and greasy all the time, time,
    time
Keep my skillet good and greasy all the time

Everyone sang along on the chorus. Jessie smiled and strummed a little before the next verse, and everyone still clapped along or slapped a knee to keep time.

Honey, if you say so
I'll never work no more
I'll lay around your shanty all the time, time, time
Lay around your shanty all the time

"Get ready, Ami. Skillet again. Come on now."

Got some chickens in my sack
Got the bloodhounds on my track
Keep my skillet good and greasy all the time, time,
    time
Keep my skillet good and greasy all the time

This time I joined in on the chorus. I felt shy and my voice wasn't too loud, but I did it. I sang along, and my reward was that big, shining smile.

If they beat me to the door
I'll sic 'em on the floor
Keep my skillet good and greasy all the time, time,
    time

Keep my skillet good and greasy all the time, time,
   time

By then, I was singing and clapping right along with every-one, and I felt happy and light.

Gonna buy me a jug of brandy
Gonna give it all to Nancy
Keep her good and drunk and goosey all the time,
   time, time
Keep her good and drunk and goosey all the time,
   time, time

Everyone laughed at poor Nancy, then we sang the skillet part one more time, and then it was over. There was more clapping and whooping, and Jessie went back to fiddling with the pegs. She must have seen me watching, because she answered the question I was thinking without looking away from what she was doing.

"This tightens the strings. When they get loose, the guitar gets out of tune and then the notes don't play true. This is a pretty old guitar, and she gets loose pretty quick, 'specially in the heat."

"Oh," I said. I wished I knew something smart to say about guitars. Luckily I was saved by Nina.

"'Brown Girl!'" she called out. I was confused about why she would holler out those two words, but then others repeated the call and I understood that it must be the name of a song.

"Dang, y'all don't let it stay happy for long, do ya?" Jessie asked, but she was smiling, and right away she began to play the notes. I expected something slow and sad, but instead there was something a little dangerous and hard about the sounds coming from the strings. She looked straight into the fire and sang.

> I'm as brown as brown can be, my eyes are black
>   as sloes
> I'm as brisk as a nighttime nightingale, as wild as the
>   forest doe
> My love, he was high and proud, a fortune by
>   his side
> But a fairer maiden than ever I'll be he took to be
>   his bride

People shook their heads and made disapproving noises.

> He sent me a letter of love, he sent it from the town
> He wrote to tell me that his love was lost because
>   I was so brown
> I sent back his letter of love, in anger I wrote down
> Your love is wasted on such as me because I am so
>   brown

"Tell 'em," someone called out. But there was no clapping or laughing now. I felt the chills run up the back of my neck as I wondered what the brown girl would do next.

> I'll dance upon your grave for twelve months and
>   a day
> I'll do as much for you as any maiden may
> I'll make you rue the very day that you were born
> I'm a bonny brown girl

Jessie glanced over at me and flashed the crooked grin.

> *I heard not another word more until six months
>   passed by*
> *The doctor said he had a broken heart, without me
>   he would die*
> *I went to his bedside, I walked and never ran*
> *I laughed so loud and then louder still, all at this
>   lovesick man*
> *"I prithee forget," said he, "I prithee forget and
>   forgive*
> *Oh, grant to me just a little space that I may be well
>   and live"*
> *I'll dance upon your grave for twelve months and a
>   day*
> *You'll die for betraying a bonny brown girl all on
>   one summer's day*

All around the circle, people made sounds of approval at her cold anger. The song faded out and people clapped, but no one louder than Nina. I had noticed that she was not the only brown-skinned person at Lake Point and that once I looked, there was pale white, golden tan and just about everything in between. But still, I could see why Nina would like a song about a bonny brown girl. I wasn't sure what bonny meant, but I guessed it was something good. Was the man in the song not brown like the girl, and that's why he left her? Papa said it was a sin to mix the races, but I guess I'd never had much cause to think about what that really meant. The girl in the song had loved the man, but he broke her heart just because she was brown. That didn't seem fair.

Jessie laid the guitar flat across her lap like she was done play-ing, at least for the time being. All around the circle, people fell into easy conversations. Someone on the other side of Jessie was talking to her, and I felt strangely left out. But then Hanna and Nina came over to where Melissa and I were.

"I'm glad you showed up tonight, Ami. We were worried about you after you ran off at lunch." Hanna was standing in front of me, her face looking down with concern but also curiosity.

"I'm sorry about that," I said. "I just . . . there's things you don't know about. And things I don't know about, looks like. It's just a lot. I needed to be alone for a while."

"You probably aren't used to having all these people around, telling you things and asking you questions, huh?" Nina said.

"Yeah. I guess I never thought that much about being by myself most of the time. It was just how it was. But now, seeing all these people, and all these people seeing *me* . . . I think maybe some of that is catching up to me. Like I'm just feeling how alone I really was, even though I thought I already knew it."

No one said anything for a minute, but I noticed that Jessie had finished her conversation and was looking at me and listen-ing to what I had said. I stared at the fire to hide how flustered I felt every time I looked at her.

"That's the thing about loneliness," she said. "It can creep up on you anytime, and sometimes it's worst when the most people are around. Don't always make sense, does it?"

"That's true," I said, looking over at her finally. "Right before I came up here, to where y'all were sitting together, I was walk-ing through the woods and down by the lake. And I didn't feel lonesome then, just peaceful. Back home, I spend a lot of time in the woods by myself, so I always feel good there. Just . . . quiet.

Settled inside. But I went out there because I was so upset and feeling like I had nobody." I let my voice trail off, not knowing what else to say.

"It's good to have a place like that," Jessie said. "For me, it's always been music. No matter what else is happening, I can get lost in the songs, and by the time I come up found again, things always seem better." We smiled at each other, and I felt warmth spreading all over my body that had nothing to do with the heat of the night. Even though music and the woods were not the same, what those things meant to Jessie and me was the same.

"Who taught you all these songs and how to play that guitar?" I asked. "Did someone give it to you?" Then it was like a cloud came over her face, and she looked away from me, toward the fire. It was dying down to embers by then, glowing red but not giving off much light or heat anymore.

"That's gonna have to be a story for another day, Ami Miles. I'm real tired right now, and I think it's time I got myself to bed." She looked up and gave me the crooked grin again, but it seemed sadder now. "I'll see you tomorrow, I bet." Then she stood up and dusted off her backside with one hand, and just like that, she was gone. She walked off in the opposite direction from the lodge, toward the small cabins, but it was so dark that she disappeared within seconds.

I realized that Nina and Hanna were still standing there and that they had been watching and listening to that whole conversation. My cheeks burned red again, but it was full dark now, so I knew they couldn't see. I saw a look pass between them, but I couldn't tell what it meant. And suddenly I was dead tired. The day had caught up with me all at once, and I was ready for sleep. I yawned big and loud, then put my hand over my mouth and laughed. My new friends laughed with me, and we all said good night and headed off to bed. When I got back to my room, I barely had the energy to use the bathroom and splash water on my face before I fell facedown on the bed and was asleep.

Thirteen

Helen had said there were about sixty people at Lake Point, and half of them lived in the lodge, mostly single adults and childless couples. Families with children lived in some of the cabins on both sides of the lake, so they'd have more room to spread out and more privacy for the business of doing what families do. There were more of them than I would have thought, and I wondered if maybe the sickness was fading away after all these years. The cabins had their own kitchens, but anyone could participate in the big communal meals at the lodge as long as they took their turns helping out.

I found Helen that third morning after breakfast, back behind the counter where I'd first seen her. She smiled when she saw me coming, which was a whole lot better than having her point a pistol at me.

"Hey there, stranger," she said, "how you been?"

"Pretty good," I said, smiling back. I got the feeling that Helen didn't like just everybody, so it made me kind of proud to have her act friendly toward me. "But I need to keep busy. I was hoping I could get on garden duty." She gave me a thoughtful look and nodded her head.

"Idle hands is the devil's workshop, that it?" she asked. This was something Ruth often said, and I felt another stab of homesickness shoot through my chest.

"Something like that," I said. "I know my way around a garden, so I won't be any trouble. And I want to earn my keep. Like you said, everybody here works to keep this place running, right?"

"Well, I can't argue with that. Go on out there, then. Just tell 'em I sent you. They can always use extra hands."

The gardens were run by a couple of older women named Hillie and Sam. Even though they didn't really look alike, their mannerisms and way of talking were so similar that I wondered if they were sisters. And they both wore their hair as short as men! They always had on old hats or visors to keep the sun off their faces, and they dressed in loose clothing that hid their skin from the sun and kept it from burning.

Hillie and Sam weren't much for talking. They seemed to be able to communicate with each other without ever saying much, and I figured they had a routine from working those same garden beds for years. That first morning when I went out there, Hillie looked me over, sizing me up.

"You ever done any gardening before?" she asked, looking like she expected the answer to be no.

"Yes, ma'am," I said, sticking my chin out. "How else can folks eat?" She looked surprised, and Sam cackled and nudged Hillie with her elbow.

"We got a live one," Sam said, and Hillie cracked a grin.

"Looks like," she said, but her voice was friendly. "All right, then, Miss Expert Gardener, this is how you'll do: Pick whatever looks ripe, pull up any weeds that's sprouted since your area was last worked over, and deal with any pests. You see any hornworms on the 'maters, pull 'em off and throw 'em in that bucket over there for the chickens. You see any aphids or whitefly infestations anywhere, spray 'em with this. You know what aphids are, don't ya?" I shifted my weight and put a hand on my hip.

"I know what aphids look like. You got vinegar and hot pepper seeds in your spray bottle?"

Hillie smiled at me for real then. "What else?" she said. "All right, then, go on and get to work. You can start over there," she said, pointing me to the tomato patch. It was satisfying to pull the ripe, red tomatoes from their vines and put them into the big basket that would take them to the kitchens. It felt good to know that I was doing something useful, and being out in the sunshine and fresh air helped me stay calm, even though it felt like my mother could show up anytime—or never.

I didn't see Jessie that day. I found myself playing her campfire songs over and over in my mind, watching her there like the moving pictures I'd heard about. I could see the way her hair and eyes reflected the light of the fire, and the way she tossed her hair back and tilted her face up to sing. It was the music, I told myself, so different from anything I knew, that had gotten itself stuck in my head. And I'd realized that she must be the Jessie Nina had mentioned in her story about Teenie and her baby. I wondered if I could ask Jessie about that when I saw her again. But it wasn't until the next day, while I was picking ripe tomatoes and singing "Good and Greasy" softly to myself, she snuck up behind me.

"Kinda sticks in your head, don't it?" I whirled around and saw Jessie standing there, smirking. I felt the flush creep up my neck and over my whole face, which only made me more embarrassed.

"I think you might need a hat or something, Ami Miles. Your face looks like you're gettin' too much sun." I started to say that it wasn't the sun, but then I realized she was teasing me. And then all I could do, for some reason, was laugh.

"Well, you're the one stuck it there," I replied too late. We stood there just looking at each other for a minute. She looked different in the sunlight. She seemed a little older than me, maybe a year or two. Her long black hair was pulled back into two thick braids, but the sun caught blue sparks wherever it touched. Her eyes were gray and rimmed by thick, short lashes that made them seem outlined in black. Her skin was tanned all over from the sun, and there was a whole lot of it showing. She had on a top that was really just skinny straps holding up a tube of fabric that clung to her chest and stopped short of covering her belly button. Her pants had once been blue jeans, but they were cut off short and frayed to strings all around the bottom, and they hung on her hips like they were made to fit someone bigger around. Her feet were bare, and a straw cowboy hat hung from a string hooked over one finger. My grandma Ruth would have had a fit and shooed her inside to put some clothes on.

"Yoo-hoo," she called out, but her voice was just loud enough for me to hear. I dragged my eyes back up to meet hers and saw that smirk again. "There we go. I'm on garden beds today. Looks like we'll be workin' together." She put the hat on over her braids and walked toward me. "I'll start on the next row." She tossed a grin back over her shoulder at me as she brushed past, her arm grazing mine. Her skin felt as warm as it looked. She grabbed a basket off the pile and went to work on her row. Pretty soon, she was humming softly, words rising up through the sound just every once in a while, singing *time, time, time, hm-mm mm-mm-hm-mm, all the time.*

I tried to focus on the tomatoes, but the work was too easy. I wondered if she had been looking me over while I was looking at her. That same uneasy thought filled my head: *What do they see when they look at me? Is there something wrong with the way I look?* I was still wearing Amber's shorts and short-sleeve shirts, washing one set out in the tub each night and hanging it over the shower rod to dry. When I got back to my room the night before, I'd studied myself in the mirror. My skin didn't tan all over the way Jessie's did; it just seemed to sprout more and more freckles. I was amazed they hadn't grown together yet. *That would be better*, I thought. I needed to change the subject.

"You ready to tell me who taught you your songs now? It *is* another day, right?" I made my voice sound steady, but for some reason, my heart was thumping in its cage. Why did I feel so crazy around this girl? Talking to her should be no different from talking to Hanna or Melissa or Nina. It was, though. It was very different, and I couldn't make sense of it. I kept my eyes on the tomato plants, but I heard the humming stop. Then she was quiet for a minute before she spoke.

"It was my daddy. He died a couple of years ago. That was his guitar, and he taught me how to play." Her voice sounded tight but not angry.

"I'm sorry," I said. "You must miss him a lot."

"He was a bastard and I'm glad he's dead," she replied. There was a hard edge to her voice, and I could not have been more shocked if she had slapped me. "But sometimes I loved him. And sometimes I miss him. Music was the only good thing he ever did." I didn't know what to say to that, so I stayed quiet.

"He was the reason my mama left," she said, her voice softer now. "He used to hit her because he couldn't make her do like he wanted. When I was about six years old, I guess she had enough. She said she was going down to the beaches to find us a place and then she'd come back for me, but she never did. Hell, she might not've ever made it that far. I don't even know if she's still alive. So then it was just me and him."

"Did he . . . ?" I didn't know how to ask the question in my mind.

"Hit me? Naw. For some reason, he never did. He used to say I reminded him of his sister that died when they was kids, so maybe that's why. But after Mama left, he stopped talking to me much. Seemed like most of the time he didn't even notice I was there, like he couldn't see me. Sometimes I wished he *would* hit me, just so I'd know I was really there. When I was little, I'd scream and throw fits and try to make him talk to me, but he always just left. So I gave up. By the time he died, it didn't hardly make no difference. I was always by myself anyway."

I tried to picture Jessie as a little girl, and my heart broke for her. I felt tears well up and spill over, and I didn't wipe them away. When I looked up, Jessie was standing stock-still, staring at me with her mouth hanging open. She looked so surprised, like I had hollered out or something. I didn't know what to say, so I just raised my chin and looked her dead in the face. I would not be sorry for feeling sad about what had happened to her. She closed her mouth, then gave her head a little shake and turned back to the plants.

"He didn't teach me all the songs I know, though. I taught myself a whole lot more than he ever knew. Made some others up myself." She grinned at me. I recognized what I saw in her face as pride, but somehow I couldn't think of that pride as sinful. It seemed to me that she *should* feel proud of what she could do.

"I'd like to hear some more of those songs," I said. "The only songs I know are church songs. That's all that was allowed back home."

"'Just As I Am,' 'Onward Christian Soldiers,' like that?" she asked.

"Yeah," I replied. "'Amazing Grace' was my favorite."

She nodded. "That's a good one. Miss Jean, you know, over at the library? She has some old records and record players. Hymnals and songbooks too. They got even more in the town library at Eufaula. I go over there sometimes and bring things back. Miss Jean keeps lists of everything we get from there. I don't know why; it's not like we'll ever need to put them back."

"Were those library songs the other night or ones your daddy taught you?" I asked.

"Little of both. He taught me 'Good and Greasy.' Used to sing it all the time when he was in a good mood. But the other ones are real old mountain songs. I found a whole book about them called *Appalachian Ballads*. These people lived up in the Appalachian Mountains in West Virginia and around there. Some of them never came down off the mountain once in their whole lives, so even though the world was changing all around them, they stayed the same. Buildin' cabins out of trees they cut down themselves, butcherin' their own meat, growin' their own food. Not too different from what we got here, really, but for them it was more of a choice to keep livin' like that even though they coulda come down off the mountain and bought a house lit up with electricity and clean water runnin' hot and cold out of the taps. Eventually they did, but not for a long time."

"Maybe they were scared to change," I said. "They felt safe

with what they knew, so they just stayed put." She nodded, and I felt a little thrill that she agreed with me.

"Maybe so," she said. "They sure kept the songs the same. There are rules for a ballad. The tune has to stay the same on every verse, and it has to tell a story—usually a terrible, sad story. Brokenhearted lovers, tragedy, sometimes murder. I guess life was hard on the mountain. Not much entertainment either. Stories and songs were it."

"I haven't been to the library or met Miss Jean yet," I said.

"Well, we got to fix that, don't we? Miss Jean knows a little bit of everything, and I can tell you're real curious." She flashed me the crooked grin. "You like to read?"

"I do, but I only ever had a few books. Some old encyclopedias and some books about a pioneer family named Ingalls."

"*Little House on the Prairie?*" she asked. "*On the Banks of Plum Creek?*"

"How did you know?" I replied, surprised.

"Shoot, Ami. All us kids here read them books. Miss Jean and her sister, Evelyn, taught us how to read and write and made a little school, like. We read those books and plenty others you might know: *The Birchbark House, Narnia, Wrinkle in Time, Anne of Green Gables, Harry Potter*. I didn't always like to go, and my daddy didn't make me, but I liked the books best."

"My . . . I wasn't allowed to read anything else. Just the encyclopedia and the Ingalls family. And the Bible, of course." We were both still working our way down our rows while we talked, but she stopped and looked up, surprised.

"Not allowed? How come? Where'd you grow up, anyway? You haven't told me about that yet."

I thought about telling her that would have to be a story for another day, but then I just started talking. She had told me about her daddy and her mother leaving, so it seemed wrong not to tell her my story. It wasn't easy to talk about, but once I got started, I couldn't seem to stop. I told her everything—about Heavenly Shepherd and Ruth and Papa Solomon, Rachel and Billie and Jacob, David and Amber. I told her how the compound came to be and how I thought my mother had to leave because of the C-PAF man but now I wasn't sure about any of that. I talked about what it had been like to grow up with all those adults and no other kids, and how I spent as much time as I could outside in the garden and the woods. And finally, I told her about *that man*, Zeke Johnson, and how my aunts and uncles had a plan for me to run away and come here.

"Ruth tried so hard to raise me up right and get me ready to do my duty," I said. "It took me five days to walk here, and that whole time I was walking, I was thinking. I thought . . . I thought maybe I could make it right and go back, but now . . . now I don't know. It's all different than I thought."

I had talked so long that the sun was straight overhead and we had finished our work. Jessie didn't say anything for a few minutes. She walked over to a little shelter nearby that had a jug of water and cups set up for whoever needed a cool drink on this hot day, and poured us both a cup. Then we sat down at the picnic table that was there, facing each other across the table. Without garden work to keep my hands and eyes busy, it was hard to know where to look. She took the straw hat off and fanned her face with it. Finally, she let out a long, low whistle.

"Damn, girl!" she said with a little laugh. "I was *not* expecting all of that!" She looked like she was thinking, making sense of everything I'd told her. "Why was the plan for you to run here, though, to Lake Point? I'm surprised they even knew about this place or knew that there were people here." That was the last part, the only part I hadn't told her. It was the hardest part for me to talk about.

"She's here. My mother. Or at least she's supposed to be here, but she's gone on a scavenging trip right now, so I haven't seen her yet. But Miss Helen figured it out from this drawing I have, so it's her."

"So you mean they knew she was here this whole time, and they didn't tell you? She was here this whole time, and she didn't go back for you?" She sounded angry. It felt good to have some-one take my side and echo the way I felt about everything. And the fact that that someone was Jessie felt even better.

"Yeah," I said softly. "Ruth always told me that my mother had to leave because of the C-PAF men, and I always thought they had somehow kept her away from me or that something might have happened to her. I thought it must be really bad to keep her from coming back. But then the other day, before I met you that night, Hanna and her friends told me about the journals in the library and how there was no such thing as the C-PAF men."

"But, Ami," Jessie said, "would your family have known that? It sounds like y'all were pretty isolated out there. Maybe they were still scared you'd both be taken."

"I know, I thought of that too," I said, "and that's probably true. But when she came here, when my mother got here and stayed here, she would have found out." I felt the pain of that knowledge wash over me just as hard and rough as it had the first time. "So why didn't she ever go back for me? Why didn't she want me when hardly anyone was lucky enough to have a baby anymore? What's wrong with me?" I wanted to stop there and not point out whatever it was that people saw when they looked at me, just in case she hadn't seen it. But the sadness was spilling out of me, and there was no way to pull it all back in.

"What's wrong with me, Jessie? That man, Zeke Johnson, when he looked at me, it was like . . . like he saw something he didn't like. And when I met Hanna and those other kids, they were nice and all, but Will looked at me kind of funny, too, like he was trying to figure something out. Do you see it? Please, don't lie to save my feelings. Just tell me!" I locked my eyes onto hers, and she did not look away. The earlier anger was still there but also something else. I hoped it wasn't pity. I couldn't stand the thought of Jessie feeling sorry for me.

"Ami Miles." She reached across the table for my hands and grasped them in both of hers. "Now you listen to me. No, don't look away, look at me and hear what I'm about to say. There is nothing wrong with you, girl, not a single solitary thing. You are *beautiful*. Don't you know that?" I started to pull away, but she held my hands tight. She caught my eyes with hers as they tried to slide away. "I think it's probably just hard for you to read people's faces and body language since you've never had any practice at it, right? I don't see anything bad or confusing when I look at you, Ami. I see your pretty face and your eyes so smart and curious, taking everything in. But it really doesn't matter what I see or what that man saw, or Will, or anyone else. What do you see? How do you see *yourself*?"

"I don't know!" I said, pulling away and jumping to my feet. "I never even saw what I look like until I got here. I had a tiny pocket mirror that I kept hidden away, but mirrors weren't allowed on the compound because vanity is a sin. And I never saw any other girls to know how they looked. I never thought about my face much at all, really."

"What did you think about, then? Before you came here, before they brought that man into your place, what did you think of when you thought of yourself?" I looked back at her, then over toward the garden beds and up at the sky. I thought about all the time I spent by myself growing up. It never crossed my mind back then to worry about how I looked, and there was no one to care anyway. Even when I peeked in my little round mirror, it was because I wanted to *know* what I looked like, not to judge it.

"I guess I didn't, really. I was just there. I just *was*. I was the only child and the only girl and the only Ami. I was at home in the woods and in the garden and with the animals. When you're all alone, you don't have to think about how you look or what people think of you. You're just yourself." Jessie stood up and came around the table toward me, smiling the big shiny smile.

"But see, Ami, when you're around other people, you *still* don't have to care about none of that. You can still be just Ami. Just yourself." She stood there giving me that big crazy smile, just beaming it in my face until I couldn't help but smile back just as big. We might have stood there smiling like a couple of crazy fools for who knows how long, but right then her stomach rumbled louder than I had ever heard a stomach do, and we both busted up laughing. We laughed until we bent double and then stood back up wiping away tears.

"Uh, Jessie, is it lunchtime, maybe?"

"I might be just a touch peckish," she said, and we cracked up all over again. Finally, we got ourselves collected and made our way to the lodge for lunch.

Fourteen

Lunch at the lodge was set up the same. There was a long line of freshly washed greens, tomatoes, peppers, cucumbers, herbs, and other stuff that people could pile into bowls to make salad. Then there were things like squash, zucchini, eggplant, and more peppers that had been cut into chunks and skewered on long, thin sticks and grilled. Fish and other meat were saved for dinner. It felt good to look at all that food and know that I was helping to grow it and feed all these people. I grabbed a couple of skewers and a hunk of the delicious brown bread they baked every day in the big kitchen, then slathered the bread with some of the peanut butter they ground from the peanuts that grew almost wild in a big field near the raised beds. It was sweet with honey from the bees, and I saved it for last.

I didn't see Hanna and the other kids sitting anywhere in the big room, and I felt a little jolt of happiness that Jessie and I could eat together, just the two of us. I wanted to ask about Teenie and her baby, but I thought we had both had enough big serious talk for one day. Jessie entertained me with gossip about different people sitting at tables around the room. I think she made most of it up, but it kept me laughing and cheered me up. Sometimes she made up silly little songs about people. She took my empty skewers and stuck a wedge of red pepper at the end of each one like feet, then made them do a kicky dance while she sang. No one at Heavenly Shepherd had been too big on silliness and laughing, except sometimes my uncle Jacob if no one else was around. It felt good to laugh.

Just as I was starting on my peanut butter bread, Will and Hanna came and sat down at the table with Jessie and me. I was glad to see them, but I also felt a little twinge of annoyance that it wasn't just the two of us anymore. I told myself it was because I felt so comfortable around Jessie and I just hadn't connected with anyone else the same way. For a second, her face looked like she felt the same way, but I thought I must have imagined that.

"Hey," said Hanna. I saw her eyes meet Will's, and he smirked. "Lunch buddies already, huh?" The blood rushed into my face so hard I thought it might shoot out my eyes, which only made me feel even more embarrassed.

"It's a good thing she wasn't waiting on y'all," Jessie replied with a smirk of her own. "You two just about missed lunch. You musta been on the *far* edge of property check this mornin'." Now it was Hanna's turn to blush. I guessed I was right about the way Hanna always looked at Will when he talked. And as usual, Will didn't seem to notice.

"We went to see Teenie, *actually*," he said. "She asked about you. What are you doing, Jessie? She needs you." *That's Will*, I thought, *straight to the point*. So much for keeping things light and easy. I looked across at Jessie to gauge her reaction, but she kept her face cool. I wished I could learn to do that.

"Well, it sounds like she's got the two of you and everybody else around here looking after her, so I don't know what she needs me for." Jessie's voice stayed even and her face was defiant, but her back was up and I could tell she didn't like this conversation.

"Jessie—" Hanna started, but again Will barged ahead.

"You're not just anyone to Teenie, and you know it. She's scared." Jessie's brave face slipped a little then, and I could tell that Will saw it. Luckily Hanna could, too, and she stopped him from going in for the kill.

"I get it, Jessie, I do," Hanna said. "You know that I of all people understand why you're so worried." Jessie started to interrupt, but Hanna put up a hand and kept going. "But what's done is done. Teenie already got pregnant again even though Margie told her not to. She already made her choice to keep it, and it's too late to turn back now—you know that. Don't *you* wait till it's too late. You need to go see her." Jessie started to say something, then shook her head and stood up to go.

"Jessie!" Hanna shouted her name and stood up so fast she almost knocked her chair over. The two of them stood there for a second, their faces angry and eyes locked. Then Jessie turned and walked away. I stood up to follow her, but Hanna put a hand on my shoulder.

"Let her go, Ami. She'll be fine; you just have to leave her alone when she's like this." I felt a definite flash of irritation at the idea that Hanna knew Jessie better than I did, but of course she did. They'd known each other their whole lives, while I'd only spent a few hours with the girl. Why was I feeling so crazy when it came to Jessie? I had never had a real friend, so I didn't know what it was supposed to feel like. Maybe this was all part of it. We both sat back down in our seats next to each other, with just Will left across the table from us now.

"Why is she so upset?" I asked. "I don't really understand what's happening. Who is this Teenie person to Jessie? Why is Jessie mad that she's having a baby?" Hanna puffed up her cheeks and then blew out a loud breath.

"It's not that she's mad—it's not that simple. Teenie is . . . was . . . Teenie and Jessie were best friends. Inseparable. When we were little, I thought they were sisters because they were just always together. After Jessie's mama left—" She stopped like maybe she was telling things she shouldn't.

"I know about all that; Jessie told me," I said. Hanna raised an eyebrow and glanced at Will, then kept going.

"After Jessie's mama left, she just ran wild. Teenie's mama, Lurene, was the only one who could get her to act halfway civilized. She and Teenie made sure Jessie was fed and stayed on her about showing up for lessons at least some of the time. Her daddy didn't really . . ."

"Her *daddy* didn't even deserve to be called that," Will practically spat. Hanna looked at him with that moony-eyed look she seemed to save just for Will.

"So anyway, Teenie was just a year older than Jessie, and all growing up, they were like two peas in a pod. But then about the time Teenie turned sixteen, things started to change." Will gave a rough little laugh, but Hanna pressed on. "Teenie started to get interested in . . . other things. She started paying more attention to how she looked, wanting to spend more time on her sewing, wanting to act grown-up. Normal stuff, but it wasn't like that for Jessie."

"Hell, it still ain't," Will interjected. "Jessie's still half-wild, and I don't see her settling down anytime soon." If I didn't know better, I would have sworn he was looking at me like that was a challenge. Just then, Ben and Nina came and sat down at the table.

"That's just because she wouldn't settle for you," Ben said as he slid into his seat. Nina nudged him roughly with her shoulder, and Hanna gave her brother a hurt look, but he just shrugged. "No sense pretending we don't all know that's true." Will looked like he was about to shoot fire out of that sunny face of his, but then he laughed.

"Yeah, well, maybe she won't grow up, but I have. That was a long time ago. I've moved on." He looked at Hanna then, and she gave him a big grateful smile. I guessed he noticed more than I thought.

"Why are we talking about Jessie?" Nina asked.

"She was here with Ami when we came in, but Will made her mad about Teenie and she left. We just went to see her this morning," Hanna said.

"*I* made her mad? Looked like it was you and her about to lock horns right over this table," Will said.

"Hanna was just telling me about how Jessie and Teenie used to be best friends, but I still don't really understand what's going on with them now," I said.

"I only got to the part where Teenie started acting more grown-up and Jessie didn't," said Hanna.

"Ah," Nina said, "well, it's pretty simple, really. Matthew came along, Teenie fell in love and got pregnant, mostly in that order, and Jessie was jealous. She felt like he stole Teenie from her and that Teenie was too young for all that. Then the pregnancy went wrong, the baby came way too early and didn't make it, and Teenie almost died. She needed Jessie then, and Jessie stepped up. She helped Lurene nurse Teenie back to health and got her through that awful grief. Lord, that girl was sad. Everybody was. Mama said having to take that little blue baby out of Teenie's arms was one of the hardest things she ever had to do." She froze suddenly, and I realized that everyone had gone still. I looked around and saw that they were all looking at Ben.

"Ben, I'm sorry. I wasn't thi—"

"It's fine," he cut her off. He looked around the table and said, "Jesus! Stop looking at me like that." I sucked in a breath; taking the Lord's name in vain was a sin, but no one else seemed shocked by it. Ben started methodically shoveling food into his mouth, and everyone looked away. I wanted to ask what any of this had to do with Ben, but I knew I couldn't. Not right then.

"Okay, that's enough of that," Will said. "Let's talk about something else. I was thinking this might be a good night for a swim." He looked around at the group like he'd just made a big announcement.

"Ooh, first night swim of the summer!" Hanna said. "I'm in!"

"Me too," said Nina. She looked at Ben, who seemed more relaxed now but was still focused on his plate. "Ben, wanna go swimming tonight?"

He shrugged. "I dunno, maybe," he said. But when he looked up and met her eyes, he smiled. "Yeah, probably." Her face lit up. *Hoo boy*, I thought. *Everybody around here is pairing up.*

"It's official," Will said. "First night swim of the summer, tonight, by the old dock. I'll tell Melissa."

"You'll come, won't you, Ami?" Hanna asked.

"Uh, I'm not . . . I don't really know how to swim, but I guess I can stay in the shallows," I said.

"Yeah, it's not deep where we go, and we've got some old tire tubes that make good floats. You'll love it!" Nina said. She was smiling at me, excited to bring me into the fun. It felt nice to be included like that, and I found myself returning her smile.

"Maybe you can get Jessie to come. If you can find her," Will said. He meant me. And just like that, whoosh! Red-hot face again. I suddenly felt like everyone was staring at me.

"Me?" I stammered. "I don't even—"

"Don't worry about Jessie," Hanna said, kicking Will under the table. "I'll find her. We'll see you back here at dinner and head down to the dock together, okay?"

"Yeah, okay," I replied. I tried to get that warm, friendly feeling back, but I felt flustered, and when I managed to drag my eyes up from the table, I caught Will giving me that curious look again. I hurried away to the quiet emptiness of my room. Being around people was still wonderful, but sometimes it wore me out. I took a quick, cool shower to rinse off the sweat and dirt from that morning's garden work and played my conversation with Jessie back in my head. I wondered if I would see her at dinner or the lake later. It was hard to believe this was the same day. I felt like more things could happen in an hour at Lake Point than ever happened in a week at Heavenly Shepherd. I suddenly felt like I needed to take a nap if I was going to get through dinner and night swimming with everyone, so that's exactly what I did.

Fifteen

There was no sign of Jessie at dinner, and Hanna wasn't there either until the rest of us had almost finished eating. We all looked at her expectantly, but she just shook her head. The rest of them told stories about other night swims from summers past, laughing about a time when Will got stuck knee-deep in the muddy lake bottom and didn't want to admit it until he finally had to ask for help or stay stuck there all night. I tried to laugh along, but their stories of growing up together always made me feel a little sad. Watching Melissa and Will rib each other, I couldn't help but wonder what it could have been like if my mama had stayed and had another baby. Hanna and Ben weren't as easy with each other, though, so I guessed that having a sibling could go different ways. When everyone was done eating, we all headed down to the lake together.

"You're gonna love this, Ami!" Melissa said, dropping back to walk beside me.

"Yeah? I've never done too much swimming, even in the daytime. I'm kinda nervous about tryin' to do it in the dark."

"Oh, don't worry, it's not real deep or anything. And we've got an hour or so before the sun sets, so that'll give you time to get your bearings," she said.

"Yeah, and no one's seen that gator in years." This was Will walking just ahead of us.

"Gator?" I asked shakily.

"Shut *up*, Will, gah!" Melissa laughed. "Don't listen to him, Ami. There's no gator. Those signs were just a joke."

"Signs?" I asked. "What signs?"

"Those." Ben pointed. We were drawing even with an old boat dock, the wood half-rotted along the waterline, and there beside it was an old hand-painted sign, faded and paint peeling. You could just make out the words BEWARE OF GATOR and a red circle with a line through it. It looked like there had been something inside the circle, but it was mostly gone now.

"Back when this place was a resort and campground, they wanted people to swim in the pool and stay out of the lake," Hanna said. "But no one has ever seen any sign of a gator as long as we've been alive. Trust me, I would *not* be gettin' in that water if there was any chance of bein' eaten by alligators!" I nodded and gave her a nervous little laugh, not wanting to seem chicken. There was a little log-cabin-looking shed near the dock, and Nina and Ben ran inside and came back out with their arms full of shriveled old black tire tubes. They tossed them on the ground, then Ben went back in for an old foot pump and started plumping the tubes up with air. As soon as the first one was done, Nina grabbed it and started running toward the water.

"Look, Ami!" she hollered before tossing the tube straight

off the end of the dock and then jumping on top of it. I was pretty sure that trick was what she wanted me to look at, but I was distracted by the fact that she was half-naked. She must have stripped off most of her clothes while I was watching the pumping, because she was down to a little strapped top like the one Jessie had worn that morning and her underpants. I looked around in shock to see if anyone else had noticed, only to see that the boys were wading in wearing nothing but shorts, and Hanna and Melissa were in pretty much the same getup as Nina. I stood frozen to the spot. Did they expect me to follow suit? I was still getting used to wearing shorts and short-sleeve shirts! They were all in the water by then, and they all turned to look at me expectantly. Will's chest was muscled and tanned, and Ben's was skinny but wiry. I felt my face turn beet red once again.

"Come on, Ami, don't be scared," Hanna called. "Look, it's not even deep!" She stood up to show that the water was only about waist-deep on her. Her top was a dark blue, practically black now that it was wet, but it clung to her breasts like a second skin. I felt my mouth go dry as I tried to look anywhere but at her chest.

"I, uh, it's not that," I muttered. "I'm not, uh, I don't think I'm dressed right." I was standing on the land end of the dock, and I looked down at my feet as I spoke. I tried to imagine taking my shorts off and having everyone see the high-waisted cotton underpants I wore. Was I wearing the ones with little faded blue flowers or the plain white ones that had been washed so many times they'd turned grayish? It didn't matter because those shorts were not coming off. Melissa waded around to the side of the dock to get closer to me.

"It's okay, Ami," she said in a quiet voice. "You can keep your shorts and everything on." She smiled up at me reassuringly.

I looked down at her sweet freckled face and thought about climbing down to wade in where she was. Then I looked toward the end of the dock, where everyone was off to one side in chest-deep water, watching me. I took a deep breath and blew it out slow, then I started running. I hit the end of the dock and launched myself as far as I could, angling away from the group. For just a second, I was flying, and I felt as free as I ever had in my life. Then I hit the water and sucked about half the dang lake up my nose when my feet slid out from under me on the muddy bottom. I came up coughing and sputtering, my hair sliding forward from its knot on the top of my head. I saw everyone's faces looking horrified, and that made me laugh. I laughed and coughed and blew lake water out of my nose, and then everyone else started laughing too. Once I could breathe again, I undid my hair and then went under, remembering to hold my nose this time, and came back up so the whole mess was slicked back from my face.

Nina handed me a tire and showed me how to sit on top of it so my bottom settled down into the hole in the center and I could lean back with my arms and legs draped over the tube. It started to feel kind of peaceful with all of us floating around the dock, watching the sun drop down toward the edge of the water. I noticed that Hanna had her foot on Will's tube so they wouldn't drift apart, and when Melissa hooked my tube the same way I felt grateful. We stayed like that until the sun touched the edge of the water and then, quicker than seemed possible, dropped below the edge of it. We were quiet, but it was a comfortable kind of quiet.

"When I was little, I thought the sun lived in a treehouse," I said. "I wonder what I would have thought if I'd seen it like this, setting into the lake every night."

"Why a treehouse?" Ben asked. His voice was closer to me than I expected, and I guess anytime Ben talked I was kind of surprised.

"Well," I said, "I don't rightly know. There were a lot of trees all around the compound where we lived, no big open spaces like this lake makes. It seemed like the trees caught the sun in their branches before it could drop too low in the sky. And Ruth, that's my grandma, she would tell me the sun was going to bed so I should too. I guess I imagined the sun going to bed in its own little house way up high in the trees since that was the last place I saw it go." I glanced sideways over at Ben, feeling a little silly and wondering why I'd felt the need to share that story. I hadn't even thought about the sun's treehouse in a long, long time. His face was in shadows now, but as far as I could tell, he wasn't laughing at me.

"Aw, I love that!" said Melissa. "When I was little, I thought that cats and dogs were the same animal, but cats were girls and dogs were boys." Will laughed and rolled his eyes, and she used the side of her hand to shoot water toward his face. He kicked his feet to splash her back but got Hanna just as much as his sister. Pretty soon, it was all-out war, with everyone kicking and splashing and slipping down under the water to stay "safe," which didn't make any sense at all but still felt like it did. Finally, the splashing and laughing died down, and we all dragged ourselves back up onto the dock and laid onto the warm boards to dry. It was full dark by then, with a sliver of moon and about a million stars giving the only light. I'd never seen so much of the night sky in one big piece like that, and it nearly took my breath away.

"Penny's gonna be so mad she missed this," Nina said. "I thought they'd be back by now, but surely they won't be more than another day or two."

"Who's Penny?" I asked dreamily, but I was thinking how it was a shame that Jessie was missing this too. I was a little glad she hadn't seen me snorting lake water up my nose and blowing it back out again, but mostly I wished she was there.

"She's my best friend," Nina said. "She's the only other girl my age around here, plus she's brown-skinned like me. Even though her mama is white." In my comfortable haze, I didn't understand what she meant at first, then shock settled over me. In my head, I heard Papa's voice saying *the mixing of the races is an abomination unto the Lord.* I started to react, but no one else seemed to think there was anything wrong, and of course they would have known about this their whole lives. I was glad for the darkness that hid my face, but I didn't know what to say. I could feel Nina beside me, waiting for me to carry on my side of the conversation.

"I hope they found some of the things on my list," Will said from the other end of the dock. "I need that stuff to get my lab set up." I felt suddenly thankful for Will's constant need to talk about himself.

"Will has been studying all the medical and science books we can find," Hanna said admiringly. "He says it's time we started making up for lost time and figuring out some of the old medicine we lost after the Break."

"Well, I hope they bring back some clothes or at least cloth," Melissa said. "I've, uh, grown out of most of my tops."

"More like *busted* out," Nina said, and all three girls started to laugh.

"Stop!" Melissa protested, but she was laughing too. "I can't help it. Mama says it's the curse of the Landry women."

"Must be nice," Nina said from beside me as she sat up and looked down at her own flattish chest. "My mama says she was a late bloomer, so I prob'ly will be too."

"Yeah, well, at least your clothes still fit," Melissa said.

"Ladies, you're embarrassing poor Ben over here," Will called.

"Mhm, *Ben*," Hanna said. I thought of Hanna standing waist-deep in the water in her wet top and felt suddenly, uncomfortably hot. I'd never thought much about my own breasts unless it was to try to imagine nursing a baby. And they definitely weren't anything Ruth or my aunts would have talked or joked about to me. Maybe Amber might've, if we'd been close like that. Thinking of my grandmother and aunts hearing this conversation sent a jolt of shame through me, and all the warmth and comfort I'd been feeling up and went in an instant. What was I doing here with a bunch of strange kids who thought it was fine to run around half-naked and joke about indecent things and didn't bat an eye at the thought of being friends with a half-white, half-brown girl whose mama had flouted the law of God? All those sermons I'd heard Papa preach about the temptations of the world, and yet here I sat, jumping in with both feet and barely a thought in my head.

I had to get out of there. Before I knew it, I was on my feet, stepping over Nina and off the land end of the dock onto the tall grass. I heard voices calling my name, asking where I was going, but I just called back that I had to go. I wondered if they could know my thoughts, and my face flamed up. But wasn't it them who should feel ashamed? Somehow it didn't feel like it, but that was confusing. Was I wrong to go along with their ways that went against everything I'd ever been taught, or was it wrong for me to judge them for living a kind of life that felt normal to them even though it was strange to me? *Let him who is without sin cast the first stone*, I remembered. I stopped in my tracks, suddenly wishing I could go back. But it was too late; the moment was broken. I would have to make up an excuse, say that I felt sick or something. *Lying is a sin*, said a voice in my head. *Sinner.* Who was I to judge anyone?

I trudged back to my room but couldn't sleep. Instead I tossed and turned on my lumpy mattress, feeling homesick for my own bed in my own little room at Heavenly Shepherd. Maybe I was lonely there and things weren't perfect, but at least they weren't confusing. I'd never had any reason to question my place or the things Papa and Ruth had taught me. But at Lake Point, *everything* was confusing. I don't know what I expected, but it wasn't this place or these people. The only two things I'd planned on were finding my mama, which I had but hadn't done, and finding a man I'd want to have a baby with, which most definitely had not happened. And why not? I had to admit, Will was pretty nice to look at, but for some reason, that didn't seem to have any effect on me, and besides, Hanna seemed to have those kinds of feelings for him. And then there was Ben, who was just fine, but he was so quiet, and again, I was pretty sure Nina had him claimed. Not that I was sad about it.

I tried to think about the other men I'd seen around the place. They all seemed so much older, even though some of them looked like they might only be in their early twenties. But that was older, wasn't it? They were nowhere near as old as Zeke Johnson, and my grandparents were ready to match me up with him. That thought was enough to turn my stomach and send me tossing and turning almost clear out of the bed. What was I going to do?

I flipped over onto my back and stared up at the ceiling in the dark. And then my thoughts went to the same place they seemed to go all the time lately: to Jessie. I played back over that first night, the way her hair hung down shiny and black by the light of the fire. I could hear her singing almost as clear as if she'd been in the room, her voice that could carry so much sorrow, then danger, then laughter.

I flopped over onto my stomach and thought about our morning working in the gardens, just that same day, which seemed impossible. I could see her standing in the sunlight, dangling that hat from her finger, so much skin showing warm and golden in the heat. I saw the straps of that thing she called a shirt and couldn't help but think of Hanna wearing almost the same thing, standing in the lake. It wasn't hard to imagine Jessie's top wet and clinging like that. But *why* was I imagining that?

Suddenly the heat in the room was suffocating, and I knew I was never going to fall asleep. I wished I could go back and jump in the lake, let it wash away all these thoughts of Jessie, then lie back under the stars and watch them until my eyes closed on their own. If I were back home, I would have taken my blanket roll and slept out in the woods, but there were too many people here, and these weren't my woods. I settled for the next best thing, standing under a cool shower. I should have washed the lake water out of my hair anyway, and I set myself the task of untangling it with the slippery soap and my fingers. By the time it was clean and rinsed, I felt cooler inside and out. I took the tangled sheets off my bed, shook them out, and put them back on smooth and straight. Feeling like my world was at least a little more orderly, I opened my window to let in the breeze, then finally fell asleep.

Sixteen

A long, low, rumble woke me that next morning, thunder so deep it seemed to rattle my bones. Rain was blowing into the open window, and I hurried over to shut it. "So much for garden work this morning," I said out loud. I didn't talk to myself as much as I used to now that I had real friends to talk to, but old habits were hard to break. As much as I hated to admit it, I'd been hoping Jessie would be assigned to garden beds again today, even though I knew the regular rotations only lasted a day. *Would she switch with someone to see me?* I wondered, and then, *Why would she do that?* I had to get out of that room! I got myself dressed and wandered downstairs to breakfast.

It was early, and there weren't many people eating yet. I guessed the rain gave folks a welcome excuse to sleep late, or at least lie around in bed longer than they usually could. I ate by myself and didn't mind it. I picked a seat close to the big windows across the back of the room and watched the rain beat against the glass. The sky was dark, and I could see trees bending and blowing in the wind, but that somehow made it feel even more safe and cozy to be inside with a warm bowl of oats sprinkled with nuts and berries. I took my time eating and watching the rain, and when it didn't let up, I decided to check out the library Jessie had told me about. I needed something to read if I was going to be stuck inside all day, and I was curious about all those other books she had mentioned reading in their little school.

I walked around until I found where the library had been set up in a row of smaller rooms along one side of the big window room. The entrance was just a little nook with a desk and rows of old wooden cabinets full of little tiny drawers, and there was a woman there.

"I—Is this the library?" I asked, even though I knew dang well the sign I'd just passed said LIBRARY in big ol' letters. I just didn't know what else to say.

"It sure is," the woman said kindly, "and I'm the librarian. You can call me Miss Jean." I nodded, feeling a little more comfortable. There was something about her that made me feel like I was welcome to be there, and I realized that was the opposite of what I'd expected for some reason.

"Yes, ma'am," I said. "I've heard of you. From the other kids, you know." I mumbled that last part, trailing off. I wasn't getting any better at talking to new people.

"Well," she said, "it's good to know my fame precedes me!" She winked at me like I was in on the joke. "Why don't I give you a little tour; would you like that?" I nodded and she started off through a doorway behind her.

"These rooms were designed for meetings back when business people used to come here for things like that. They were all connected to each other with doorways, but we took the doors out and put in shelves, and *voilà*, the library was born!" I stopped and stared. Someone had used plain boards to build in shelves from floor to ceiling and corner to corner on every wall in each of the rooms, and on all those shelves were books! So many more books than I could have ever imagined, right there for anyone to borrow and read.

"Now this first room is the children's section," she said, stopping so I could take it in. The room was small but cozy. There was a rag rug on the floor, bright strips of colored cloth braided together into a big oval. I'd never imagined there could be a whole room of books just for children. I walked over to get a better look at one shelf. Most of these books were wide and flat, their spines looking worse for wear but still holding together. I slid one out, and it was full of colorful pictures with just a few words on each page. It made me sad to know that these books had existed when I was little but that I never saw them or got to read them then.

The next room was full of "young adult" books, which Miss Jean said meant teenagers like me but that a lot of adults liked them, too, because they were fun to read. In that room and the room labeled ADULT FICTION, there were smaller signs over each section that said things like FANTASY, SCIENCE FICTION, ROMANCE, REALISTIC FICTION, MYSTERY, and THRILLER. Miss Jean talked as we walked, explaining what each label meant and telling me examples like "This will be your wizards and dragons and vampires and such." I still didn't understand a lot of that, but I tried not to ask too many questions.

Then there were rooms with labels like HISTORY, SCIENCE, PSYCHOLOGY, MYTHOLOGY, and RELIGION above the shelves. It seemed funny to me that the religion section could have any books besides just the Bible, but Miss Jean said those shelves were full of books about how different people understood the Bible, which I guess I had never thought about before, and others with titles like *Major World Religions*, which was also a new idea to me, that there could be more than just the one I knew. I decided I would spend a lot of time in that room, starting as soon as the tour was over.

When we came to the last room, I saw a sign over the door that said ARTIFACTS, and Miss Jean walked in ahead of me.

"Well, hey, Jessie. I didn't even realize you were back here. You must've snuck right by me!" she said, wagging a finger but not seeming at all bothered or even surprised to see Jessie there. I wasn't that surprised either, to tell the truth, and if I'm really telling it, then I guess I had hoped she would be there. "I was just givin' our visitor the tour. Have y'all met?" She stepped out of the way so Jessie could see me. She did look surprised but in a good way. She flashed me her big, pretty smile.

"Why, yes, ma'am, we have. Hey, Ami."

"Oh good!" Miss Jean said. "Well, I've got books to shelve, but you couldn't get a better guide to this room than Jessie. She's in here more than anybody." I was still behind her, blocking the doorway, so she stepped around me and was gone. Then it was just the two of us.

"Hey yourself," I said back. I took another step into the room and looked around. When we came in, she was sitting on the floor in the corner, looking at something that looked a little like the children's books but even flatter and more square. After Miss Jean left, she stood up and took a step toward me but then stopped and looked down at the floor. We both stood there not knowing what to say, listening to the sound of rain hitting the roof high above our heads. Then there was a flash of lightning, and thunder boomed quick behind it. We both jumped a little and then laughed.

"Hey, listen, I wanted to say I'm sorry," she said.

"About what?" I asked, confused. Far as I could remember, Jessie hadn't done anything she needed to apologize to me for. She looked up at my face like she was trying to tell if I was serious.

"You know, about yesterday. I shouldn't have run out like that. We were having a good time, least I thought we were, and you told me all about your family and everything. It was just . . . that stuff Hanna was sayin' made me so mad, and I . . ." She crossed her arms over her chest and looked up at the ceiling, and it looked like she was about to get mad all over again.

"Yeah, I could tell," I said, stepping closer and dipping my head to get her to meet my eyes. She looked back at me and grinned. "But that wasn't nothing you need to apologize to me for. That's between you and them. We don't need to get into all that again right now." The truth was, I was curious, but Ruth always said curiosity killed the cat, and right then I wanted to get back to how things had been between us yesterday a lot more than I wanted to hear about Teenie and her baby. That could wait. She looked relieved, and I took that as a sign that I was headed in the right direction.

"What is all this stuff, anyway?" I asked, looking around the room again. "Miss Jean said you would be my guide. Better not make a liar out of her."

"Oh, better not," Jessie said with pretend seriousness. She made her voice sound a lot like Miss Jean's. "Now, this room has the records and record players, along with old electronic things that don't work anymore. You can see these little signs that say what they are." We walked around the room, picking up folded cards that said funny names like COMPUTER, SMARTPHONE, TABLET, and GAME CONSOLE.

"The computer can even turn on if it's plugged in, but it don't do much besides light up blue and show a few words and pictures scattered around the screen," Jessie said. "Miss Jean thinks it's a waste of solar power, so she keeps it unplugged most of the time. The record players are unplugged, too, but she lets me plug one in whenever I want." I could see that it was those record players that kept Jessie coming back to the artifacts room.

"This is the best part!" she said, sounding like herself again. She was bouncing up and down on her toes as she tried to decide what to play first. I didn't understand how the record player worked or how music could come out of those flat, shiny black circles.

"I don't exactly understand it either," Jessie admitted, "but it's something to do with these grooves, see?" She held a record out toward me and I stepped closer, suddenly aware of the little bit of space still between us. "They just look like little lines going around to us, but Miss Evelyn, that's Jean's sister, she says if we could shrink down to the size of ants and walk around inside the lines, we'd see a lot of bumps and stuff, and somehow that's what holds the music. Then the needle on the record player reads those bumps, and the speaker plays the music. It's science." I still didn't understand, but she said that luckily I didn't have to understand for it to work. Jessie finally decided on a record and showed me the cover. It was all bright blue-and-orangey background with a picture of five women wearing nothing but towels wrapped around their bodies and another on their heads. Something white covered their faces except for their eyes. Nothing about the image made sense to me, but I kind of liked it for some reason.

"Okay, this isn't an old one like the songs I sang the other night. I mean, it's old, but not old-old like the ballads. This is an all-girl band from the 1980s, and it's something called rock music. Get ready to rock, Ami! I promise you have never heard anything like this." She slid the record out of the flat cardboard cover, set it carefully on the player, and gently dropped the needle into the outer groove. Instantly sound was raining down over me. I don't know what I was expecting, but it wasn't that flood of so many different sounds all stacked and piled on top of one another. There was something that sounded a little like Jessie's guitar but lower and more solid, and it was playing the same seven notes repeatedly and really fast. There was another sound like someone hitting something with a stick that reminded me of the way we had all kept time by clapping during "Good and Greasy." And then someone started singing, maybe one of the women wrapped in a towel on the record cover, and her voice sounded kind of sped up and sharp but also happy, and she sang about people walking down the street in time because *they got the beat.*

At first, Jessie just watched me and laughed at my stunned reaction, but after a few seconds, she grabbed my hands and started jumping up and down, dancing me around the room. I couldn't help but follow her lead. It was like the music got inside me and made my body move. I felt like I would burst with the energy of it all. Then that song ended, and the next one was slower. It reminded me a little of the sad ballads, but Jessie picked the arm of the player up and over to the side, then replaced that record with another one that had a laughing brown-skinned man on the cover. This one had us dancing again even though I was puzzled by the man proclaiming that he had soul and was super bad. Didn't everyone have a soul, and wasn't being bad, well, bad? I couldn't think about it too hard, though, because Jessie had let go of my hands and was doing a funny shuffling dance all around me, swinging her hips and turning in circles. Without her lead, I just stood and kind of swayed in time to the music, but my eyes followed her everywhere.

She went on playing songs, sometimes letting one record play through several songs, sometimes changing them after just one song. Everything she played was fast and rhythmic, and we kept on dancing. There was something called jazz, and some of it was slow, but she played me swingy songs on a record by a man named Oliver Pleasant, who looked old on the cover but sounded young. Finally, we were too tired to keep it up, and she chose a record with a plain white cover that folded out wide because there were two records inside instead of just one. She studied the list of songs carefully and set the needle somewhere near the middle of one of the black discs, and then she sat down on the floor and patted the space beside her. The song that came out was as simple and spare as the others had been complicated and busy, just a quiet guitar and one voice singing about a blackbird flying away on broken wings. It made me think about my flight from Heavenly Shepherd—in the dead of night, just like the song said. Had I been waiting for that moment all my life, and I just hadn't known it? Or was it this moment, here in the library at Lake Point with Jessie, that I'd been waiting for? The answer felt like yes. I knew that I had never felt more awake and alive than I did in that moment.

Jessie seemed to know what I was thinking, because she reached over into the small space between us and took my hand. She didn't squeeze it or even look at me when she did it, almost like she didn't even know she was doing it. Her hand in mine felt like the most natural thing in the world. We were connected,

Jessie and me, in ways I still couldn't understand but that I knew were real and true, so holding her hand just seemed to confirm that connection in a physical way. I searched my mind for another connection like ours but couldn't find it. Even though we'd just met a few days ago, I felt like I had known her for a long time. I trusted her enough to tell her the whole story of why I was there, and she repaid my trust by listening and responding in just the way that I needed.

When that song ended, Jessie pulled away just enough to kneel by the player and jump the needle forward to the groove closest to the end of the record. It was another quiet, slow song, and the man singing was telling someone named Julia that his words were meaningless, but they were just for her because she's an ocean child with seashell eyes and floating sky hair. I figured he was right about the meaningless part because I couldn't picture the girl he was describing at all, but I still liked the song. After that, she took that record off and put it back in its case, then scanned the shelves thoughtfully, looking for something.

"*Yesss*, here it is," she said mostly to herself. The record she held was mostly black, with a photograph of a brown-skinned woman near the bottom. She had some kind of paint around her eyes that made them look big and pointy at the edges. I saw that her name was Nina, just like the Nina here at Lake Point. I wondered if her mother named her after the singer. Jessie put the record on, then set the needle down carefully and sat back down in her place next to me.

This song started out with just the woman's voice, which was richer and deeper than the woman's on the first song we listened to. She sang slow and deliberate about birds in the sky knowing how she feels because it's a new day for her. Then the music came in behind her, not guitars but something harder and different-sounding, dropping deep notes that made me picture stair steps going down. Her words were about feeling free and starting new, but something about the way she sang them and the music behind made me think that freedom was being said like a threat to someone who didn't want her to have it. It was my favorite of all the songs we'd listened to, and I closed my eyes to hear it better. At the end, the woman sang a bunch of nonsense sounds strung together, but somehow they made sense as part of the song.

Finally, I opened my eyes and saw that Jessie had scooted around so she was facing me. We both sat with legs crisscrossed and folded onto themselves, and our knees were as close as they could be without touching. I was self-conscious realizing she had been watching me while I was listening so intently, and I felt the red-hot flush creep up my neck and over my face. I gave an embarrassed little laugh and looked down at my lap, but when I looked up again she was still watching me.

"Ami," she said, but no words followed. I felt overwhelmed by the music and the newness of everything in this place, but also, I couldn't deny it anymore, by Jessie and the closeness of her body to mine. Our eyes were locked onto each other, and it almost felt like some thread ran between us that was pulling us in closer to each other until finally there was no way to stop it and our lips touched. It was a simple kiss, just stillness and pressure, but there had never been anything warmer or softer than Jessie's lips on mine. *All my life*, I thought, *I was only waiting for this moment to arrive.* And that thought lasted exactly as long as the kiss did, until Jessie pulled away just a little and I opened my eyes and saw her beautiful face so close to mine, and I panicked.

Seventeen

Ami?" Just my name again but this time loaded with questions, and before I knew it, I was up and running. I could hear her calling after me, but I didn't look back or slow down. I had to cross the width of the big room, but luckily the library rooms were up near the front door, so there was no one in my path. I kept running down the hallways and up the stairs until I finally reached my room. Once I was inside, I leaned back against the door like I expected someone to come break it down. Was I expecting Jessie to follow me? Was I hoping she would? My heart was pounding from running as much as it was from panic, and I was breathing hard. I slid down to sit on the floor while I waited for my body to calm down and get back to normal. My mind would not stop racing, though.

What had I done? I wasn't sure if I was more upset that I'd kissed Jessie or that I had run away. Why did I kiss Jessie? Or did she kiss me, or was it both of us at the same time? Who had ever heard of such a thing? Who had ever *done* such a thing? I was supposed to be here looking for a partner, a *husband*, so that I could be the godly woman Ruth raised me to be! I needed a husband if I ever wanted to be able to go home again. *If I ever wanted to go home again.* Maybe that was the real question, the real reason I felt so scared and lost. How much had changed in just a few days? When I stopped believing my mother could help me and that new Ami was born, what happened to the old Ami? Was she still me? Did I want to be that old Ami anymore?

Running away and getting to Lake Point all by myself was the beginning. Being on my own and taking care of myself, making my own choices about the best way to get myself where I needed to be, had shown me how strong I really was. I never would have thought I was capable of any of that, but I was. And then being here, meeting all these new people, finding kids my own age who could become friends, seeing how much bigger the world was than I had ever known—it was all just so big! And it all made Heavenly Shepherd look mighty small. How could I fit myself back into that little closed-up life?

And then there was Jessie. Had I really only spent a few hours with her? That day in the garden, just then in the library, and the other night around the fire—that was it. But in the spaces in between, I'd thought about her almost constantly. How could I feel the way I felt about her after such a short time? I didn't even *understand* how I felt about her, but I did know that it was strong and would only get stronger.

Without meaning to, I thought about the kiss. When I closed my eyes, I could still feel her soft lips on mine. I could still see her eyes opening so close to mine and hear the way she asked my name like a question, and I did not feel like I wanted to run away from her at all. Even though my mind said that I should and that kissing her was wrong, my heart and my body wanted to get that close to her again as soon as I could. But I *had* run away from her, and I was afraid she'd be mad or worse, hurt. Maybe this was as confusing for her as it was for me. I had to go back.

When I got back to the library, though, she was gone. I didn't know how much time had passed, but I didn't think it had been long enough for her to get very far. I realized that I wasn't sure exactly where Jessie lived, so I couldn't go to her room. The rain had stopped sometime during all the music, so I figured she might have gone outside. On a hunch, I crossed the big room to get out to the patio and walk down toward the lake, but I didn't see her. Instead I saw Will, and before I could turn around and pretend I hadn't, he saw me.

"Hey, Ami. Looking for somebody?" He smirked as if he already knew the answer to that question, but how could he?

I reminded myself that no one knew what had happened between Jessie and me, though my cheeks burned at the thought. Will watched my face turn red and laughed.

"Nope, just taking a walk. What about you?" I refused to let him get me flustered.

"Just takin' a walk, seein' if that storm did any damage. Want to walk with me?" I didn't know why I always felt kind of on edge with Will, but I did. It was still strange for me to be around any other kids my age, but it seemed easier with the girls. A little voice in my head was whispering that Will was a boy my age, a potential mate, and that I should try to get to know him. Especially after what happened with Jessie, it felt important for me to push forward in the search for someone I could choose. Someone who was a boy. What did I really know about him and Hanna, after all?

"Okay," I said simply. He looked surprised but then happy.

"Have you been around to the cabin side yet?" he asked. I

shook my head no, and he nodded like he thought so. "There are the cottages right around the lake, which are newer than the cabins but, you know, still old. They were designed to be a little more fancy and nice when the resort was trying to get more rich folks to come here. But they're also smaller. We live in one of the bigger cabins since there's four of us. But we'll pass the cottages on our way. I want to show you something." I glanced over to see if I should be worried about the *something* he wanted to show me, but I couldn't judge his expression. Will, the golden boy. He always seemed so sure of himself, of his *rightness*. I wondered what that was like.

We followed the path around the opposite side of the lake from where the gardens were, and soon we came upon a long row of cute little cottages. Each one had a peach tree in front of it, loaded with ripening fruit. Most of the peaches were still green yet, but soon they would be bursting with sweetness and juice. My mouth watered a little just thinking about it. I loved peaches.

"These are Miss Hillie's babies. Sam helps her, but it's Hillie who gives the orders. Did you know a peach tree can only bear fruit for about twelve years? They grow new ones from the pits in a little nursery over by the greenhouses so they can keep the line going. By the time these stop producing, there'll be new ones to take their place."

"Kind of like people, I guess. Or like people used to be," I said. "We have some peach trees back home, but they grow wild. Nobody takes them down when they stop producing, so they just get old and gnarled until they finally die. But they drop more fruit on the ground than we can gather, so new trees spring up on their own anyway." We just stood there, thoughtful, looking at the trees loaded with fruit.

"I guess the government thought they could fix things by cultivating us like these trees," Will said, "but it didn't work like that. People ain't trees; I guess they had to learn that the hard way. But it looks like we're more like those wild ones of yours, coming back anyway. At least some of us." It was easier for me to talk to Will when we didn't have to look at each other. We looked at the trees.

"My papa . . . my grandfather told me that there used to be chemical companies that messed with the seeds of different crops so they couldn't reproduce," I said. "They wanted all the farmers to have to buy seeds instead of saving them from one year to the next the way they had always done. He figured that might have had something to do with why we stopped being able to have babies. Like the chemicals worked too much or something, maybe. But then he would say the barrenness was God's judgment on us, so I'm not sure if that meant God made the chemical companies mess with the food or what. I tried to ask him, but he would just say the Lord works in mysterious ways and ours is not to reason why. He liked to say that a lot." I let my voice trail off. How had I ended up rambling about Papa Solomon and God from a conversation about peach trees?

Will barked out a laugh. "You don't still believe all that, do you?" Now he did turn and look at me. "About God making everything happen like some big puppet master in the sky? You know that's just a story, right?" This was so shocking to me that I thought I must be misunderstanding what he was saying. The look on my face must have said as much, because he shook his head and laughed again. "Ami, God's not any more real than the C-PAF men. That's just a story people made up a long, long time ago to try to figure things out. Didn't you ever read about the evolution of species or how the universe was really formed?

Scientists figured most of it out a long time ago. They went into space, and they sent satellites and telescopes up there to take pictures and measure things. The universe is infinite! It goes on and on with no end. The earth is just one of billions of planets, just like the sun is just one of billions of stars with their own solar systems. People used to claim that God made us special, but by the time the Break happened, hardly anyone believed that anymore."

"Then why are there all those books in the library here about world religions and understanding the Bible? And what about the Bible, do you think it's all just lies?" I felt light-headed.

"Well," he said, kicking at the dirt, "of course there are hold-outs. Some people can't handle the idea that we're on our own and it's all up to us. And, you know, religion was a big part of the history of the world. We can't really understand history or art or music or anything without understanding the people who made all that stuff happen and what all they believed in. Religion is still something people can study just like we study history or science, but that don't mean we have to believe in it. Shoot, the more you learn about religion, the more you start to see that hardly anybody ever agreed on anything about it from the very first. Most of the wars that were ever fought in this world were about religion; did you know that? People used to kill each other to try to prove they understood God better than the other guy, if you can believe it." I could believe it. Papa Solomon loved the Old Testament stories, which were full of the word *slew*.

"But still," I said, "you don't really *know* that God isn't real, right? That's just what you think." I felt defensive and wrong-footed. I wished I had studied all that stuff Will knew about science and space and that other thing he'd said about "species." How could I argue with him when I didn't know what he knew?

Papa and Ruth had tried to keep my faith strong by hiding things from me, but all that ended up doing was making me feel doubtful and weak. I wanted to go back to the library right that minute and start reading all those books on the shelves. I needed more information. Until then, I needed to change the subject.

"You said these trees are Miss Hillie's babies. Is that because she couldn't have any real babies of her own, or did she have some and they're just grown up now?" Will gave me a confused look and then laughed.

"Well, I don't know, Ami. I reckon Hillie never knew if she was able or not, seeing as how Sam couldn't exactly get her pregnant." He raised one eyebrow and watched my face like he wasn't sure how I would react. Mostly I felt like I was missing something.

"What?" I said stupidly. "Sam?"

"Sam and Hillie are married. We just threw them a big thirtieth anniversary party a few months ago. Far as I know, neither one of them ever tried out being with a man. They fell in love pretty young." Now it was my turn to laugh. I was sure Will was pulling my leg.

"Riiight," I said. "Sam and Hillie are married. Are you and Ben married too? No, I know, you and Melissa are getting married, since anybody can marry anybody! I think I'll marry that peach tree right there!" I realized I was moving around a lot, like I do when I get agitated, but Will was just standing still, watching me with that eyebrow cocked. He didn't look so amused anymore.

"Ami, do you really not think that Sam and Hillie can be married? Gay people have been gettin' married for, hell, at least a hundred years. And before that, really, it just might not've been strictly legal. Where is it you come from, Ami Miles?" But

I couldn't answer him. My mind was a whirl, and I had to sit down right there where I stood.

"But," I asked, my mind grasping at one of the million thoughts that were flying around in there, "but *why*? Why would they want to do that? I thought the whole point of getting married was to try to have babies."

Will sat down next to me. We were looking out at the lake now. I couldn't have this kind of talk with him looking right at me. "Now who in the world told you that? That's the kind of backward thinkin' that made people give up on life during the Break, Ami."

"But people gave up because babies are the whole point!" I said. "There was nothing left for them to live for . . ."

"They ain't, though," he said. "Not everybody chose to have them even back when they could, you know? But some gay couples did adopt." This sounded like some of the things Ruth had hinted at, about people not wanting to follow the natural way and follow God's plan, and not wanting to keep some of the babies they had. It was still hard for me to wrap my mind around. I wasn't ready to ask Will about the mechanics of it all, though.

"*Gay*, that means women who love other women and . . . men too?" Out of the hornet's nest of thoughts in my head, one little thought was breaking free and flying straight toward my heart: There was a word for what had happened, was happening, between Jessie and me. It was a thing that was done. Miss Hillie and Sam were not sisters; they were a couple, and they had once been young like Jessie and me. They had fallen in love and gotten married. And other people like them had been doing the same thing for *a hundred years*. And even before that, maybe not out in the open, but in secret. Probably ashamed and scared like I had felt just a few hours before, after that kiss. Ruth had known about this; I was sure of it now. My family had kept secrets from me about something as big as this.

"Well, not everybody fits into neat categories like men and women, but—" he started.

"Thanks, Will. I gotta go," I said, jumping up and heading back the way we'd come. He called after me, but I just waved and said I'd see him later. I couldn't take any more talk just then. I needed to think, but I needed *not* to think too. This was all too much, and I needed a break from it. I made for the cool quiet of the woods on the other side of the lake. I had to round the point that curved in front of the lodge, but no one was down that close to the water, and I kept my head down and tried to look unwelcoming to company. Soon I was on the path, under the green-lit canopy of leaves and branches. I forced myself to slow my footsteps. I realized I was breathing heavy and fast, so I took a few slow, deep breaths. Slowing my mind was a lot harder.

All those talks about the way of things, about finding a partner and carrying out God's plan and hopefully making a baby, and not once, *not once* had Ruth ever mentioned that sometimes it happens in a different way. Not once had she ever told me that those feelings I was supposed to feel for a man might end up being for a woman instead. I guess if I had grown up in a more normal way, around other kids my own age, I would have figured it out on my own. My only ideas about courting had come from Laura Ingalls and her Almanzo. No wonder those were the only books Ruth let me read. There must be books with gay love stories all over the place. Everybody knew about this but me! There was so much I didn't know, and I felt my foundations cracking. Papa Solomon loved to preach about how the man who has faith builds his house on a rock and everything else was shifting sand, but what happened when it was faith itself that was built on sand? I needed a rock to carry me through all this, not half-truths and secrets and outright lies!

My footsteps had sped up again to match my racing thoughts, and soon I was coming out of the woods to the place where I could see the gardens off in the middle distance. There were the shapes of Hillie and Sam. They were not like any of the other women I knew, but they were somehow like each other, and that had made me think they were sisters. But now that I knew, I could see it; the easy way they had together, the way they barely needed more than a nod or gesture to know what the other meant. I wondered if they both wore their hair short because it was cooler and easier for the hot outdoor work they did or if they just didn't care about any of that stuff at all. What had Will said right before I left? *Not everyone fits into neat categories.* I wished I could ask them, but I felt too shy and afraid. What if I said the wrong thing? What I needed was information, and I thought I knew where I could get it.

Eighteen

When I got to the library, I saw a few people reading in some of the rooms, but I didn't see Miss Jean. Jessie wasn't there either, and even though I knew we needed to talk, I was a little bit relieved. I needed time to figure out what I wanted to say to her, and I needed to understand some things better. I found the religion section again and read the titles, wondering at how many books there were. Each one of those books showed that there was a person who had spent enough time thinking about this stuff to at least feel like they had figured a little piece of it out. They must have studied a lot of these other books before they felt ready to write their own. I had never really thought about the idea that people might live their lives that way, studying and thinking over ideas until they had something that seemed new enough to want to write it down for other people to read.

"Hello?" I turned around to see a woman standing behind me. I figured she must be Miss Jean's sister, Evelyn. It was hard for me to guess her age because her dark curly hair hung loose past her shoulders like a girl's, but it was sprinkled with gray. She had only a few lines at the corners of her eyes, and somehow I knew that smiling had made them.

"You must be the new girl Jessie told me about. I'm Evi. My sister and I are the librarians here." *Jessie talked to her about me?* The thought made me smile, but I needed to focus.

"I'm Ami." I wasn't sure what else to say, but Evi seemed willing to wait. She looked at me expectantly, then smiled as the wait stretched into an uncomfortable silence. Finally, she decided to take the lead.

"Well, Ami, is there something I can help you with? I see you're in the religion section. Is there something specific you want to look up?" She smiled.

"I . . . well, uh, I'm not sure. I just, I was talking to Will? And he said, well, he told me that . . . some things that were . . . different. From what I was taught." I looked at the floor, my cheeks burning. I was still bad at talking to people. Evi probably thought I was some kind of fool.

"Ah, I see. Will!" She gave a low little laugh. "Yes, he has *a lot* of opinions about these things. And I'm guessing that maybe where you come from, there was only one opinion. Am I right?" I looked up and saw her friendly smile, and I burst into tears. *Don't be nice to me!* I thought, but I didn't say it. I needed my anger as something hard to push against. I wished the earth would open up and swallow me whole.

"Oh boy, okay, hey, Ami? It's okay. Here, let's go over here and sit down for a minute. It's going to be all right." She led me through a doorway into a nook near some windows that contained a few squishy-looking chairs, handed me a clean hand-kerchief out of her pocket, and told me she'd be right back. I sat there trying to get ahold of myself, but the embarrassment just piled on top of everything else and made me feel even worse. I couldn't stop crying. Pretty soon, she came back with two cups of hot tea and a plate of butter cookies.

"I know a nice cup of tea can't fix every problem, but it sure never makes one worse, does it?" The tea was milky and sweet, and I did feel a little better after a couple of sips. We never drank it that way back home, but I liked it.

"That's honey from my bees making it sweet. It's all the clover around here that keeps the bees so happy." She watched approvingly as I took a bite out of one of the cookies and made an involuntary *mmm* sound. "That's right, you eat up. I just baked those last night. Baking relaxes me, and it gives me something to do when I can't sleep. I'm a little bit of a night owl, myself. How about you?"

"Me? Um . . . I guess not too much. I like to get up real early before everyone else. That way I can get my chores done before the heat of the day sets in, too. I guess it's cooler at night for baking, though?" She smiled and nodded.

"That's right. Doesn't heat up the house as much. So, who is 'everybody else' back at home?" Something about Evi made me feel comfortable, and before I knew it, I was telling her everything. She reacted to the story of my family and Zeke Johnson about the same way that Jessie had. When I told her about waiting for my mother, I saw a look pass over her face like pieces fitting together, and she frowned. And then I told her about Jessie and the kiss, even though I felt my face burning and couldn't look at her while I said the words. I told her about how Will explained about gay people and told me about Hillie and Sam, and how that made me feel a little better but also a lot worse in some ways because it just made the whole mess even more complicated. And then about what he said about God just being a story that people had outgrown and how I didn't know about any of the science and history things he talked about.

"And you think that maybe if you could figure that part out, then you would know what you should do?" I nodded, feeling miserable again and looking down into my empty cup.

"Did you know that some people used to think that looking at the tea leaves after you drank a cup of tea could tell the future?" she asked. I shook my head no. "Sounds kind of silly, doesn't it? Other people tried using a special deck of cards called the tarot or throwing different versions of dice or bones or sticks. I tend to think of all those different things as prayer. It's all just asking, isn't it? For answers, for guidance, for help deciding what to do?"

"I guess that makes sense. But then, how can we ever know which is the right way? Is the answer in some of these books?"

She gave me a sad little smile and shook her head slowly. "I wish it were that simple, Ami. The truth is, we really *can't* know, not for sure. Of course, I think it's wonderful to read about the different ideas and religions and ways that people have come up with all over the world since the beginning of time. I've done quite a bit of that myself, as you can imagine. But after all that, I think what I've decided is that it must not matter what we believe. If we can't know the truth, how can that be our fault? Maybe God is real and maybe He's not, but I have to think that if He is, or if *She* is, because that's a possibility too, you know, then such a God wouldn't hold a little thing like being wrong against us poor, confused human beings."

"But then . . . what's the point? If it doesn't matter what I do, then what's to keep me from just doing whatever I want?"

"Well, what if you did? Why would that be a bad thing?" Her grin was a little mischievous now.

"Well, what if I wanted to do bad things? Why should I stop myself, if it's not because God will punish me?"

"Is that the only reason you don't do bad things to people now? Are you thinking about conking me over the head right now and stealing my books?"

"Well . . . no. But, but what if I was?" I felt like I needed to get up and pace, but I made myself sit still.

"Well, then I guess I'd be in trouble. But mostly, I think people don't really need to be threatened with punishment or bribed with rewards to behave reasonably well. And even having those threats and bribes has never really kept the truly bad people from doing their bad things, has it? Maybe we just like feeling like we have some control in spite of all evidence to the contrary. And then, plenty of people who didn't believe in all that stuff have done wonderful, beautiful things."

"So how am I supposed to know if I'm doing what I'm sup-posed to do and choosing what I'm supposed to choose?" I asked. I felt more frustrated and confused than ever. I wished that someone could just tell me the right answers to all of my questions.

"Maybe the real question is this: Why do you think there is something you're *supposed* to do or choose? *Supposed to* according to what? If there's some big divine plan laid out for you, Ami, then do you really have any choices to make?" She waited a few seconds to let that sink in. "What if there is no *supposed to*? What if we all just have to live our lives and make our choices and make the best of wherever those choices take us? Would that be so terrible?"

"But what if I make a mistake? What if I choose wrong?"

"What if you do, Ami?" She smiled and shook her head. "Do you really think anyone has ever made it all the way through life without making a mistake? Mistakes are in the eye of the beholder, if you ask me. Sometimes we make choices and things don't work out; that's true. And then do you know what happens? We just move on. We survive. There are plenty of people here at Lake Point who could tell you some stories about surviving if you need proof. Sometimes it's other people's bad choices we have to survive. Your friend Jessie knows something about that. And based on what you told me about your family, you know something about that yourself. It's just that you haven't come out on the other side of it yet. You still don't *know* that you've survived." I didn't know what to say to that, so I just sat and thought about it.

"You know, I do have a book for you, Ami, but it's not what you came looking for. Let me go get it." I ate another cookie and let my eyes wander to the window, where I could see what was left of that morning's rain dripping from the trees. The sun had come all the way out now, and the world looked washed and bright. I felt like my brain was shutting down from having too many things to figure out, and it felt good to focus on the world outside. Pretty soon, Evi was back, holding one of the flat, wide children's books I'd noticed on my first visit. Instead of being bright and colorful, though, this one was mostly brown like old paper bags and boxes.

"*Christina Katerina and the Box*," she said, looking at the cover lovingly. "This was always my favorite. You know, mine and Jean's mama was the librarian before us, and her mama before her. I grew up in this library. This is the first book I can remember sitting and reading to myself. I must have read it hundreds of times. Sometimes I wonder if it didn't have a bigger influence on me than any of these other big grown-up books." She handed the book to me. "You can't take it out of the library, but why don't you sit here and read it? I think you'll enjoy it, and that might be just what the doctor ordered right about now."

The book was about a girl named Christina Katerina whose mother gets a new refrigerator and gives her the box to play with. She drags it out under an apple tree in the yard and turns it into her play castle. Then a mean boy called Fats gets mad and tips it over, so she makes the box into a clubhouse. Then they fuss again, and Fats sits on top of the box and caves one end of the roof in, so she makes it into a race car and pretends to drive it around the tree. Every time something bad happens to the box, Christina turns it into something else. Finally, it becomes a ballroom floor for a fancy party until they try to wash it and it falls to pieces. And then she isn't even upset! I was surprised about that until I found out that Fats's mama just got a new washer and dryer (whatever those were) that came in not one but *two* big boxes, and they turn them into sailing ships right there under the apple tree.

I finished the book and then read the whole thing again two more times. I loved the way all the pictures looked like they were drawn with a pencil and some were filled in with brown paper. Something about the story made me feel happy. I wasn't sure why Evi would say that it mattered more to her than all the big books she'd read, but I thought it might have something to do with the way Christina saw the box. She didn't need it to be just one certain thing, and she didn't even need it to stay the same. Whenever something happened to the box that wasn't what she expected, she just decided to try something else. She didn't waste time crying over things that couldn't be undone. That seemed like it might be a good way to be.

Nineteen

The next morning, I went back to the gardens to work. I hoped Jessie would show up, but she didn't. Hanna and Nina were there, though, and I was glad to see them again. They were good about making me feel included in their conversation without me having to say too much myself. That morning, they were both excited about something they kept calling "the Fourth." I was tired of feeling like everyone else knew things that I didn't, so I tried to just listen and hopefully figure out what this meant, but eventually I had to break down and ask.

"The Fourth?" Hanna replied, confused. "You know, the Fourth of July. The Fourth!" When I still looked lost, Nina jumped in.

"Wow! Did you celebrate any holidays where you come from? Christmas, Easter, Thanksgiving?"

"Well, yeah, of course!" I said, not bothering to mention that I'd never heard of Thanksgiving. "We celebrated religious holidays. But I never heard of this Fourth of July thing."

"It's America's birthday!" Hanna exclaimed, laughing. "It's the day we declared our independence from England in 1776 and became our own nation." No wonder we didn't celebrate it on the compound. I could practically hear Papa spitting out *government holiday*.

"Oh, well, yeah. I read about that in my old encyclopedias, I guess. The date just didn't really stick in my mind, and we never did anything special to celebrate it. What do you do on the Fourth?"

"We have a big cookout and make ice cream and play music and just generally make a huge racket. People used to shoot off these things called fireworks to make it like the rockets and all from the Revolutionary War, but we don't have a way to make those anymore, and all the ones we've ever found don't work for some reason. But still, it's fun." Hanna never missed a beat pulling the tassels off corn plant after corn plant, which was our job that morning.

"You forgot about the parade," Nina said. "Everyone dresses up in red, white, and blue, and people decorate bicycles and whatever else they can rig up to roll along, and we all march in a big parade around this end of the lake. It's kind of silly, I guess, but getting everything ready and trying to outdo each other is a lot of fun."

"Ooh, Ami, you have to ride on our float!" Hanna said. "The boys are building some kind of rolling platform for us to decorate and ride on while we're all dressed up. It'll be fun!"

"Not just the boys," said Nina. "Melissa and Jessie have been helping too. And Melissa is the one who drew the design for it."

"Jessie?" I asked, knowing it wasn't really a question but not able to figure out what else to say. Nina and Hanna exchanged a look. "I guess that's where she's been lately." Hanna frowned but then quickly recovered her smile.

"Yeah, she's helped work on it some, and she's gonna play her guitar so we can all sing as we go rolling along. Say you'll come and ride with us!" I didn't know what else to say, so I just said okay. Hanna and Nina gave a little cheer, then went back to talking about what they would wear and how they could get everyone's costumes to match up in different ways. All I could think about was Jessie. I needed to find her and apologize for the way I ran off after we kissed. My heart sped up just thinking about that kiss, and I had to turn away before the other girls could see my face flush red once again.

"Where are they building it?" I asked, trying not to sound too interested.

"Over behind Will and Melissa's cabin. There used to be one more past theirs, but it burned down at some point, and someone built just a roof over the foundation to make kind of a covered work area. It's the perfect spot!" I nodded and kept working, but I knew where I'd be headed as soon as I could get away. Which turned out to be after Hanna and Nina dragged me to lunch with them. I had to admit that I was hungry, and if I missed lunch, I'd have to wait all the way until dinner. Still, I skipped the salad and stuffed down a peanut butter and strawberry sandwich before making my excuses and all but running away toward the cabins. Neither of them said anything, but I had a feeling that Hanna and Nina both knew where I was going. It seemed like my secret wasn't so secret after all. I wasn't sure how I felt about people being able to see that I liked Jessie in that way, but I also wondered how *they* felt about it. If I could believe Will, no one should think anything of it, but Will couldn't really speak for everyone.

I made my way out the back door of the big room and around toward the cabin side. It was a cloudy day, and a breeze blew across the lake to make the heat feel a little less sticky. I kept myself from running and took deep breaths to try to slow the galloping of my heart. I thought about the things I wanted to say to Jessie and imagined different ways that she might react. Was she mad at me, or upset? Had I hurt her feelings by running away? Or worst of all, did she not really care that much? Maybe she was just waiting for me to go back home so she could forget all about me.

In the end, all that worry was wasted because she wasn't there. I could see the work area and the float sitting there with no one in sight from a pretty good ways off, but for some reason, I kept walking toward it. I just couldn't think what else to do. So far, the float just looked like a shallow wooden box. I guessed they planned to attach wheels to it somehow, but it was hard to picture it rolling along with people standing on it. Would they attach ropes so someone could pull it? I stood there trying to look like I was really interested in it for as long as I could, but there wasn't too much to be interested in, and eventually I gave up and walked back toward the lodge.

When I got to the other end of the row of cabins, I noticed a path that I hadn't seen or paid any attention to before and decided to follow it. It turned out to be pretty short, just a little way around a clump of trees, really, and it ended at something I'd never seen before. There were all kinds of metal ladders leading up to little platforms and playhouses, with slides and swings and old tires hanging off different sections. It looked strange and wonderful to me, but even more strange and wonderful were the children playing on it.

There were three or four little kids climbing and swinging and running all over. One little boy was so small I couldn't believe that he could walk around on his own. A huge smile lit up his face, and he was laughing and clapping his chubby little hands as he ran away from a bigger girl who pretended to chase him. When she got close, she would pretend to fall, and he would squeal and clap with happiness that she'd missed him. A woman who must have been the little boy's mother sat on a bench off to the side, watching him and smiling. I was supposed to want that. Why was I looking for Jessie like everything would be okay if I could just talk to her? I couldn't have a baby with Jessie, and that was God's plan for my life. Wasn't it? I stood there watching the little boy, probably staring, lost in my own thoughts and confusion until he turned and ran straight for me.

Just as he reached the spot right in front of my feet, he stopped and looked up at me. He glanced back over his shoulder at the girl who was chasing him, then held his hands out toward me.

"Up!" he said, giggling. I just stood there looking at him, then he said it again. "Up!" He was bouncing up and down, wanting me to be part of the game.

"It's okay," his mother said from her spot on the bench. I guessed she thought I was worried that she wouldn't want me picking up her baby, but the truth was that had nothing to do with it. I'd never held any kind of baby. I didn't even know how. But it looked like this little boy wasn't taking no for an answer. And as it turned out, there was nothing special I needed to know. As soon as I bent over toward him just a little, he jumped up into my arms.

"Go!" he squealed, laughing. So I did. It felt good to give myself over to *doing* after all that thinking. I took off in a shuffling run, dodging around the swings and bars to keep the girl from catching us. He clapped his hands and screeched every time the girl almost caught us, bouncing up and down on my hip. His little body felt so solid in my arms, so warm and real, that holding on to him was as natural as breathing. We ran like that for a good while without him ever getting tired of the game, but finally my arms got too tired and I was out of breath. I slowed down enough to let the girl catch us. She tickled him, and he slid down my body and ran over to his mama, giggling and reaching his little hands out for her until she scooped him into her lap. He got quiet and still faster than I would have thought possible, then laid his head against her chest and popped his thumb into his mouth.

"Somebody's ready for a nap," she said, smiling. "Thanks, girls," she said to us as she stood up, shifting his little legs around so they straddled her waist and his head was on her shoulder. "I don't have the energy to keep up with him like that!" They walked off down the path toward the cabins, and the little girl wandered away. I sat down on the bench, still catching my breath from all that running, and felt how tired and shaky my arms were. The boy had been so small, but he seemed to get heavier and heavier the longer I held him.

Just think, Ami, I heard Ruth's voice in my head. *A little baby of your very own; can you imagine?* Could I imagine it, I wondered, now that I had seen and held that tiny boy? I tried to picture myself as the woman on the bench, watching her baby play and laugh, feeling thankful for the bigger girls keeping him entertained for a few minutes. But if I went home and had a baby at Heavenly Shepherd, there would be no bigger girls. It would be the same for that baby as it had been for me, living in a world of grumpy adults. Maybe I could have more babies, but maybe not. I thought of Teenie and the baby she lost, her own life in danger if what the others said was true. I needed to find out more about that. Maybe I'd ask Nina to bring me to her midwife mama so I could ask her some questions.

And none of that even mattered, I knew, if there was no
father to bring back with me. I'd tried to make myself think of
Will or Ben as possibilities, but deep down, I knew they weren't.
I didn't know why not, but I knew that what I felt around them
was nothing like what I felt around Jessie. I didn't know why
that would be, or even if it *should* be, but I knew that it was.
And I knew this wasn't something I could solve by running away
again.

Twenty

The next morning, everything changed. I was just walking into the big room, wondering if Jessie would be there to eat breakfast with everyone, when I noticed it was a lot noisier than usual in there. Before I could get far enough in to see what was going on, Miss Helen came around the desk and made a beeline for me like she'd been waiting to catch me walking in.

"What's—" I started to say, but Helen put her hands on my shoulders and kind of spun me around so I was walking back the way I'd come in.

"Come with me," she said. I tried to turn around to look at her, but those bony hands of hers were too strong, and she marched me into one of the little meeting rooms up near the front doors. "Wait here," she said, and before I could ask questions, she was gone. *What in the world?* I thought, but I didn't have to wait long to find out. A few minutes later, she opened the door again, but instead of coming in, she just stood there in the doorway.

"Ami, there's somebody here I think you should meet," she said. She smiled at me encouragingly, then stepped back and out of the doorway. For a second, I didn't see anyone; then a woman stepped into the room.

She was a little shorter than me and so small and slight that at first she looked like a child. Her straight blond hair was cut just above her shoulders, shorter than Papa and Ruth ever would have allowed. It looked bleached out by the sun, while the rest of her was tanned a deep reddish gold. She took a step toward me, and I could see lines fanning out from the corners of her eyes, showing that she was not a little girl, as I'd first thought. She had fine wrinkles at the corners of her eyes and mouth, but all at once, I knew I was looking at the face from my drawing. I felt the floor drop out from under me and reached out for the wall to keep myself standing.

"Ami." It was my mother's voice, saying my name for the first time that I would ever be able to remember. Not a question, a certainty. She knew me as soon as she saw me. I started to cry, and so did she.

"Mama?" I said, and before I could stop myself, I flew into her arms. She wrapped them around me so tight, saying my name over and over again. The name she chose for me, when I was her baby.

"You're here; you're finally here. I knew you would come; I knew it!" It was the happiest I'd ever felt in my life. As long as we stood there, nothing bad could happen. Gradually we broke apart, wiped our faces, laughed like we were embarrassed. She took a step back.

"Let me look at you," she said, putting her hands on both my shoulders. Her eyes moved over my face and hair, and she never stopped smiling. It was nothing like the way Zeke Johnson or

Will had looked at me, making me wonder what they saw. There was nothing in my mama's eyes but pure love. "You're so grown up," she said, "and so beautiful!"

"I wish I looked more like you," I said, not really thinking before I said it.

"Oh hush," she said, "don't be silly. You look like . . . well, you look just perfect. Those curls! I'd kill for those curls," she said, reaching up to touch the curls that had sprung loose around my face. She reached behind me and pulled my braid forward over my shoulder. "It's so long, though," she said quietly. "I guess . . ."

"Yeah, Papa would never let Ruth cut it," I replied. Her smile seemed to freeze for a second at the mention of her parents, but then she laughed and reached down for my hand.

"There's someone I want you to meet!" she said. She turned and started through the door, pulling me after her. Back out in the big room, the noise had died down a little. I guessed it had been all the excitement of the travelers returning and that the crowd had thinned as people found their families and went back to their cabins and cottages and rooms. We made our way toward the back of the room, but about halfway there, we stopped. There was a man coming toward us. He stopped and looked at my mother like he was waiting for something.

"Ami, this is Marcus," my mama said. Her voice seemed to shake a little. She kept ahold of my hand and turned to look at me. "My husband." Marcus's skin was a smooth, dark, even brown. It was darker than Nina's skin, and his eyes were a deep, dark brown. His hair was bound close to his scalp in tight braids that ran from front to back. He was looking straight at me, watching me take him in. What was it that I saw in his face? Happiness, yes, but also something that looked a lot like fear. *The mixing of the races is an abomination unto the Lord*, I heard Papa say. I looked from Marcus to my mama, not knowing what to say or how to react. She reached out for his hand, and he looked over at her and smiled reassuringly. *He loves her*, I thought. I opened my mouth to try to at least say hello, but then I noticed someone else standing behind Marcus, a girl maybe a little younger than me.

"And this is your sister, Penny," my mother said, her voice shaking for sure now. I felt like I'd had the wind knocked out of me. The husband I was ready for because of what Helen had told me, but a sister? Nobody had said anything about a sister! The name Penny did ring a bell, though, and I remembered Nina's words. *Penny's gonna be so mad . . . I thought they'd be back by now . . . Even though her mama is white.*

"Hey," the girl said, and then we just stood there looking at each other. Her skin was lighter than her daddy's but not as pale as Mama's. There were freckles sprinkled across her nose, and her eyes were hazel like mine but more gold than green. Her face looked almost familiar to me, and I was surprised to realize that we looked a little alike. We both had our mama's nose and the shape of her eyes. Even her dark hair had a coppery shine to it like mine, but I could tell hers was cut shorter, and she wore it pulled up into a puff at the crown of her head. *I have a sister*, I thought, and tried to return her smile.

Then I remembered Nina had said that Penny was the same age as her, so that meant she was, what, fourteen? Which meant my mother had her when I was about two, barely older than that little boy on the playground. It had never crossed my mind that my mama might have had another baby after me. All those times I'd wished for a sister, but just then it was hard to feel happy like I'd always imagined I would. There was a buzzing in my ears, and my vision started to close in. I felt myself sway, and my mama cried out my name. Marcus stepped forward and helped her walk me over to a chair, then squatted down beside me.

"Put your head down between your knees," he said, and I did. "Take slow, deep breaths. Count five in and five out, okay?" I nodded to show that I'd heard him. His voice was gentle but firm. I stayed bent over for a minute, counting out breaths the way he'd said, then slowly sat up. Marcus was still kneeling beside me, and my mother was watching me with a worried face. Penny was looking around at the curious faces of some of the other people in the room who were starting to drift toward us.

"Can we do this at home?" she asked my mother. *Our mother*, I thought, and almost laughed. It was that crazy kind of laughter like when Amber and I looked at the huge pile of stuff on her couch before I ran away, and I knew that just like that time, if I started to laugh, it would turn into crying. Beside me, Marcus nodded.

"I think that's a good idea. Ami, do you feel okay now? Can you walk a little? I think some fresh air might be good, and we can all go home." *Whose home?* I thought, but I just nodded and stood up. My mother stepped forward like she wanted to take my hand again, but I took a step back without thinking and she stopped.

"Yes," she said, "let's go home! I swear, these trips feel longer and harder the older I get. We just need to get our bags." She was already moving toward the back of the room, where a few other travelers were still sorting through a mishmash of bags and cartons. It looked like they were taking their personal things but leaving most of the stuff they'd found on their trip, and I guessed there was a system of dividing it all up or putting it to use fairly. My mother had two bags, and Penny had just one. The three of them each took one, leaving me with nothing to carry. Mama and Marcus talked softly on the walk back to their cabin, and they would both glance back at me or Penny or from one to the other of us from time to time. I looked straight ahead and didn't say anything the whole way, though I could see Penny looking over at me a few times from the corner of my eye. Finally, we reached their cabin, and we went inside.

The door opened into a cozy sitting room, with a little kitchen off to the side. I hung back in the doorway, not really knowing what to do with myself while the three of them moved around, putting the bags in their bedrooms. *This is their home*, I thought. *They live here together.*

My mother got us all glasses of water, and we sat down to talk. She and Marcus sat together on the couch, Mama looking nervous now, clutching his hand to steady her own. She looked at me, and I saw that her eyes were grayish blue. *Couldn't tell that from my drawing*, I thought. *At least Penny doesn't look more like her than I do.* I knew it was ugly to think such a thing, but I thought it would just be too much if she got to look like our mama on top of getting to be raised by her.

"I just *knew* if you ever came, it would be while I was out on a trip," my mother said, breaking the silence that was about to stretch out too far. "Every time I left, I was afraid I'd miss you. I'd tell Marcus what to do, to wait till I got back if he could. So when he came to meet me when we got back today, as soon as I saw his face, I knew!" She was smiling at me as she talked. For some reason, that didn't sit right with me.

"I've been here more than a week," I said. My voice sounded flat. "I showed Miss Helen your picture, the drawing you left? She told me she talked to your husband, but she didn't mention Penny to me. I didn't know anyone here." I stopped, not sure what else I wanted to say. My mother frowned, then quickly forced her face back into a smile.

"Oh, Helen can be a bit gruff, but she's got a soft heart. I'm sure she made you feel right at home. Did you meet some of the other kids, make some friends?" I could see her straining to keep a smile on her face, but her eyes were darting from me to Penny to Marcus like they couldn't find a safe place to land. Part of me wanted to be that safe place, but another surprising part of me wanted to see her struggle the way I'd been struggling while I waited for her.

"I met them," I said. "I'd never met anyone my age before I got here. I've never known anyone younger than Amber." I let the name hang there, a challenge. Amber meant Heavenly Shepherd, something only my mother and I shared. She was the one my mother sent the Lake Point brochure to and trusted to keep her secret until I needed to know. I stared into my mother's eyes until she looked down at her lap. I didn't know what had gotten into me. A few minutes ago, I'd felt so happy, but that happiness was being replaced by angry questions.

"Why did you leave?" I asked bluntly.

"We all have to go out on supply runs when it's our turn. There are things we need sometimes that we can't make or grow here. We could get along, I guess, but there's still so much out there, it seems silly not to make use of it." She looked at her husband's face for agreement. Somehow that made me even madder.

"No," I said, "why did you leave *me*?"

"Ami," Marcus said gently, "there's plenty of time for us to talk about all that later." He moved his eyes from me to Penny, like he thought maybe she didn't need to hear all of this.

"No way," Penny said. "I want to hear this too. I'm not a baby anymore." Mama and Marcus looked at each other and seemed to speak with just their eyes. My mother sighed like she'd just lost a fight.

"What did they tell you, your grandparents?" she asked me.

"I asked you first," I replied. They both gave a little laugh. They seemed less surprised by my stubbornness than I was.

"I guess that's fair," my mother said in a voice barely louder than a whisper. I knew this must be hard for her, but it was hard for me too, and she was the one who created this whole mess, not me. But it was Marcus who spoke next.

"Look at me, Ami. Now think about your grandfather Solomon, and I think you'll be able to answer your own question about why *we* had to leave." I peeled my eyes away from my mother to look at him. The expression on his face was patient, like he was just waiting for me to get it. And then I did.

"You were there? At Heavenly Shepherd?" I asked. The pieces were starting to fall into place. "But you're not . . ."

"Your father? No, I'm not. I met your mother when you were about a year old." I looked from Marcus to my mother and tried to imagine them younger, back at the compound with the rest of my family. If there was one thing my papa Solomon had, it was opinions. Ideas about right and wrong, about *should* and *must* and *must not*. Of course I had heard him preach about brown and white people mixing in marriage many times. It was one of his pet subjects, but it didn't really need to be, did it? It wasn't like there were a lot of different kinds of people coming down the hi-way anymore or living on the farms around us or coming to visit at Heavenly Shepherd.

Except one time, there was. One time a man with dark brown skin came down that hi-way, and he and Elisabeth Miles fell in love.

My face must have shown that understanding settling in,

because Marcus smiled sadly and nodded. But that was just the answer to the first part of the question, the part about why they left. The second part was about why they didn't take me with them. My mama must have realized this because she started trying to answer it. But that meant . . .

"Wait a minute," I said slowly. "How can that be? You left right after I was born! You ran away from the C-PAF man."

She shook her head sadly. "I figured that's what they'd tell you. There never was no C-PAF men, Ami. That was just a story—"

"Yeah," I said with a hard little laugh, "I found that out after I got here. Which I figured out you must have too. But I thought you still believed it when I was born, so it still made sense that you thought you had to run to keep from getting taken."

"Ami," she started, her voice not sounding very sure. "When we left the compound, I was a scared, pregnant girl. I was barely sixteen when I had you; did you know that? Your daddy, well . . . he wasn't . . . he didn't stick around. He was a lot older than me, and he just showed up at the compound one day. At first, I thought he was a traveler passing through, but then it seemed like my parents had planned it." Her voice trailed off.

"That sounds about right," I said, my voice angrier than I meant it to be. I felt like I might be sick. My mother looked down at her hands and nodded. I saw a tear spill over and slip down her cheek.

"When you were born, oh, Ami! You were just like the sweetest, most perfect little angel. And my mama and daddy, well, they acted like I'd performed a miracle. They fussed and carried on over you like you was the last baby on earth, which I guess to them you were. And Billie and Rachel and Jacob too. It was like you were everybody's baby. If I wasn't the only one that could nurse you, why, I don't think I would've ever even gotten to hold you! I was so young, and Ruth was always so much stronger than me. Before long, it was like you were another of *her* babies. They treated me like I was just your big sister, not your mama at all. And I guess after a while I just went along with it. I wasn't . . . it wasn't like I had decided I was ready to be a mama. I was just a child myself in a lot of ways. But I always loved you, Ami." She looked hard at me, searching my face to see how I was taking all this.

"Not long after your first birthday, I met Marcus." She looked at him then and smiled through her tears. He nodded, and she looked back at me and kept going. Every once in a while, her eyes would shoot over to Penny, to see how she was taking all this, I guess. I could tell that it hurt her to tell this story, and part of that was having to let Penny hear it.

"Marcus, he came down the road looking for survivors. It's hard out there, harder than you might think, and he was coming south from what was left of the cities. I know you've been sheltered, protected from what all is out there, Ami, but some of it is bad. There's bad people up around where the big cities were. It's . . . it's not like what you've known." Marcus looked serious and nodded, prompting her to go on.

"So he wanted a safer place, where people were kind and he could pitch in, help out, maybe find someone special to keep him company." She smiled over at him, and I saw how young she still was. I tried to imagine her as a girl of seventeen, just barely older than I was then.

"But my daddy, well, I guess you know how that went. He wasn't having it. You'd think, in all this big, empty world that has more than half fell apart, that he could find it in his heart to make a place for a healthy young man just wanting to be part of something, but you'd be wrong. I begged my mama to speak for

Marcus, but of course she would never go against her *husband*." That last word sounded so bitter I wondered if it left a bad taste in her mouth.

"It was too late for me, though." Marcus spoke now. "As soon as I saw your mother, I knew she was meant for me. And I knew that she knew it too. So I moved on down the road like Solomon said, but I didn't go far. I set up camp on an old abandoned farm a couple miles down the road. Couldn't risk him or your uncles finding me in the woods when they went hunting, and that farm was pretty well picked clean of anything useful, so I didn't expect any company there. I got some, though." Now it was his turn to smile over at my mother. *Courting*, I thought. *That's what that looks like.*

"Oh, you knew I'd come," she replied, swatting at his broad shoulder. "You only picked that old place because you could see I'd been there." She turned her eyes from him and spoke to me now. "That farmhouse was all caved in and rotted even back then, but the barn was in pretty good shape. Had a metal roof on it. I'd go there sometimes to get away from my family. It was my own secret place, and I hid my treasures there." She spoke like she knew I would understand exactly what she meant. I'd had the same family, after all, the same upbringing. The same kinds of innocent little-girl secret treasures. In all the years I'd been missing my mother, I'd thought of her as an adult, tired and bitter like Rachel and Billie, steady and sure like Ruth. But she had been just a girl, after all, when she had me, more like me than the adults who'd raised me. *How would I handle the same situation?* I wondered. How *had* I handled it when Zeke Johnson had shown up in the yard? I'd run, just like she did. But I hadn't left a daughter behind.

"I started sneaking over to that old barn every chance I got," my mother said. "We tried to figure out what to do. I knew how much my parents wanted babies to carry on the family line, so I thought if I could have another one, my daddy would soften toward Marcus and his . . . being different. I didn't understand back then that it was about more than that for him. He wanted control, just like always. He didn't want it to be my choice; he wanted it to be his." Now it was my turn to look at my lap, thinking about my big plan. I had told myself that if I could find a husband on my own and bring him back to the compound, Papa Solomon would accept that and forgive me for running away. But hearing my mother now, I knew that deep down I'd always doubted that plan. It was Papa's way or the hi-way, always. And I had chosen the hi-way, just like my mother had. He would never forgive that.

"When my pregnancy started to show, I knew I couldn't hide it from the family for long. My sisters saw it first, and even though they didn't tell, I knew they wouldn't stand up to Daddy for me. I begged them to help me think of the best way to tell our parents, but they said there was nothing they could do. We were all scared of what my daddy would do. Amber was sweet to me about it and helped me cover it up as long as I could, but she was just a girl herself and an outsider with no sway over anything. Finally, one day I saw my mama looking at me funny, staring at my little round belly starting to push against those awful dresses we had to wear. Then she looked me dead in the eye and asked, 'Is it him?' I knew who she meant, and I told her yes." She started to cry now, but she kept talking.

"My own mama, Ami, she just looked at me so cold and told me I had to go, said not to even think about tryin' to take you with me. My own baby girl! She said . . ." She was crying so hard then that she couldn't talk for a minute. "She said I was a filthy whore, that they wouldn't let me 'contaminate' you with my filth. She said if she'd had any other choice, she wouldn't even have let me nurse you because . . ." She broke down again, and Marcus put his arm around her and made soft shushing noises into her hair. I looked over at Penny and saw that she was watching her parents and crying. But I just felt numb. It was like I was hearing and seeing everything from far away. She shook her head and started again.

"Because she knew I was a common slut when I didn't complain about . . ." She stopped and looked at Penny. Then she took a deep breath and sat up straighter. "Because I didn't complain when they brought your daddy in to mate with me." Her voice turned bitter and hard, and it was like she was spitting out the words. "They bred me to a stranger like I was some *dog*, their own daughter. Told me a lot of pretty stories about how it was God's plan. Then my mama had the gall to say I was no better than a bitch in heat because I did *my duty* without complaining." Her words were like knives in my heart.

"I wanted to take you with me, Ami; you have to know that. But I knew they'd never let me. And after all the ugly, hateful things my mama said to me, well . . . I didn't think I deserved to have you. I'm stronger now, but back then . . . all I had ever known was them. I told myself I would come back for you once we found a safe place and this baby was born, but part of me knew they'd never let you go. That night while everyone slept, I packed the few things I had and ran to Marcus. We knew we couldn't stay there, but we didn't know where to go. Marcus had heard about a settlement in Georgia, so we planned to go east and look for it."

She stopped and looked at Marcus, like he knew this part was too hard for her to tell. He put his arm around her shoulders and took over telling the story. "We thought we knew where we were going, but we got lost. I had an old map, but some of the roads had crumbled, and the turnoffs were grown over. It's not easy to find your way from one place to another when you can't stick to one main road like the one you took to get here. We ran out of supplies and had to scavenge. Your mother was just a skinny little thing to begin with, and she was losing weight. We were worried about the baby getting what she needed to grow and be healthy. I was able to hunt a little, but it was winter, and a colder one than usual. Then it snowed, a big heavy snow that lasted for days. We were lucky enough to find an empty house in decent shape to stay in and ride out the storm. We holed up in the den with the fireplace and managed to stay warm, and there was plenty of snow to melt for water, but we just about starved. Your mama was weak and sick and scared. I was out of my mind with worry, going out in the snow to try to find food. One day, I managed to shoot a rabbit that I cleaned and boiled in melted snow over the fire."

"I could barely get him to eat any of it," my mother broke in. "He kept trying to give it all to me. Finally, I told him that if he starved to death, I would soon follow since I was pretty much bedridden by then. That got him to eat a little and drink some of the broth." He shook his head but smiled at her and said his piece.

"Finally, after about five days, the snow stopped and the sun came out and melted it all away. By then, your mama was too scared to leave that house, afraid of giving birth on the road. The sun brought all the animals out of their hidey-holes, and I had a little more luck with hunting. We stayed there through the spring, getting by on dandelion greens and wild lettuce and berries, whatever else I could scavenge and hunt, and then, finally, Penny was born.

"I had never seen anything so beautiful," he said. He looked at Penny then, and she smiled at him. I felt a stab of jealousy so deep it almost bent me double. "You were just this tiny, perfect little person. You never fussed, either, just nursed and slept. We stayed there through the spring and all through the long, hot summer. Once your mother had her strength back, I felt better about exploring a little farther out, and I found us a fishing hole. Some days, we'd all go and sit under the big, shady trees and fish for our supper. I wished it could stay like that forever. But I knew it couldn't." Marcus was looking at Penny, but my mama was watching me. Her eyes filled with tears and spilled over, and mine did the same. Didn't Marcus understand what he was saying to me? He looked back at me then, and I knew that he didn't. He couldn't see how his words cut into me, telling me how fast my mama had forgotten all about me, but she could. She took over telling the story, maybe thinking she could tell it different somehow, soften it for me so it didn't hurt as much.

"I missed you every minute, Ami. You can't imagine what it was like, to look at that sweet baby and love her so much but also to feel my heart ripped to pieces over leaving you behind." She stopped, tears pouring down her face, her eyes begging me to understand. I wasn't sure if I did or not, but I could see that she meant what she said. It hadn't been easy for her to leave me.

"Pretty soon, the air took a chill and the leaves started to turn. We had barely managed to keep ourselves alive during that last awful winter, and I knew I couldn't risk putting the baby through another one like that now that she was out in the world. The last thing I ever wanted to do was go begging back to my daddy to take us in, but I had to. I told myself stories, oh, about how once he saw her, all would be forgiven. I'd be back with you again, and you'd have a sister to play with! The two of you would grow up together and be best friends. I thought they'd want that for you too. Your sweetness had worked on them like magic, Ami. I thought it would be the same with this baby, that she could fix everything. So we set out for home before the weather could get any colder. The closer we got, the scareder I felt, and the more I told myself and Marcus that everything was going to work out. By the time I got there, I had convinced myself it was true. Which made what happened even harder." She broke off.

"I don't think we need to go over all that right now," Marcus said in a low voice. But my mama shook her head.

"If I don't get this out now," she said, "I never will." She wiped tears off her face with both hands, then pressed her fingertips into her closed eyes for a minute. No one moved or spoke.

"Billie was out in the yard when she saw us coming up the road, and she ran inside hollering. By the time my daddy came out, I was halfway to the door. I looked down at that little baby in my arms, so tiny and precious. She was everything my parents claimed to want. I was such a fool." Marcus put his hand on her arm, and she covered it with her own but kept going.

"Do you know what he did when I held my precious baby up in my arms for him to see?" I dreaded hearing the answer. I could imagine all of Papa's ideas about sin and abomination directed at that little baby, and it made me wince. "He took one look at her and then spit in my face." Penny and I both sucked in our breath. Marcus made a hissing sound, even though he knew the story. He was there and saw it happen.

"He asked me what I thought I was doing there with that . . . well, I won't say the ugly words he used. He said I had defiled myself and flouted God's will just like the whore of Babylon. He said I was 'damaged goods,'" my mama spat out. "Said he wouldn't have me around to contaminate you any more than I already had with my ungodly filth. He turned us away, wouldn't even let us step foot inside the house after we'd traveled all that way. I called out to my mama, thinking she'd talk sense into him, make him show some mercy. I begged her to bring you out so I could see you one last time. She wouldn't even come outside. She just stood there inside the door, shaking her head at me. I called out for Billie and Rachel, for my brother, for anybody. But they wouldn't cross my daddy to help me."

It was quiet for a few moments after that. I think we were all just trying to take it in.

"I felt like I had no choice but to leave you there, Ami. They wouldn't let me near you, and it wasn't safe to take you anyway. Life outside the compound was so much harder than I ever imagined it could be. We'd nearly died out there; I just couldn't take that kind of risk with you. I wouldn't have risked it with Penny if I'd had any choice. And as much as my daddy seemed to hate me then, I knew he couldn't be bothered with enough baby raising to do you any real harm. He'd hand you off to Ruth and my sisters, and I could see already how they loved you. Billie and Rachel had already been married a few years, with no luck making a baby. You were all they'd ever wanted."

"But how come you never came back?" I blurted out. "You could have done like you said, found a place for our family and come back for me so we could be together. I thought you must be dead!" My mother's tears spilled over afresh.

"After we . . . we left you there, we headed south down the hi-way, but we didn't find Lake Point right away. You had that brochure I sent you, with the map on the back?" she asked, and I nodded. She gave me a sad little smile and shook her head. "We had no idea where we were going or what we might find. It was sheer luck that we eventually stumbled upon this place. We were traveling with a newborn baby, and it was already too cold to sleep out in the woods with her. We had to find places to sleep, old barns and houses, whatever we came across. When we found a good one with most of a roof and a place to make a fire, we stopped for the winter. By the time we got here a few months later, I was sick. Not just in my body but in my mind too. In my spirit. I . . . I couldn't stop going over and over it all, how I'd lost you, how my own mama and daddy hated me and called me filthy and damaged. I missed you so much, Ami; you can never know how much. But something else was wrong too. I had seen something like it with May . . ."

"Jacob's wife?" I asked, surprised to hear her name. "No one would ever tell me about her. What do you mean you'd seen something like it with May?"

"Ruth called it the baby blues," Mama said. "Later, a lot later, once I got better, Evi gave me some books about it from the library. Postpartum depression, they called it. Sometimes after a woman has a baby, her hormones go kinda haywire. I think leaving you and having a new baby while you were still so little, that made it worse. My breasts got infected, too, that was the body sickness. *Mastitis*, that's another word I learned from Evi's books. Big red, shiny lumps that made me shiver and run a fever. We spent a week just camped out, waiting until the infection ran itself out and I was strong enough to walk again. But the spirit sickness only got worse, not better. As soon as we found this place and Helen took us in, I went to bed, and I didn't really get out again for about a year. I saw the same thing happen to May, except her baby died."

"What?" I exclaimed. "May and Jacob had a baby that died? I never knew that." I thought about my poor sweet uncle Jacob. This was why they'd all acted so funny whenever I asked about May.

"Stillborn, just about a month before she was due. Cord got tied in a knot. May knew something was wrong even before the contractions started a month early. He'd stopped kicking." She shook her head sadly. "May never got over it. She killed herself six months later. We tried everything to cheer her up, help her snap out of it, but nothing worked. Jacob promised her they'd try again, have more babies, but she wouldn't hear of it. She stopped speaking to him after that." She paused, then looked up at me and then Penny with a sad smile. "But my babies didn't die, neither one of you. You were perfect and beautiful, and I knew you were safe at Heavenly Shepherd, Ami, even though it killed me to leave you there.

"Marcus took such good care of Penny and me. He convinced me that I had to fight the sadness, for both of you. So I got out of bed, but I wasn't . . . I wasn't the same. I wasn't right in my mind for a long time after that. And by the time I started to come back to myself, you weren't a baby anymore, Ami. And Penny was big enough to need me in a way that you never would have, not with my mama and sisters around." She looked down at her hands then, like she was ashamed. For a minute I didn't know what to say, then I exploded.

"So what!" I said. "You still could have come back for me. I needed you! I waited and waited for you to come home! They told me that story about the C-PAF man and how you had to run off so he wouldn't catch you. When you didn't come back, I thought maybe he had. I thought you were *dead*! Do you know how it felt when I got here and they told me there had never been any C-PAF agents?" I was crying hard now, unable to take those crazy up-and-down feelings I was having. I had been so happy just an hour ago, and now I was on fire with anger. I couldn't reconcile the story my mother was telling with the imaginary mother I'd mourned and needed all my life. She was crying, too, and so was Penny. Marcus's face was unreadable.

"I didn't know what they'd told you, Ami! You were a little girl by then, almost five years old. What if they'd told you I died? What if they told you that Rachel was your mama, or Billie? How would you handle it if I just showed up out of the blue and turned your whole little world upside down? I felt so weak and ashamed about everything that had happened. I felt like I didn't deserve you. Even before I left, my mama had taken you from me. Marcus and I stayed up late so many nights talking about it, trying to figure out what was right. This place, Lake Point, it wasn't as solid then as it is now. There had been some kind of big falling-out just before we got here, people fighting for control. A lot of people had left, and after five years, the place was just getting strong again. The crops had failed from drought two of those years. We went hungry some days to make sure Penny got what she needed. At least at Heavenly Shepherd, I knew you were safe. I knew you had enough to eat and a roof over your head and that Ruth would teach you."

"Oh, she taught me all right," I said, my anger still burning. "She taught me all the parts of things that she and Papa thought I needed to know. How to read the books that they chose for me, how to be a godly woman so I could one day grow up and give them another baby to carry on the precious family line. Do you know why I finally found you, why I had to run away?" My mother's eyes were afraid now, her hands clutching Marcus's so tight I thought she would break his fingers. "They found me a man, Mama. Just like they did for you, sounds like. I thought he was old enough to be my daddy, but now I see he was much older than either one of you! I came back from a trip to the woods, and they were all there waiting for me. I felt like . . . like I would just die if I had to let him touch me. And then I felt so ashamed for thinking that way, for *not* doing my duty like I'd been taught!" My mama bent forward till her head almost touched her knees, sobbing. She grabbed fistfuls of her own hair and rocked back and forth, helpless.

"Ami," Marcus said, his hand up like he wanted me to stop. But I was going now, and it was all going to come out.

"You knew! You knew that would happen to me, just like it happened to you. You knew and you left me there anyway. You just gave me away!"

"That's enough." Marcus's voice was low and even, like he had to fight not to yell. But I still wasn't done. Then my mama sat up and looked at me, her eyes begging me to understand.

"At least you sent that paper about this place," I said, the fire going out of me fast and sudden. "You should've seen your sisters and Jacob and David, Mama. You were right about them; they did love me. And when that man came, they protected me. They put on a whole show at that dinner, Rachel and Billie falling all over themselves to butter Papa up and set him at ease. Jacob knocked over his tea and Papa lit into him about not being a man, and he just sat there and took it. They said Amber was poorly and sent me to her trailer with a plate, and she told me their whole plan. Before I knew it, I was wearing pants and fancy shoes and a pack on my back, walking all the way here to find you."

"You're so strong; I can see that, Ami. Stronger than I ever was," Mama said.

I laughed.

"Yeah, well, I guess you're not the only fool in the family, Mama. I walked all that way imagining how you would help me, that we'd be together and you would know what to do so our family could be together again. But you have your own family now. You left me, and then you just forgot all about me!"

"That's not fair!" Penny said, jumping up from her chair. "You heard what she said—she never forgot you. Look at her, Ami! Does it look like this is easy for her?"

I looked from Penny to my mother to Marcus, but all I could see was a family that I wasn't part of. My mother had been so happy I'd found her—we both had. But this was all too much, and I'd ruined everything.

"I have to go," I said. "I'm sorry."

"Ami," my mother called out, but I was already gone.

Twenty-One

The next morning, I woke up to the sound of someone knocking on my door. I had the feeling I'd slept for a long time, but instead of feeling rested, I felt groggy and confused. I wondered if I'd missed breakfast. I couldn't remember why I woke up so suddenly, then the knocking came again. I stumbled over to the door and opened it, wondering if Hillie or Sam had sent someone to get me because I was late to work in the gardens.

It was Jessie.

"Mornin', sunshine," she said with that crooked grin I'd been missing. Then she made a point of looking up at my wild nest of hair and pushed past me into the room. I reached up and tried to smooth it down, but I knew it was no use.

"Jessie," I said stupidly. "I wasn't . . . what are you doing here? Hang on, give me a second, please." I practically ran into the bathroom and closed the door behind me. I could hear her low laugh through the door.

My hair was worse than I'd feared. There was more of it sticking out of my braid than staying in, and it stuck out in all directions. I untied the end and raked my fingers through it, then smoothed it all back from my face and twisted it into one big knot at the back of my neck. It wasn't great, but it would have to do. I splashed some water onto my face and rinsed my mouth out, and then I was out of excuses to hide in the bathroom. I looked my mirror-self in the eye. It was still hard for me to think of her as just my own self reflected back at me. *Come on, Ami girl*, I told her silently. *You can do this*. I opened the door and saw Jessie sitting on the edge of the bed, waiting. There was nothing to do but go to her.

"I been looking for you," I said, "since about five minutes after . . . the last time I saw you."

"I was tryin' to give you some space. You ran off so quick, I thought . . ."

"I'm really sorry about that," I said, sitting down next to her but facing the room. As with Will, I found it easier to have this conversation if we didn't have to look right at each other. "I was . . . I didn't understand what happened. But as soon as I ran away and caught my breath, I knew I needed to go back. Because as confused as I was, you were the only person I wanted to talk to about it. But you were already gone, and then I haven't seen you anywhere since then, so I thought maybe you were mad at me about it." She didn't say anything for a minute, then I heard her take a deep breath and let it out.

"I wasn't mad, Ami. Least, not at you. I know how new all this is to you and how overwhelming it all must be, and I shouldn't have . . . I didn't mean to take advantage." I shifted on the bed so I could look at her then.

"What do you mean? You didn't take advantage!"

"Didn't I? All of this here, the people, the books, the music, it's nothing new to me. I've been here all my life. And one of the things Miss Jean and Evi always told us about in school was how it is out there, how lucky we were to be in this safe place and to have one another. We read the journals about the way it is for people out there. I *knew*, Ami. I knew it must be too much, but I just . . . I told myself it wasn't. Because I liked you so much." I felt my face instantly flush bright red and hot. I looked away in embarrassment, but we both laughed. *Because she liked me so much*, I thought. Butterflies filled my stomach.

"I like you so much too," I said quietly. "And it's not your job to decide what is too much for me, miss. That's for me to decide." She gave me the big shiny smile I remembered. "Where I come from, there wasn't . . . I didn't know about, you know, gay people. That there was any such thing. So when you, when we kissed, it seemed impossible to me that such a thing could happen. But then after I didn't find you that day, I ran into Will." She made a sound in her throat, like a cross between a groan and a laugh. "No, it was good. I didn't, you know, I didn't tell him what happened. We were just walking and he showed me the cottages and he was telling me about the peach trees, and he said they were Hillie's babies and I asked was it because she couldn't have any, and he said he didn't think she'd ever tried since she and Sam fell in love so young, and I couldn't believe it! I thought he was pulling my leg." I laughed.

"I never even thought of that," Jessie said. "Sam and Hillie have been married since before I was born. It wasn't something I ever thought much about. But also, Ami, since this is new to you, I feel like I should tell you that kissing one girl doesn't mean you're gay, really. I mean, it might? But not everyone falls just to one side or the other, you know? You might like a girl one day, and later you might like a boy. That's more common than you might think." That was a whole new twist to an already complicated and confusing situation for me. I'd always been given the idea that you met someone, fell in love, got married, and tried to have a baby. There was never any talk about even liking more than one person, much less more than one *kind* of person! And for some reason, it hurt my feelings to hear Jessie say that.

"Well, thanks a lot," I said. Jessie looked surprised. "Don't worry, I won't get any big ideas that you only like me." I started to stand up so I could move away from her, but she grabbed on to my hand and made me look at her. She looked confused for a second, then started to laugh.

"Woo, girl! You are somethin' else, you know that? I was tryin' to let you off the hook! I know you have all these ideas about how you have to have a baby, and as I'm sure you know, I can't make that happen for you. And just for the record, while we're on the subject, I think you are way too young to be worryin' about babies and marriage like you are. What's the big hurry?"

When I didn't answer, she went on. "I *do* only like you, Ami. And I'm glad you like me too. And who knows, maybe that will go on and on and turn into something big, something that lasts our whole lives. But maybe it won't, and that's okay too. People around here, they couple off and then break up pretty regular. And when you read some more books besides Little House on the dang Prairie, you'll see that people have always fallen in and out of love. And I don't know, maybe that's a good thing and maybe it's not, but it seems to just be the way things are for most people. Just . . . all I'm sayin' is you don't have to decide everything about the whole rest of your life right this very minute! Okay?" I wasn't ready to answer her yet. I didn't know if it was okay with me or not. I'd just never thought about things in that way before. And I was stuck on something else she'd said.

"What about you?" I asked.

"What about me *what*?" she replied.

"You said everybody couples off and breaks up all the time. What about you?" Suddenly the thought that Jessie had kissed someone else, maybe Hanna or even Will or Ben, made me feel kind of sick. But she just gave a little laugh and shook her head.

"Nah. It's hard when you ran around in diapers with somebody. All these other kids feel more like brothers and sisters, or at least cousins, to me. They don't seem to mind it, but I've always—I just feel different, I guess." I felt an unreasonable amount of relief to hear her say that. It made me silly.

"Oh, I see how it is," I teased. "You just like me 'cause I'm fresh meat!"

She made a surprised face, then stood up and put her hands on her hips in pretend outrage. "You take that back, Ami Miles."

I closed my lips tight and shook my head no. "Make me," I said, and that was all it took. She tackled me and pinned my shoulders down to the bed with her hands, leaning all her weight against me.

"Take it back, or else!"

"Or else what?" I asked, then flipped us over so she was the one pinned to the bed. Her surprise looked real then.

"Well, aren't you the strong one?" she said. We laughed, and then we stopped laughing. This time, I wouldn't be caught off guard or overwhelmed or confused. This time, I knew exactly what I was doing. I took my hands off her shoulders and lowered myself down so my elbows were propping me up. Our faces were so close together, and she was smiling at me, but I still felt like I should ask. "Is this okay?"

She nodded. I brought my face even closer, so our lips were almost touching, and she brought her face up the rest of the way to mine. Her lips were exactly as soft and warm as I remembered. I felt her arms wrap around my waist and then her hands on my back. That went on for a little while, but then I thought of something.

"Why'd you come here this morning?" I sat up next to her on the bed. It seemed to take her a minute to get herself together and switch directions, which I kind of liked. Finally, she sat up facing me with her legs crisscrossed underneath her.

"I heard . . . Nina saw you. With your mama and them."

"Did you know?" I asked. "Did everybody know except me?"

"Now, how would any of us know Lissie Hawkins was your mama, Ami?" I shrugged, wanting to pout. *Lissie Hawkins,* I thought. *I didn't even know my own mama's name.* I felt so touchy about the whole thing still. She sighed. "Okay, if I'm tellin' the whole truth, I had a hunch that she might be. The timing made sense, and you kind of reminded me of Penny, even though I couldn't quite put my finger on why. But I never said so to anybody, and I never heard any of them say anything that made me think they had the same idea."

"Why didn't you tell me?" I wasn't upset, really, just wrongfooted. It seemed like every time I started to think I knew where I stood, something came along and shook the ground underneath me again.

"I wasn't sure, and besides, I didn't think it was my place. If you had asked me if I knew who your mama was, I probably would have told you Lissie was my best guess. But since you didn't, I figured it was best to stay out of family business." When I just nodded, she put her hand on my knee and added in a quiet voice, "But now that you know, I'm here. I came to see how it went. How you're doing."

"Well . . . it went," I said, and she laughed. I wasn't sure I was ready to go back over the whole thing again just yet. "Finally finding my mama, and then finding out about Marcus and Penny and why they left, it was all just . . . a lot. I feel like I need to break off pieces of all that new information a little bit at a time, you know?" She nodded, and I went on. "All these years, my whole life, I've been imagining what it would be like when I finally got to meet my mama. And I never imagined it would be like that. I was so mad! All that time I spent wondering what happened to her. I guess I never let myself think she just didn't want me."

"Oh, Ami," Jessie said, her eyes shiny. I must have looked surprised, because she said, "What, you think you're the only one who can feel for other people? Now go on."

"It was . . . I felt so happy at first. I ran to her and she put her arms around me, and we just stood there hugging and crying. But then she introduced me to Marcus. And then Penny, and I . . . well, I almost fainted." I laughed a little, feeling embarrassed at the memory. "Then once we got back to their cabin and she told me the whole story, I felt so . . . well, I felt a lot of different ways. She was about my age when she had me, and she met Marcus a year later. I tried to make myself think of her like that, like *me*, just scared and confused about what to do. But all this . . . anger and . . . hurt, it was like it was bubbling up from inside my chest. I think I wasn't very nice to her. I'm ashamed of how I acted."

"Well, I think that's only natural after everything you've been through. She owed you some answers."

"Yeah, and I asked for them too. But the answers weren't what I expected to hear." I told her the whole thing, everything about why they had to run away, how they tried to come back with Penny before winter came again so she would be safe and we could all be together but Papa Solomon wouldn't let even my mama see me before he sent them away because Marcus and the baby weren't white. And how she got sick and so sad after they left, and then Lake Point wasn't steady enough to bring me here until they felt like it was too late to uproot me. Telling it all to her the way my mama had told it to me was strange—it made me see it through her eyes a little more, maybe.

"I was just little then, so I don't remember when they got here, but I have heard a lot of stories about those bad years of drought and big fights that split up the community," Jessie said. "And then they seemed like everyone else to me, like they had always been here, and Penny was just one of the littler kids running around. Your mama did always seem kinda sad and real quiet all the time, but maybe less and less as time passed." I nodded and tried to push down the anger I felt.

"I should be glad about that, I know. But it still hurts."

"I think that's understandable, Ami," she replied.

"You know what?" I said. "I don't want to talk about this anymore right now, okay? I just want to think about something else for a while." Jessie nodded and lay back against the pillows.

"Okay," she said, "what would you rather think about?" I looked at her hair fanned out so black and glossy against the white of the pillow. Her pretty gray eyes looked back at me like she knew exactly what I wanted to think about. I stretched myself out beside her, and there wasn't much more talking for the rest of the morning. Neither one of us knew too much about what we were doing, and we took it pretty slow. There were some bumped noses and foreheads, and a few times we broke out laughing, but no one panicked. And I didn't feel the slightest urge to run away.

After a while, when we realized we had missed lunch and our stomachs were growling, Jessie had the idea of making a little picnic by the lake. She grabbed some food from the kitchen for us, and we headed down to the same dock where we'd all gone swimming a few nights before. I remembered how that had ended, with me flustered and confused.

"Jessie, can I ask you something?" I thought her shoulders stiffened a little, and she looked out at the lake instead of at me. "You know how there's a lot of things I don't know about because of how I was raised?"

Her shoulders relaxed, and she turned her face to look at me. "You mean like kissing girls?" she teased, waggling her eyebrows up and down. I felt my face flush, but I laughed and shook my head.

"Well, yeah, like that. But that was something that just never came up. *At all*. But there was other things that . . . that did come up. That my papa preached about and said was wrong. And I guess I never really—" She was looking at me and nodding like she understood where I was going, but she didn't cut in. She waited for me to get it out.

"I just never thought to question the things he preached about. But now I don't know how to . . . I don't know if that means I really believed all of it myself or if I just accepted it because I had no reason not to. Not while I was still there."

"But now you are questioning it?" I shrugged my shoulders and looked out at the water, finding it hard to meet her eyes.

"The day that you got mad at Hanna and Will about Teenie and left, that night they brought me here to go swimming. And it was . . ." I tried to think of the words ". . . it was kind of shocking to me how, uh—" I heard her laugh softly beside me.

"How everybody got kinda naked and then got wet and they looked even more naked?" I turned to look at her then, my eyes huge in my face.

"Were you watching?" I asked, and she laughed again.

"Nah, but I can imagine. Just 'cause we ran around together our whole lives, that don't mean there's nothing new that comes up. We grew up swimmin' in this lake like that, together, but it feels different now. We all look different, and we all notice it." I thought of Jessie noticing Hanna's wet chest and felt a stab of jealousy. Then I remembered how *I* noticed it and decided it wasn't worth mentioning.

"Yeah," I said, "there was that. And how they talked about it *out loud* and made jokes about it! That never would have happened back home. But also, that was the first time I heard about Penny, even though I didn't know she was my sister yet. Nina was wondering when she'd get back, and when I asked who she was, she said something about her also being brown even though her mama was white. And she just said it like it was nothin', but . . ."

"But you thought it was somethin'?" Jessie asked.

"I don't even know, that's the crazy thing. I was just always *told* that it was wrong for people to do that. But now, I don't know if that's what *I* think. Hearing my mama tell about how it happened and seeing her with Marcus, I mean, anybody can see they love each other. And I guess seeing that, it's a lot different from hearing about it when there's no real people to put with the idea. Does that make sense?" Jessie nodded and gave me a sad little smile. "And when she said her own daddy spit in her face and called Penny an ugly name, even though she was just a baby! How can a person who does a thing like that claim to be a man of God? How does he claim to be any kind of man at all?" I was getting upset again just thinking about it. I jumped up, needing to pace.

"I mean, all that talk about babies being precious gifts from God, what about all that, huh? Was that little baby not precious just because her skin was darker than his? She's his own flesh and blood! And Ruth . . . I can't hardly believe she would do her own daughter and grandbaby that way." I thought of something and then turned to look at Jessie. "How am I supposed to believe they ever really loved me or cared about me, knowing they wouldn't have if I just *looked* a little different?" I sat down again, feeling the truth of what I'd said wash over me.

"I don't know, Ami," she said. "If you're askin' me, I'd say what they did to your mama and Marcus and Penny was wrong. And what they did to you was wrong too. Seems to me like your grandpa didn't practice what he preached, in more ways than one. My daddy used to say 'talk is cheap.' Not that he was a great one to talk, but that time he was right. It's easy to spout a lot of big talk about knowin' what God wants and followin' his will, but I ain't seen the man yet who don't do just exactly as he pleases when it really comes down to it. It's just that some of 'em admit it, and some of 'em don't."

Part of me wanted to argue, to defend my grandparents even after everything that had happened, but I knew she was right. I tried to think of any Bible verse Papa might have quoted to back up his claim that the mixing of the races was wrong, but there was nothing. Once again, it was my faith that was built on the shifting sand of his teaching. I looked down at my hands and saw they were clenched fists in my lap, like I thought if I closed them tight enough, I could hang on to something, anything, that had tied me to my family and our life at Heavenly Shepherd. I looked at Jessie and then up at the sky, so clear and blue and open. *Is God up there, looking down at me?* I wondered. If I prayed for help, would I get it? Or was that all just a story like Will claimed? Or was Evi right, and maybe God was there, but He or She or whatever They might be was not anything like the God my papa claimed to know so well? I looked down at my hands again, and I opened them. Whatever I'd been trying to hold to, deep down I knew that it was already gone.

Twenty-Two

After that, I knew I needed to go back to my mama's cabin and talk to her. I was still mad and hurting and confused, but I wanted her to know that I was trying to understand. And underneath everything else, I was still the same little girl who'd grown up missing her mama. Now that I'd found her, I wasn't willing to give her up again without a fight. So I headed down the path to the cabins, trying to think what I would say when I got there, and then I met Penny and Nina coming the other way.

"Hey, Ami," Nina said, looking at me and then Penny in a nervous way.

"Hey," I said. I'd been so focused on myself and my mama, I hadn't really thought much about Penny or how she felt about all this.

"You comin' back to yell at my mama and make her cry some more?" she asked. Nina looked like she had to bite her tongue to stay quiet, but she just shook her head and looked at the ground.

"Penny, I—" I started, but what was I going to say? I almost hoped she would cut me off and fuss at me some more, but she just stood there, waiting.

"I'm sorry," I said. "Believe me, all the times I imagined what would happen if I ever saw my mama again, I never imagined what happened yesterday."

"Yeah, well, it wasn't what any of us imagined either. I don't know why I thought you'd be different from *those people* who raised you."

"What? Penny, that's not—I'm not like that," I said. "None of this, how mad I got and how upset I was, it wasn't about *that*. It was wrong for them to turn y'all away; I know that!" She stood there looking at me, trying to decide if I was telling the truth. She was stubborn. "When Papa and Ruth turned you away, they took my mama from me. And I've spent my whole life missin' her. I didn't even know they took my sister from me too."

"So you don't care if your sister looks like this?" she asked, moving her hands so they pointed from the top of her head down to her feet. Her voice was still angry, but her face looked hopeful. I didn't know what I'd say until I said it.

"Well, I mean, it's bad enough you got to have Mama to yourself all this time; you didn't have to be so much prettier than me too," I said, and grinned at her. Her eyes got big, then she threw back her head and laughed.

"I told you you'd like her," Nina said. Penny took a step closer to me and studied my face, looking serious.

"Hmmm," she said. "I'm not *that* much prettier." She cracked a big smile, then reached behind me and pulled my braid over my shoulder. "And I could never grow my hair this long."

"I wouldn't be too sad about that," I said. "It mostly just gets in the way and drives me crazy."

"You should cut it, then," she said, like it was nothing. I wondered if Mama had held on to any of the ways she'd been taught by Papa and Ruth.

"Is she home?" I asked. "I was comin' to apologize to her too. And just . . . to talk to her."

"Yeah, she's wanting to make us both new dresses for the Fourth." I must have looked surprised in maybe not a good way, because she pointed a finger at me. "This means a lot to her. And Mama is an amazing seamstress! So be nice." I nodded, and she turned to look at Nina. "I think I'll go back with Ami. Catch up with you later?"

"Sure," Nina said, looking relieved. "I'll see you both later." Penny and I started walking back to her cabin together, but before we got too close to the door, she stopped and turned toward me.

"I get it, you know. Why you got so upset. I can't imagine what it must feel like to miss your mother and think she might be dead, then find out that she's been living this whole new life with her new family. And I know you never even knew about my dad or me. But I always knew about you, Ami." I was surprised. I guessed I just figured I would be something they didn't talk about.

"I know she mentioned her depression and having to come back from that and take care of me, but I'm not sure you really understand what it was like for her. None of this has been easy, and she never forgot you. When I was little, I had an imaginary friend named Ami. Then when I got older, I thought of you as the ghost who haunted my mama." I tried to read her face when she said this, but she gave me a sad little smile that hid whatever else might have been there.

"I'm sorry." I didn't know what else to say, but she shook her head.

"It's not your fault. I just wanted to make sure you knew. That she missed you and talked about you and mourned all that time she lost with you. But we never stopped hoping you'd come. And I know you never stopped hoping she'd come back. So now that you're here, I really hope this can work. That's all." It felt good to hear her say that, and without thinking I reached out and took both of her hands in mine.

"I hope so too," I said. "I'll try." She squeezed my hands and nodded, and then we went inside. My mother was standing at a table, sorting through pieces of cloth and old clothes she'd collected on her trip.

"There's someone here to see you, Mama," Penny said. She looked up and gave me a shaky smile.

"Ami!" she said happily. "I wasn't sure—"

"I'm sorry," I said, cutting her off. "I shouldn't have acted like I did. It was just a lot to take in, and so different than I thought."

"Oh, honey," she said, stepping toward me. "You don't have anything to be sorry for. I know it was. I think maybe . . . well, maybe there was no way for it to go different than that. But I hope we can move past all that now." She reached up and brushed a stray curl back from my forehead. "I've missed so much time with you, and no matter how much I wish I could, I can't get it back. But we have now, don't we?" I could only nod, tears running down my face, and step into her arms. We stayed like that for a minute, then broke apart. I wasn't sure what to say after that, but Penny broke the silence.

"I told Mama we had to be on special lookout for anything red, white, or blue on this trip, and we brought back all kinds of stuff! There's plenty for you to use too, Ami," she said, moving toward the table covered with scraps of fabric. "Nina said you're going to be on the float with us. What were you planning to wear?"

"Uh," I said, looking down at the clothes I had on. "I don't really . . ."

"I was thinking maybe a sundress out of this for you, Ami," my mother said, pulling out a big folded piece of light blue material covered with tiny white and red flowers. "There's enough for both you girls, if you don't mind matching." I looked at Penny and she shrugged her shoulders, but I could see all over her face that she hoped I'd say yes. I guessed maybe matching dresses was a sisters kind of thing.

"Sure," I said, wondering what a sundress was. They both smiled like I'd said the right thing.

"Mama is real good with designs. Everyone asks her to help them when there's something special they want to dress up for or when they want to learn a new quilt pattern. Don't they, Mama?" Our mother looked embarrassed. *Pride is a sin*. It might as well have been stamped across her face, but I could see her determination not to pass that on to Penny. Better never to learn some lessons than have to try to unlearn them.

"I think that's great," I said, giving my mother a smile. "You should be proud of your talents and hard work." She looked at me, surprised, but then nodded and gave a shy smile.

"Thank you," she said, "but we won't have much to be proud of if we don't get to work. Too much talking and not enough sewing, I'd say." She sounded just like Ruth but in a good way. I still missed my grandmother, even knowing everything she'd done. Or *hadn't* done. "I'll just need to take some measurements," she said, holding up a well-worn yellow measuring tape and taking a tentative step toward me. I felt suddenly shy.

"Oh! Um, okay. Just . . . what do you need me to do?" Penny

looked down like she was trying not to laugh, but our mama was all business as she had me stand with my arms down, then straight out to the sides. I felt my face turn red when she measured my chest, but she acted like it was nothing.

"Just be glad she doesn't have anything to compare those numbers to," Penny said, smirking. "Otherwise you'd get to hear how you're turning into a woman right before her very eyes!" She laughed, and Mama rolled her eyes.

"Well, you are!" she said. I felt a twinge of jealousy, but I tamped it down. I was here, I reminded myself, I was part of this. After the measurements, I watched Mama take big sheets of old, crinkled paper and cut a pattern, then lay out the pieces on top of the bits of material she planned to use and pin them before cutting. Her hands were swift and sure. *Not everything we learned at Heavenly Shepherd was wrong and useless*, I thought. But she'd gone beyond that same old pattern we'd been taught and learned to put her own shape to the things she made.

"I can help sew once you get it all cut out. If you want," I said. "I don't know that I'm much of a designer like you, but I can sew. Do you have one of those old machines like we had at home?"

Mama nodded. "We do, and thank you, Ami. But this light isn't the best for detail work, and Marcus should be home soon. He's been over at the lodge doing repairs for Helen. Why don't we stop for now and pick up sewing in the morning when the sun shines right in this window behind me? I've got some of Evi's cookies; we can have a little snack now and wait for him to get home. I know he'd like to see you." For some reason, my instinct was to run away again, but I stayed. This was my family, I reminded myself. We needed to get to know each other. I'd never have a chance to know my own father, but maybe Marcus and I could figure out a way to be family to each other.

"That sounds nice," I said, and she smiled again. We settled in the front room with cups of mint tea from a mix my mother grew and dried herself in her little kitchen garden behind the house. I wondered if she missed the white sugar she had growing up or if she'd gotten used to using honey or nothing at all.

"So you're going to be on the float with the other teenagers. I guess that means you've made some friends?" she asked. I nodded, and she went on. "That's good. I've watched most of those kids grow up since they were little bitty things. I'd see Hanna and Melissa getting taller, seemed like a few inches every time I saw them, and think about how you must be growing too. Sometimes it helped; sometimes it made it worse. But I never stopped missing you, Ami. I hope you believe that. I know it must be hard for you to understand."

"I know," I said, looking down into my cup. "I believe you. It's just . . . it's still a little bit hard for me. I'm trying." She just nodded and looked down into her own cup.

"I've been thinking about what you told us, about how you ran away and your aunts and uncles helped you. I knew Amber would, but I wasn't sure about my sisters. Jacob always was softhearted, though." I laughed a little in agreement. "I'm just surprised they haven't . . . I mean, do you think they're looking for you? I keep half-expecting to see my daddy walking up to the house."

"I thought they might. I stayed off the road most of the way here and kept hidden in the woods alongside. Amber said they'd try to throw him off, tell him I probably went north thinking to find you in one of the C-PAF places, but she wasn't sure that would work. But I don't know." I shrugged. "I've been here a week now, and they haven't turned up, but part of me can't stop thinking they'll be here any minute. I 'magine he's pretty mad that I left like that. Embarrassed him in front of *that man*."

"Oh, I just bet," my mother said angrily. "Can't have your womenfolk *disobeying* you in front of company, can you?" She looked up at me now, so I raised my eyes to meet hers. "You did the right thing by leaving, Ami. He had no right, *no right* to expect such a thing of you. Bringing in some man twice your age and expecting you to just . . . *breed* with him, like cattle!" *Like they did to you*, I thought, but there was no need to say it. "I've got half a mind to go back there myself and tell him just what kind of man he really is!" I must have looked surprised, because she laughed and shook her head. "But I won't, though. No use poking the bear while he's settled in his den. If he comes out of there, well, that's another story. But I don't know . . ."

"What?" I asked.

"Well, you know Solomon. *It's my way or the hi-way*. He may not come after you at all." I should have felt relieved at the thought that Papa would decide I wasn't worth coming after, and I was, but it also hurt.

"When I was walking," I said, "on the way here, I thought . . . well, I thought if I could just find you, then everything would be all right. And I thought that maybe I could find my own . . . partner, to try to, you know, have a baby with. And that I could bring him home and Papa and Ruth would take me back and everything would be the way it was before, except better, because I wouldn't be alone anymore. But then when I got here, everything was so . . . you weren't here, and being around other kids my age was . . . also not like I expected."

"I'm sorry I was gone when you got here. And about the way you found out about me being married," she said. "And then

I came and threw in a sister!" She looked at Penny, and we all laughed.

"It's funny, but I think you girls do look a little alike," Mama murmured. "Except I never let that river of curls grow past her shoulders. That must be a mess to try to keep up." She eyed my braid, which had lost control of most of the curls around my face. "Why don't we cut it?"

"What?" I said, even though I'd heard her perfectly well. "I don't know. I've never . . ."

"I know, they never let you cut it because the Lord has given it to you as a covering, blah, blah, blah. Who wants a cover in Alabama in July? We won't do anything too crazy, just to your shoulders, so it's easier to pull up. You can wear it pulled up high, like Penny."

"I was thinking I'd ask Daddy to give me cornrows now that we're back," said Penny. "They're so much easier in the summer."

"Marcus . . . does *hair*?" This seemed so funny to me. I couldn't imagine Papa or even my sweet uncles braiding my hair.

"Men can do all kinds of things you've never seen them do! Around here, men who are lucky enough to be fathers take that luck seriously. And even without kids, it's not all 'men's work' and 'women's work' the way we grew up knowing. Everybody pitches in and does what needs to be done."

"Yeah, I've noticed that a lot of things are different." I gave a nervous little laugh. "I thought Hillie and Sam were sisters until Will explained to me about . . . you know, gay marriage and all that."

Suddenly her smile disappeared, and her lips pressed together in a line just like Billie's and Rachel's used to do when they didn't approve of something. "Yes, well. Not all changes are for the best," she said. I felt my stomach flip over.

"What do you mean?" I asked, caught off guard again. "Will told me that gay marriage has been legal for a hundred years. And Sam and Hillie, they keep this whole place fed! They've been married almost as long as you've been alive. You . . . you think that's wrong?" She sniffed and looked away.

"Oh, Mama," Penny said, shaking her head and looking up at the ceiling. "We've talked about this . . ."

"I guess it's not for me to judge what other people do. Maybe there's some things I just can't understand or some of the old teachings I can't shake as easily as others. It just don't seem natural to me."

Penny let out a disgusted sigh, and I must have looked shocked, because our mother shook her head and smiled like she wanted to brush her comments under the rug.

"I guess I just think it would be such a waste if you were to take it into your head to do something like that. You and Penny, you might be fertile still! You can't just throw away a gift like that." My hands started shaking, and I tucked them under my legs to hold them still. Did she already know about Jessie and me, or was she just talking? I wasn't ashamed of my feelings for Jessie now that I'd had a chance to figure out what they were, but the whole idea of it was still so new to me that it was hard to think about how it would seem to other people. Especially my own mother.

"But, Mama," I said, keeping my voice as low and calm as I could, "what about loving someone and having them love you back? Isn't that gift too precious to throw away?"

"I guess I just don't understand that kind of love," she said. "Or whether it's a gift or just confusion."

"But . . . how can you still think that after . . . after the way they put you out because of who you 'took it into your head' to love? I guess Papa and Ruth, they thought the chance to make a pure white baby was too good a gift to throw away, didn't they?"

"It's not the same thing, Ami," she said.

"How is it not?" Penny asked. "Did you choose who you loved? When you saw how hard it was going to make things for you, why didn't you just *choose* to stop loving Daddy? Would that have been so easy for you?"

"No, of course not. Maybe you're right," she said quietly, looking up at Penny and then me and trying to smile like everything was fine. "I guess you can take the girl out of the compound, but you can't take all of the compound out of the girl. But let's not borrow trouble, okay? Not when we're all just getting to know each other." She looked at me hopefully, and I nodded, trying to relax my face and shoulders from the clench I was holding.

"Maybe Ami and I can get dinner started?" Penny asked, and I knew she was trying to change the subject before things got any worse. "Daddy should be home soon. You're staying, aren't you, Ami?" I wanted to say no. I wanted to hightail it out of there, but I knew that I shouldn't.

"Sure," I said. "What are we making?"

Mama smiled, and I could see the tension leave her. "Marcus said he'd bring home fish, so let's hope they're biting!" she said. "I'll put some of those little potatoes on to go with it. Why don't you girls see what looks good in the garden for a salad?" I followed Penny around to the back of the house where their little kitchen garden grew, but once we were back there, she turned around to look me in the eye.

"Well, I guess you're not the only one who has to apologize for your family's backward beliefs," she said. She looked upset. "I'm sorry she said all that stuff, Ami. I know you . . . well, I mean, it seems like . . . you and Jessie?" I felt my face flush, but I made myself look her in the eye.

"I guess everybody knows, huh?" I said. It wasn't really a question.

"Nina told me," she said, grinning. "And I think it's great! I don't think Mama knows, though. If she did, she wouldn't have said all that stuff." I raised my eyebrows and gave her a questioning look. "Well, maybe she would have," Penny admitted, "but I like to think she wouldn't. She's not a bad person, Ami. It's just, it's like she said—some of that stuff she grew up with is still stuck in her head. But I think that's just because she hasn't had anyone close to her to knock it loose."

"So that's what I have to do, knock it loose for her?" I asked, and she laughed.

"Yep! If Jessie makes you happy and she has to accept that to keep you around, then that's what she'll do. She's so glad you're here, Ami. And I am too." She gave me a shy smile, and I couldn't help but smile back.

"Me too," I said. Was this what it meant to have a sister? At Heavenly Shepherd, I always felt like there was one opinion—Papa Solomon's—and the rest of us had to fall in line. But here Penny was taking my side even though she wanted me to believe that our mother could change. I decided that a sister might be a pretty good thing to have, and I felt a tiny seed of love for her plant itself in my heart.

We gathered greens, tomatoes, and cucumbers for the salad, and pretty soon Marcus came home with fresh fish that he cooked over a little firepit he'd built. Their cabin and yard were tiny compared to the compound, but there was something homey about it all. The garden was laid out in neat rows, and it was separated from the firepit by a little patio paved with old bricks fitted together in a pattern. They even had a little rough-built table and chairs out there. There was an orderliness to the whole thing, like someone had put a lot of thought and time into making things just so. *Was that my mother*, I wondered, *or Marcus? Or was this a home they could have only made together?* When everything was ready, we sat down at the table on the patio to eat.

"I hope you don't mind if we eat out here, Ami," my mother said. "I know it's hot, but at least there's a little breeze. It's just so stuffy in the house this time of day."

"I don't mind," I said. "I'm always happier outside than in." I looked up to see them all watching me, and suddenly I felt awkward. My mother must have sensed it because she started fussing over filling everyone's plates.

"What was it like—" Penny started, but Marcus cut her off.

"I don't think Ami wants to talk about that now, Penny," he said. My mother looked at him gratefully, but Penny rolled her eyes.

"It's okay," I said. "What was it like growing up on the compound, is that what you wanted to ask, Penny?"

"Well, yeah. You don't have to talk about it if you don't want to, though," she said. "I just wondered . . ."

"I don't mind talking about it. It wasn't all terrible or anything. I mean . . . the way I left was, and I always missed you," I said, looking at my mother, "but mostly it just felt . . . like normal life, I guess. I was safe and I had enough to eat, like you wanted, Mama. Ruth took good care of me, and Billie and Rachel and Amber and Jacob and David played with me and taught me things. I learned to read, even if I wasn't allowed to read a lot of different books." Penny made a surprised face, and I realized there was a lot we still didn't know about each other.

"And how to sew and grow food and even hunt a little bit, even though I didn't like it. My uncle Jacob took me fishing a few times," I said to Marcus, "but the river is a couple days away, so I couldn't go with the men anymore once I got older. I fished on the way here, though, caught my dinner my last night on the road."

"Maybe you'd like to go with me sometime?" he asked. He kept his voice light, but he looked hopeful. "It's pretty good here at the lake, but I've been working on a boat so we can go out on the river sometimes too. But your mama and Penny aren't much for fishing."

"It's just so boring," Penny said. "You have to be so quiet, or you'll scare the fish. And we have to get up too early." Mama nodded and laughed.

"I don't mind the early part; I'm not a night owl like Penny, but I like to putter around the house awhile before I have to go out or see anyone."

"Well, I like to be out in the mornings, and I don't mind the quiet," I said, but I felt suddenly shy. What would it be like to do things with Marcus, just the two of us? Having a good reason not to talk might be good. That way we could ease into things, get comfortable with each other. "I'd love to go with you sometime." Marcus smiled, but Mama's and Penny's faces both lit up, and they looked at each other like they'd won a prize.

"The girls are planning to ride on that float the kids are building for the Fourth," Mama said to Marcus. I had a feeling she didn't want to hear any more about Heavenly Shepherd just then.

"Mama's gonna make us matching dresses to wear," Penny said, practically bouncing in her seat. Then she looked at me all embarrassed like she'd been caught, so I smiled and nodded like

I was excited too. The truth was, I didn't know how it felt to be excited about a dress, but I was open to the possibility. Mama started talking about fabric she'd brought back, which led to general gossip from their scavenging trip, and I felt grateful to let the focus shift away from me. I ate and let their talk wash over me, watching their faces and the way they leaned toward one another and away depending on who was talking. It still hurt a little to see them together like that, a family that had gone on without me all those years I spent missing my mama and wondering if she was alive, but it was a dull ache now. *I'm here at this table*, I told myself whenever I felt it throb. *I'm part of this family; they want me here.* It helped. Mostly.

When we finished eating, we all helped clean up, even Marcus. That was something new for me. I tried to remember if I'd ever seen Papa Solomon or my uncles clear a plate or wash a dish, but I couldn't come up with a single time. I wondered if Mama had asked Marcus to help with those things back when they first set up housekeeping together, or if he just did them. Either way, I was proud of my mother for doing things different now that she had the chance. She must have seen me watching him at the sink, because she smiled, and said, "Nothing in the Bible says a man can't wash dishes, far as I know," and winked at me. Marcus didn't turn around, but I heard him laugh.

Once the dishes were done, we all went into the little den and sat. I started feeling antsy—how would I excuse myself and go back to my room? Would they ask me to spend the night there? I couldn't guess where I'd sleep, and even though things were going better, I knew I was getting close to my limit for togetherness. Even back home, I always liked my quiet time in my own space. But almost as soon as we sat down, my mother started to nod off.

"Mama," Penny said, "you're fallin' asleep. Why don't you go on to bed?"

"Oh," I said, jumping up, "don't let me keep you up. I'm just about ready for bed myself."

She got up and waved Penny away. "Don't rush off on my account, Ami. I guess I'm still not caught up from travelin'. But y'all don't mind me," she said. Her eyes took in the three of us. She kissed Marcus on the cheek and hugged Penny, then stopped in front of me with a questioning look before hugging me too. "I'll see you tomorrow," I said. She patted my cheek and shuffled off to bed, and I excused myself back to the lodge and my own little room.

Twenty-Three

When I told Jessie what my mother had said about some kinds of love being *unnatural*, she didn't seem too surprised. "Just because people can see things their way," she said, "don't mean they want to see things your way." It was the morning after, and we were tending the corn, beans, and melons in the "three sisters" patch. The runner beans climbed the tall, straight corn plants, and the melon vines grew lush and wide-leafed along the ground, covering the soil to keep it cool and hold in water. When I asked her why this arrangement was called "three sisters," she told me it was an old Native American way of growing three of their most important crops, except they usually did squash down low instead of melons. Jessie seemed to know all kinds of interesting little bits of information. She said she learned a lot of it in school or on her own in the library, which, according to her, was kind of the same thing—it was all Evi and Miss Jean. But she'd also learned things from Hillie and Sam and from her father and from all of the adults living around her in the compound.

"Did my mother ever teach you anything?" I asked. She was quiet a minute before she answered.

"I went to some sewing lessons she did for all of us kids, boys and girls. I was never much good at it. But she . . . I don't know, I always kind of felt like your mama wasn't too crazy about me."

"What makes you say that? Was she mean to you?" I asked, feeling defensive.

"No, it was nothing like that. I'm not sure I can even put my finger on it. She just didn't talk to me if she didn't have to, I guess. At the time, I thought maybe . . . well, my daddy wasn't the most well liked of men around here. Most people didn't seem to hold that against me, but I thought maybe that was it. Except now . . ."

"Now, what?" I asked.

"Well, now I wonder if I didn't remind her too much of you. Another little girl whose mama ran off and left her, you know? Maybe I brought up too many bad feelings for her." I looked at Jessie, smiling, until she gave a nervous little laugh, and asked, "What?"

"You," I said. She made a face and shook her head. "No," I said. "You're just so . . . where I come from, there's a lot of blaming. If you do something wrong, there's no wondering why, just punishment, or at the very least, you're made to feel ashamed. But you try to understand why people make mistakes instead of just getting mad about it. And it seems like you're usually right about why too." She shook her head and looked embarrassed.

"Yeah, well, it's easy to be understanding about things that don't really hurt you. You've heard me talk about my daddy. How understanding did I sound about him?" she asked. I thought for a second and nodded.

"Yeah, that makes sense. I guess that's another good thing about having somebody who can help you think about things a different way. When it's hardest to be understanding, they can do it for you, maybe." I smiled, and she gave me one of her big smiles back. My stomach felt fluttery, and I wished we were somewhere more private.

"I guess so," she said, still smiling. Then she looked down at the ground and pointed. "Hey, look at that!" she said.

"What?" I asked, not seeing anything.

"Right there." She pointed. "Here, come look." She dropped down onto all fours so she was shaded by a wall of corn and bean plants. I dropped down beside her to see what she wanted to show me, but I still didn't see it. "Right here," she said more softly, then pressed her lips to mine. "Tricked you," she said in a quiet, teasing voice, then she laughed and jumped back to her feet. She lightly tapped a big watermelon with her foot. "Looks like these'll be ready to cut right on time for the Fourth," she said. "Guess you better make sure you have somethin' to wear. Can't have you looking unpatriotic on my float."

"Oh, it's your float now, is it?" I asked. My stomach was still doing flip-flops, but if she could play it cool, so could I. Maybe. She laughed.

"Okay, *our* float," she corrected herself. "Still, gotta go back over there and help your mama sew that dress."

"I know," I said with a sigh. "I'm planning on going back over there after lunch. Since you're so anxious to get rid of me."

"Can't give ol' Lissie another reason not to like me, now can I?" she said, moving along the row. I shook my head, feeling torn. I wanted to spend time with my family, of course I did! But giving up time I could be spending with Jessie was hard.

"Speakin' of places we need to go, I've been meaning to ask you about all that stuff with your friend Teenie." I saw her back go all stiff, but then she turned to face me and put her hands on her hips.

"Is that so?" she asked. I was nervous about upsetting her, and I guess she could tell because she smiled, and said, "It's okay, Ami. I'm not gonna get mad just because you ask me a question." I blew out the breath I'd been holding and nodded. She turned back to her work and started moving down the row again, but she talked as she did it.

"I did go over there to see her. She's . . . it don't look good. Margie wants to use herbs to make the baby come on, but Teenie won't do it because it's so early. She said she can't take losin' another one."

"Did you try to talk her into it? Will and Hanna seemed to think she'd listen to you." Jessie gave a sad little laugh and shook her head.

"Teenie don't listen to nobody. She didn't listen to Margie about not havin' another baby. She didn't listen to me way back when Matt first got here and started sniffin' around. I tried to tell her he was no good, that he wouldn't be good for her. Then after what happened last time, I thought maybe he'd stay off her, but that'd be too much like right. When she got pregnant again, I tried to get her to get rid of it, but she wouldn't listen to that either, and of course he didn't try to talk sense into her."

"What do you mean, get rid of it?" I asked. She stopped and looked at me.

"Yeah, I guess you wouldn't know about that," she said softly. "Well, it don't always work, and it's tricky, especially if you wait too long. But Margie has some herbs and a way to . . . to make you not pregnant anymore if you don't wanna be."

"What?" I was shocked. "But . . . why? Why wouldn't anyone want to be pregnant now, after everything that's—" I couldn't wrap my mind around such a thing.

"Well, mostly it's like this thing with Teenie, where it's too dangerous for the mother to carry a baby. Even that doesn't happen that often. But believe it or not, some people just don't want babies. Some people aren't fit to be parents, and they at least have sense enough to know it. They used to have pills and things that could keep you from gettin' pregnant if you didn't want to, but now . . ." She shrugged.

"So the baby just . . . dies?"

"Teenie might die! And anyway, she would've had to do it way back when she first started missin' her cycle. It's not really a baby then. You can't even see it. It's just like you take the herbs and you start your cycle a little later than you would've."

"But it's *going* to be a baby!" I said. "You can't say it's not a baby just because you can't see it yet."

"Well, that's always been the part folks disagree on. There's whole books about it—"

"Gah! There's books about everything around here, seems like. I just—I don't know, Jessie. It seems like if we have a chance to bring new life into this world, we ought to do it."

"What if bringin' that new life takes away the life of the one who's carryin' it? Doesn't her life matter? She's already here in the world, a whole person with people who love her and don't want her to die!" Jessie's eyes filled up and spilled over, and I knew we weren't just talking about ideas and right and wrong. This was about a real person. A person she cared about. I went to her and hugged her. She buried her face in my shoulder and let it out.

"Of course it does," I said into her hair. "Of course her life matters. I'm sorry, I didn't mean to—"

"No," she said, straightening up and taking just a small step back, "I know you didn't mean it like that. It's just—it's hard to love somebody but have no control over what they decide to do, even when you can see they're hurtin' themselves. I just feel helpless. When she started spendin' all her time with Matt instead of me, it felt like I lost her. But at least she was still here, and after a while things settled down and we sorta figured it out, how to still be friends even though . . ." She looked up at me but didn't go on, and understanding settled over me.

"Did you like Teenie in a way that . . . wasn't just friends?" I asked. My heart was thudding in my chest, but I could see that Jessie needed to be able to tell me this. She ducked her head and shrugged her shoulders but didn't move away.

"Maybe. I mean, I didn't really think so until Matt came around. We had just always been so close, and I was slow to . . . to grow up, I guess. But Teenie wasn't, and by the time I started to catch up, she took up with Matt and I got left behind. But the way I felt then . . . it was worse than it shoulda been, maybe. If she was just my friend." She looked up at my face to see how I was taking all this. The truth was I didn't like it. But I also knew it didn't really have anything to do with me or the way Jessie felt about me. I tried to imagine what it would be like if I felt this way about Jessie but she didn't have those same feelings. It would be awful.

"That must have been hard," I said, and I meant it. I hated to think of Jessie hurting like that.

"It *was* hard. But I got over it, I really did. I started spending more time studyin' all those old ballads and stuff, listenin' to all the records I could get my hands on, writin' songs of my own. I found other things to take up my time. And then I met you." She smiled and reached out for my hand.

"Do you think I could go over there with you next time?" I asked. "I'd like to meet your friend."

She nodded and stepped closer, then wrapped her arms around me and rested her forehead against mine. "Thanks," she whispered.

We finished up and headed toward the lodge for lunch. She didn't bring up my mother again, and I didn't ask any more questions about Teenie. We talked and laughed while we ate, like always. Then, just as I was chewing my last bite of food, Nina and Penny came and sat down.

"Hanna said to tell y'all they're working on the float and to come help. Tomorrow is the Fourth! We've gotta finish it," Nina said. "Everybody else is over there already."

"That sounds fun!" I said, jumping at the chance to spend more time with Jessie. But she nudged my knee with hers, reminding me I had other plans. "But I said I'd go back and help Mama sew. I was just about to head back to your house," I said to Penny.

"Oh, don't worry about that," Penny said with a little wave. "She was up at the crack of dawn like usual. She's practically done with your dress and halfway through mine. As long as you let her do a final fitting on you, she'll be happy." I felt a little guilty at how relieved I was. "Anyway," she said with a big grin, "I already told her I was taking you with me." I couldn't help but smile back at her.

"Well, then I guess we'll see y'all there," Jessie said, hopping up and pulling me after her. She didn't let go once we got outside, and we walked along with our hands swinging between us.

Twenty-Four

I guess everybody knows now," I said, but when Jessie raised her eyebrows and looked at me sideways, I hurried to add, "that me and Penny are sisters, I mean. That her mama is my mama and that's why I'm here?"

"Yeah, word spreads pretty fast around here. Everybody knows all your business whether you like it or not. That bother you?" she asked, and I got the feeling we weren't just talking about my family business.

"Nah," I said, looking straight ahead. "I got nothin' to hide. Do you?" I asked, wondering if it wasn't just my business she was worried about. That swarm of butterflies was suddenly back in my stomach. She stopped and pulled me around to face her.

"Nope," she said, grinning. "But I don't want to rush you. I already did that once and almost ran you off." She laughed, but I thought it sounded just a little bit shaky. "I'm trying to do better about rememberin' how new this all is for you. Take it slow and all that." She was looking down, embarrassed, and I stepped a little closer to her.

"It's me you're worried about, is it?" I asked softly. She brought her eyes up to mine. My heart was thumping, and I grabbed her other hand to keep both of mine from shaking. "Well, I feel fine," I said, fighting to keep my voice even. She was just the slightest bit taller than me, and she tilted her face down toward mine.

"Yeah?" she asked, so soft I felt it more than heard it. I nodded and brought my face the rest of the way to hers until our lips touched, soft and still like that first kiss. It was still overwhelming but in a good way. I made myself step back, and we started walking again, my knees shaking just a little.

"Don't let me cramp your style, though," I teased. "That reminds me—am I crazy, or did I hear somethin' about Will being a little sweet on you?"

Jessie snorted. "Oh Lord, that was a million years ago. And the feeling was not mutual, in case you didn't hear that part," she said.

"Yeah, that sounds like what I heard," I laughed. But remembering that conversation made me think of something else I'd heard. "Speakin' of, what was all that with Ben, when y'all were talking about Teenie? And Hanna saying she understood better than anybody?" Jessie made a little *oof* sound.

"Their mama died," she said, "giving birth to Ben. Lost too much blood; Margie couldn't stop it. Hanna was just a baby herself." I felt sadness for Ben and Hanna shoot through me. And fear—I was still learning that having babies could be so dangerous for the mother. And for everyone who loved her.

"Is that why Ben's so quiet?" I asked. Jessie nodded.

"Probably. But who knows? They've got a good daddy, and he's been with this woman named Faye since they were still little. You can't replace a mama, I guess, but she's done her best. But yeah, I think Ben blames himself." I nodded, almost sorry I'd asked. We were quiet the rest of the way, but we still held hands. And we were still holding hands when we got to the little covered work area. I saw Melissa notice, and she and Hanna smiled at each other and then at me. I felt myself blush, but I didn't let go of Jessie's hand.

They had just finished getting the wheels attached to the upside-down box I'd seen when I came looking for Jessie that day, and we all had to grab hold to help flip the whole thing over.

"Now we gotta attach the rails," Melissa said.

"Yeah, don't want clumsy over here fallin' out and gettin' run over," Will said, pointing a thumb at his twin.

"That only happened once!" Melissa objected, and everyone laughed. Nina and Penny got there not long after we did, and I guessed they hadn't taken their sweet time walking over after lunch the way Jessie and I had. I tried not to cling too close to Jessie as we worked, but she never seemed to stray far from my side. She talked and laughed with the rest of them, but I could feel at least part of her attention on me the whole time, like she wanted to make sure I felt included. It was nice, but at the same time, I didn't want her to feel like I couldn't take care of myself. I made sure to do my fair share of the work, and I tried to speak up some instead of just listening to everyone else talk.

"So this foundation is from a cabin that burned down?" I asked after a while, remembering what Hanna and Melissa had said about the covered work area where we were.

"Ooh, that's a good story! You tell it, Will," Hanna said, smiling at him. I saw him roll his eyes, but Nina and Penny looked at each other and smirked.

"Actually, I think Jessie tells it better," Will said, and Hanna made a pouty face.

"Will passed up a chance to hear himself talk," Ben said. "Somebody write it down!" I expected Will to get mad at that, but he was laughing along with the rest of us.

"Yeah, yeah," Will said. "Go on, Jessie, you make it spookier than I can."

"Aw, now, I don't know about that—" Jessie started, but everyone cut her off, begging her to tell it. "All right, all right, sheesh!" She laughed. The railing was finished by then, so we all climbed into the boxy platform and sat down inside. We just barely fit in a tight circle with our legs crisscrossed, and my right knee was touching Jessie's left. She looked over at me and winked. The sun was past the treetops, and the shade of the roof above us made the shadows deeper.

"Way I heard it," Jessie started, "this spot right here was really the very first cabin built, not the last one on the row like we call it now. And the people that built it were the first ones here." We were all leaning toward her a little, and I thought about the way everyone had gathered 'round to listen to her sing that first night I met her. She was like a magnet, pulling us in.

"The man was some kinda politician, and he'd gotten this land in a government deal, all around both sides of the lake. But the family fortunes weren't what they used to be, and he needed to make some money, so this man . . ."

"Mr. George," Penny called out.

"That's right," Jessie said. "So Mr. George, he packed up his wife and little daughter and brought them out here to live in a cabin by the lake while he built this whole place. He had the idea that folks would come out here for the peace and quiet."

"And the fishing," Ben added.

"And the fishing," Jessie said, nodding. "Problem was, Mother Nature didn't want to cooperate. Seemed like she didn't care for them big machines tearing up her skin to lay all these concrete foundations, nor the buzz saws clearing so many trees back from the edge of the lake." The others were nodding in agreement, and I wondered how many times they'd all heard this story. "No sooner had they built this first cabin than she sent the storms, terrible storms with thunder and lightning, and they didn't let up all summer long. It terrified the wife and daughter, who were already kinda nervous-like on account of they were city folks. And it slowed the whole operation almost to a standstill. Meanwhile, poor Mr. George was still havin' to feed and house and pay all them workers he'd brought out here and set up in tents."

"Then the tornado struck!" Penny said.

"That's right," Jessie went on. "That tornado was the last straw. Twenty men died with nowhere to hide, no protection but canvas tents. It was a miracle Mr. George and his family survived it, but that twister skipped right over their cabin. I guess that was his one piece of good luck. The workers that survived it packed it in and left, claiming the whole place was cursed."

"Because of how they stole it," Melissa put in.

"Stole it how? From who?" I asked, but it was Will who answered. *So much for him passing up the chance to hear himself talk*, I thought.

"Lake Eufaula is man-made," he said. "The Army Corps of Engineers dammed the Chattahoochee and flooded out a whole town of Creek Indians."

"Well, they moved them off the land first, but yeah," Ben said. "Just one in a long list of land grabs by the US government." Will looked at Ben admiringly. I didn't know what they were talking about, but hearing them criticize the government gave me a little pang of homesickness.

"Let me guess," I said to chase it away, "there's a book about all this in the library?" They all laughed and nodded. I liked making them laugh, especially Jessie.

"Where was I?" she asked. "Oh right, so Mrs. George and her little daughter went back to her family up north after that, but Mr. George refused to leave. He'd sunk every penny he had in this place, and he wouldn't give up on it. Some folks said he kept on working, trying to build a row of cabins by hand so he could get paying guests rollin' through, but nobody really knew what he was up to. Winter set in, and it was just as bad as summer had been, but with snow and ice instead of lightning and tornadoes. There wasn't a good road out here yet; the hi-way was a few years off. It was spring before anybody could come check on him, and by then all they found was the burned-out husk of this one cabin and a row of concrete foundations with nothin' on 'em.

"They say his bones were half-laid over the doorstep, like he tried to get away but the fire got him anyway. And on a stormy night, you can still hear him howlin' over his lost fortunes." It was full dark by then, and no one said a word for a few minutes. I felt the hairs on my arms stand up, I was so spooked.

"Boo!" Nina said, breaking the spell. We all jumped about a mile, and then we were laughing. We climbed out of the float, stretching our legs and admiring our handiwork.

"She looks pretty good," Will said, "maybe a little plain."

"Yeah, we need to weave some colorful material through the rails, maybe," Melissa said. "Make it look more festive."

"We brought a bunch back from this last trip," Penny replied. "I'm sure there's something there we can use. Y'all wanna come look?"

"Sure!" Hanna said. *All of us?* I thought. I looked over and caught Jessie's eye.

"I don't know, Penny," Jessie said, "your mama might not want all of us bargin' in on her and riflin' through her stuff with no warning. Maybe we should do it another time, after you ask if it's all right."

"Nah," Penny said. "She won't care. And besides, it's my stuff too! I helped find a lot of it." Jessie looked at me and shrugged, and I smiled and shrugged back. So far my new friends and my new family had been mostly separate for me, but it looked like they were about to come together whether I was ready or not. We cleaned up the work area a little, putting tools back in their places and stacking the extra scraps of wood over to one side, then started walking behind Penny toward her house. I could tell she liked being in the lead and figured it didn't happen much since she was one of the younger ones in the group. I didn't want to take anything away from that, so I dropped back until I was at the tail end with only Jessie beside me.

"You okay?" she asked, looking at me from the corner of her eye.

"Me?" I asked, stalling. She gave a low little laugh. "I'm fine," I said. "I guess I'm just not sure how to act when we get there. Am I one of the family or one of the visitors?" I turned my head to look at Jessie. She shrugged and laughed again, then took my hand, and we walked along without talking for a minute before she spoke.

"We don't have to . . . I don't want you to feel like I expect you to do this"—she lifted our hands up a little—"in front of your mama. I know things are already a little touchy between you and her, and then she said that stuff about not understanding *that kind of love* or whatever. And I know you're still figuring out . . . what you want to do about everything, with going back home and all that." She let her voice trail off. It felt like my heart dropped through my feet straight into a hole in the ground, but somehow, I was still walking and holding Jessie's hand.

"I don't . . . I don't know what to say," I managed. "I don't want you to think . . . I'm not . . ." She laughed again, maybe a little bit sad, but not angry at least.

"It's okay, Ami. Really. We've got time. *You've* got time. I'm not about to be another one that's rushin' you to figure out your whole life this very minute, okay?" I looked at her, and she looked me in the eye and smiled. "Okay?" she said again, and I nodded and squeezed her hand. We didn't say anything else, and when we got close to my mama's house, she let me go. I felt like I wanted to cry, but I knew she was right. I wasn't ready.

It turned out that I was mostly worried for nothing, though. It was almost dinnertime, and Mama and Marcus were in the kitchen together chopping vegetables. They said hi to everyone, and she wiped her hands on a towel before giving me a hug, but then they went back to their cooking and let us be. We all went on to the den and picked through the pile of fabric scraps, pulling out any little bit that was red, white, or blue, planning to go back and finish decorating the float after dinner at the lodge. I hoped I'd get a chance to be alone with Jessie sometime before the night was over, but just as we were getting ready to leave, Mama came out of the kitchen again.

"Are you girls running off again? Ami, I was hoping you'd stay for supper?" I looked at Penny, who had clearly been on her way out the door to eat with her friends, and saw her shoulders sag as she gave me a little nod.

"Oh . . . are you sure there's enough?" I asked, not sure what else to say.

"Lissie performs the loaves and fishes miracle on a daily basis," Marcus said, laughing. "There's always enough."

"Don't worry," Melissa said as they left. "We'll get it all fixed up, and then y'all can be surprised tomorrow when you see it!" I caught Jessie's eye and she gave me her crooked grin, and then they were gone. I wanted to be with them, but I knew I should be thankful to be spending this time with my family. I forced myself to pay attention to where I was and quit moonin' over Jessie.

Supper was fine, and we all let Penny carry the conversation. She was excited about tomorrow, and I was learning when Penny got excited, she talked. That was good because I could tell that we were all still a little raw and careful with each other after the disaster of our first day together and my mother's comments the day before. I wondered if she had told Marcus about all that.

After we ate and cleared away the dishes, Marcus said he'd handle the washing so Mama could finish fitting our dresses. They were the same material but slightly different styles, and Penny pranced around in hers, twirling to show off the full skirt. The top of mine felt tighter and closer to my body than anything I'd ever worn, but Penny said it looked a little loose through the waist, and Mama clucked and pinned, trying to get it just right. I guessed she'd had a lot more practice sewing for Penny. It didn't take her long to take in the waist, though, and I was just about to head back to my room with it draped over my arm when Penny stopped me.

"Hey, um, are you in a hurry to get back?" she asked, sounding a little bashful. I shook my head no and waited. "I just thought maybe, you know, you might want to hang out? With me? I wanted to show you . . . something." She let her voice trail off and looked down at the floor, embarrassed. "But I mean, if you're tired or whatever, it's no big deal."

"I'm not tired," I said. "I'd love to hang out."

"Great!" she said, leading me down the hall. "You've never seen my room and I just thought, well, that seems weird? And also I wanted to show you this." We had reached her room, and she gestured to the walls. They were covered with drawings, or maybe one big drawing, depending on how you thought of it, that covered almost every inch from corner to corner and floor to ceiling.

"What is it?" I breathed.

"It's my city," Penny said. She was watching my face to try to tell if I liked it or not. Penny had imagined a city with buildings of all sizes and shapes, all in scale, with roads crisscrossing in between.

"Penny, it's . . . it's amazing! I've never seen anything like it. You drew all this?" She nodded her head, pleased that I liked it.

"I've been working on it since I was about twelve. Daddy is an artist, too, so everyone tries to bring him back colored pencils and paints and things when they go out scavenging. Some of this is crayons that we've melted down and re-formed."

I stepped into the little room, speechless, and tried to take in all the details. There were tiny people walking on sidewalks and cars driving on the streets. Clustered together in one section were tall towers, all corners and sharp edges, that almost reached the ceiling.

"That's downtown," Penny said when she saw me studying it. "Big cities had a part called 'downtown' where all the offices and things were. So, like, every morning the people got in their cars or took trains and buses to work downtown, and then at night they went home again." She pointed to another section that looked like little houses lined up on a grid.

"I saw something like that," I said, "on the way here to Lake

Point. A whole empty town. Have you seen it, too? How did you . . . ?" She shook her head.

"No, I've only read about it. And I've seen some pictures in books. I've probably got it all wrong, but this is how I imagine it would have looked. Before." I pulled my eyes away from the walls to focus on my sister.

"Well, I've never seen a big city like this, but the part with the houses looks like what I saw. Except these houses don't have trees growing through the roofs." I laughed, but it didn't sound right.

"Was it terrible?' she asked in a quiet voice. I nodded, surprised to feel a tear slip down my cheek.

"It was so empty," I said. "In a sad, lonesome, terrible way." Penny hugged me.

"I'm sorry," she said. "I didn't know . . ."

"Don't be silly!" I said, stepping back. "How could you have? And besides, this is so . . . I can't imagine being able to do something like this. I'm no good at drawing, but even if I could do that part of it, I don't think I could imagine all this the way you have."

"I bet that's not true," Penny said. "Everyone's got an imagination. All that time you spent with no one to play with, you never imagined friends for yourself or anything like that?"

"I did," I said. "I forgot about that. But an imaginary friend is nothing like all this."

"Sure it is," she said. "And besides that, everyone can draw. It just takes practice. *A lot* of practice if you want to get good at it."

"I wouldn't know where to even start," I said.

"I could show you some things. To get started, you know? If you wanted." She was bashful again. Here was this amazing girl who imagined whole cities and made them real on her walls, and she was shy about wanting to spend time with me.

"I'd love that, if you're sure you want to waste your time with a hopeless case." I laughed. She rolled her eyes, but her voice sounded serious when she answered.

"There's no such thing as hopeless, Ami."

Twenty-Five

The next morning, I woke up early, too excited about the day to go back to sleep. I showered quickly, then stood in front of the mirror, combing my wet hair into long, straight strands that fell to my hips. When it dried, it coiled up and shrank to hit right at my waist, but combed out wet I could see its true length. After we finished working on the float the day before, I had seen a pair of scissors lying forgotten on a bench. Without thinking too much about it, I'd scooped them up and stuck them in my pocket. Now they were on the edge of the sink in front of me. I wondered if I could do what I was thinking of.

I had what Jessie would call a love-hate relationship with my hair. It had always been there, fighting its way out of my braids and buns. It was hot and unruly and it got in my way, but it was part of me. Papa preached that a woman should never cut her hair, but no one at Lake Point seemed to believe that. My mother's hair barely brushed her shoulders, and I wondered how long she'd been here before she was brave enough to cut it. She had tried to talk me into doing the same. Maybe if I cut it, she would feel like I had taken her advice. Maybe it would remind us both that we didn't have to keep following the old ideas we'd learned at Heavenly Shepherd. *Knock it loose*, I heard Penny say.

I gathered all the strands into a loose tail at the nape of my neck and tied it. My hair dried quickly, as thick as it was, and it was already starting to curl up. I didn't want it to be too short, so I slid the tie down until it hung between my shoulder blades when I let the bundled hair drop. Then I picked it up again, grabbed the scissors, and before I could change my mind, I cut just above the tie. The scissors were old but had been recently sharpened, so it was surprisingly easy to saw through all the gathered hair, and then I was holding my ponytail in my hand. It felt strange to see a part of me cut off like that. I felt faint and had to sit down on the lid of the toilet and put my head between my knees for a minute. *It's okay, Ami*, I told myself over and over, *you're fine.*

I wasn't ready to look in the mirror yet, though, so I went back into the bedroom and put on my dress. It had little white buttons up the front, and I admired my mother's skill at sewing buttonholes. *I'll have to get her to teach me that*, I thought. Once I was dressed, I paced back and forth, trying to work up the courage to look in the mirror. My damp hair still covered my shoulders, but I knew that when it dried completely, it wouldn't quite reach them. Finally, I took a deep breath and went to look.

I hardly recognized myself! It wasn't just my hair, although that was part of it. I hadn't worn a dress since the night I ran away from home, but this dress was nothing like the long, loose shifts I'd grown up in. It had narrow straps that went over my shoulders, and my mother had sewn them from a different white material than the blue flowers she'd made most of the dress from. The white also outlined the top where the straps attached, and the bodice was fitted in a way that showed off the curve of my chest. The skirt flared out from my waist and ended just above my knees, and there was a narrow band of the white material sewn all around the bottom. It was the prettiest dress I'd ever seen, and for the first time, I understood how Penny could get so excited about clothes.

I want Jessie to see me in this dress, I thought. My hair curled softly around my face, and I imagined that it was somehow happy not to be scraped back into a braid for once. Maybe once it dried, I would pull it up into a puff of curls at the crown of my head, but I wanted to see what it would do if I left it alone. My chest and shoulders looked pale and blank compared to my face, but I knew that within a few hours they would be covered with freckles of their own. Kisses from the sun, Ruth called them when I was little. But I wasn't a little girl anymore. I looked grown-up, and that made me feel grown-up.

Finally, there was a knock at the door. I had been impatient for Jessie to get there, but suddenly I felt shy. What if she didn't like my short hair? What if she didn't like my dress? But then I remembered what she'd said that first long day we spent together: *You can still be just Ami. Just yourself.* I took a deep breath and opened the door. Jessie opened her mouth like she had been ready to say something as soon as I opened the door, but whatever it was, she forgot it when she saw me.

"Ami Miles," she said finally, "just *look* at you." She stepped into the room, grabbed both of my hands, and spun me around. "You're off the compound now, ain't ya?" Jessie laughed, then stepped back for another look. "Your hair looks real pretty like that," she said softly. By then it was mostly dry, and it puffed out around my face in a wild ball of curls that stopped above my shoulders. "It's like . . . *happy hair*," she said. I laughed and told her I had thought the exact same thing. "I guess I shoulda paid more attention at your mama's sewing class too. I want a dress to fit me like that!"

"Well, I'm glad you appreciate the *dress*," I said, smiling.

"Oh, I appreciate it, all right," Jessie said, pulling me close. "But that dress wouldn't look half as good on anyone else." She reached up with one hand and lightly traced my collarbones, bared for someone else to see for the first time I could ever remember. Then she ran both hands over my naked shoulders. "Beautiful girl," she whispered, and then she kissed me. By the time we made it out of that room, we had missed breakfast, and I'd had to get dressed all over again.

"There you two are," said Hanna as we walked up to the work space. "We were about to give up on you!" Then she took a closer look. "Wow, Ami! You look amazing! Look at your cute hair! And that *dress*!" I felt my face flush bright red and looked down at the ground to try to hide it.

"Don't be shy, Ami, you look really pretty!" This was Penny, and I smiled at her gratefully. I guess she had changed her mind about having Marcus braid her hair—she was wearing it down, so our hair looked a little alike now. She saw me look at hers and smiled.

"Y'all match!" Nina said, and it felt good to know she was right.

"All right, all right," Will said. "Enough with the gooshy-girl lovefest over there. Let's get this thing moving!" Everyone grabbed one of the ropes tied to the railing, and the float moved easily off the concrete pad and onto the path.

When we got to the starting area for the parade, I saw my mama and Marcus standing under the shade of a big old live oak. Penny saw me notice them and smiled at me.

"Come show Mama your hair!" she said, and before I could answer, she was pulling me by the hand. I looked back over my shoulder at Jessie, but she just waved me on.

"Look at you!" Mama exclaimed when she saw me. "I love it," she said softly, reaching out to touch it. "It suits your face real nice. Don't it feel good to have all that weight off you?" She was smiling because she already knew the answer. I nodded and reached up to touch it myself, still feeling a little shocked that so much of it was gone. "And your dress, do you like it?"

"I love it," I answered honestly. "Maybe you can teach me how to make a pattern sometime. I've only got this dress and the few things of Amber's that she gave me before I left. I'll be needing some more clothes." *If I stay*, I didn't say. Was I planning on staying? Would I have that choice, or would Papa show up and drag me back to the compound?

"I would love that, Ami," she said.

Soon it was time for the parade to begin. While I was with my family, the horses had been hitched to our float. It was the only float, as it turned out. A few other people rode horseback, and there were a handful of old bicycles and wagons, but most people just walked. Everyone was decked out in red, white, and blue. People had made crazy hats and fancy outfits, and everyone looked happy. I had never been a part of anything like it, and I loved the way the excitement was catching.

On the float, Jessie played her guitar, and we sang "America the Beautiful," which I'd had to learn, having never heard it back home. Watching her stand tall in that float, playing and singing in front of all those people like it was nothing, she took my breath away. We rolled along, singing and waving, and I felt as full and happy as I had ever felt in my life. I still didn't know what I *should* do, but I was getting an idea of what I *wanted* to do. It wasn't going to be easy, and there was no way I could do it alone, but I was pretty sure I wouldn't have to. *I'm not alone*, I thought, *not anymore*. I just wondered if there was a way I could do right by the family I'd left and still hold on to this new life I'd found.

After the parade, there was a big meal on the patio behind the lodge. It reminded me of the first day I came to Lake Point, walking out with Helen and seeing, for the first time, the miracle of all those people. Before I knew it, the sun was setting and people were lighting little smudge fires to keep the mosquitoes away. Everyone broke off into groups around each fire, and I found myself in a circle with Jessie and her guitar. It was just like the night I met her, except this time, I knew that my place was beside her. She still made my heart beat fast and filled my stomach with butterflies, but now I understood why, so I didn't get as flustered as I had been then. We sang patriotic songs like "The Star-Spangled Banner" and "This Land Is Your Land," but Jessie also played and sang "Little Sparrow" when I asked, and everyone called for "Good and Greasy" too.

After a while, people drifted off, back to their cabins and cottages and rooms, ready for sleep after all the excitement of the day. I was tired too, but I was hoping for time alone with Jessie. After she sang her last song and our circle broke up, she looked at me with a sleepy smile.

"Can I walk you back to your room?" she asked, and I blushed, right on cue. She laughed.

"That might be my favorite thing about you," she teased. "You can't hide nothin', girl!" I shook my head, laughing, and leaned my head back to look up at the stars.

"Yeah, well," I said, "I'm glad you think that's funny." She was on her feet by then, and she reached down to pull me up.

"Where do you live, anyway?" I asked as we walked.

"Well, it's funny you should ask that," she said, "because I'm about to need to move, I think." I waited, quiet, until she was ready to say more. "I been living in our same cabin since my daddy died, but it's not really right for me to stay there now that it's just me." I knew that most single people lived in rooms at the lodge, but it still didn't seem right for Jessie to have to leave her home, and I said so.

"Aw, nobody's gonna run me out; it's nothin' like that. I just thought, well . . . if everything goes okay, Teenie and the baby and Matthew need the space more than I do." She looked at me sideways to see my reaction.

"What about her mama?" I asked. "Doesn't Teenie live with her now?"

"Yeah, but they're in one of the little cottages that's really just one bedroom. My cabin's got two. And besides, Lurene's got the palsy and it's gettin' worse. My cabin is closer to the lodge where they got the infirmary, plus Margie is just a couple doors down."

"Margie the midwife?" I asked.

"Well, yeah, but she's also Margie the nurse, Margie the doctor, and Margie the all-around healer," she said, flashing me a grin. "She'll be able to look in on Teenie, the baby, *and* Lurene more often this way." We'd made it up to my room by then, and we stopped and looked at each other shyly.

"Come in?" I asked, but it was barely a question.

"You sure?" she asked. "I mean, I said I didn't want to rush you into anything."

"Yeah, you talk a good game," I said, smiling, and I opened the door and pulled her in behind me.

Twenty-Six

I woke up that next morning with Jessie beside me, and just like that, I knew what I needed to do. Once I told her my plan, everything would change, so I just lay there watching her sleep until she opened her eyes and caught me. She laughed and rolled over, hiding her face.

"I wasn't droolin', was I?" she asked.

"Only a little," I said, and she sat up and threw her pillow at me. I sat up to face her and hugged the pillow to my stomach, suddenly nervous.

"Uh-oh," she said. "Serious face." She was trying to joke, but she looked scared.

"Jessie," I said quietly. "I need to go home." She looked away and then back at my face, searching. "But I'm coming back," I said quickly.

"You don't have to say that," she said, turning her back to me so her feet touched the floor on the other side of the bed. "I understand."

"You don't, though," I said. "Come here. Please?" She twisted around until I was looking at the side of her face, but she kept one foot on the floor.

"When I came here," I started, "I was runnin' away. I was scared, and I had just found out my mama might still be alive, and I had no blessed *idea* that there could be somebody like you in the world." She looked up at the ceiling and then back at me, letting out a shaky breath. "But now that I've been here," I went on, "now that I've met *you* and felt what it could be like to have this . . . this *whole life* instead of just a little piece of one . . . well, I'll never be the same. And I don't want to be. But the way I left things at home . . . it's still pullin' on me."

"So what does that mean, then?" she asked. "What are you gonna do?"

"I'm gonna go back and face them, Papa Solomon and my grandma Ruth, and I'm gonna take my mama and Marcus and Penny with me. And we're gonna ask them all to come back with us." I waited for her to laugh or to tell me I was crazy for think-ing that would work, which I probably was, but she just studied my face and then nodded.

"What if they say no?" she asked.

"Then I'll know I tried, and I'll come back here and get on with my life," I said. It sounded simple, but I knew it wouldn't be.

"I wish I could go with you," she said.

"I wish you could too. But you probably don't want to be there when I tell my mama about us, anyway," I said. She let out a little laugh.

"You don't have to, Ami. I told you. There's no rush."

"I know I don't have to," I said. "Just like you don't have to keep tryin' to protect me." She started to say something, but I kept going. "I heard what all you said about not having to decide my whole life right this second, and I get that now, I do. I know there's no way I can even start to imagine all the things that might happen or how I might feel in a year or two years, or ten. But the thing is," I said, turning her to face me the rest of the way, "right now it's even harder for me to imagine not wanting you with me while I figure all that out." She closed her eyes for a long second, and then opened them again.

"You talk a good game," she said, and then she tackled me.

About an hour later, Jessie left to talk to Teenie about moving into her cabin, and I went to talk to my family. We tried to keep our goodbyes light, promising we'd see each other again soon, but we both cried anyway.

Convincing my mother to go back to Heavenly Shepherd was even harder than I expected.

"You know they won't come, Ami," she said. "There's just no point to it."

"They probably won't," I admitted, "not Papa and Ruth, anyway. But what about your sisters and brother? And Amber and David? They're just wasting away on the compound when they could be here with all these people!"

"They could have come here anytime after I sent word," she said, digging in her heels.

"No they couldn't, Mama. Not without leaving me behind. And they don't really know how it is here. Maybe they're just stuck and they need us to come and, and . . . knock them loose," I said, smiling at Penny.

"I want to see where you came from," Penny put in, "you *and* Ami. And I want *them* to see how good we're doing even though they turned us away." She stuck out her chin, and I knew she was remembering that awful story.

"Oh, it's just too much, girls," my mother said, "it's too far. How would we even get there?"

"We could take my boat," Marcus said. We all turned to look at him, and he smiled.

"A little fishing boat isn't gonna hold us all for a trip upriver, honey," Mama said, "or carry any extra people back."

"About that . . . ," Marcus said, "I might not have told you the whole truth about how little it is. I wanted it to be a surprise, but now I think it's time."

It turned out that Marcus's *little fishing boat* was a big old pontoon boat that he'd patched up, with a big solar-powered motor attached to the back of it. There was plenty of room for ten people on that thing, with bench seats and a plastic roof overhead.

"I saw something kind of like this on my way here," I said. "It was more like a big raft, but it had a motor like yours, and there were some rough-lookin' men on it. Four of them." Marcus nodded.

"Runners," he said. "Probably the Barnett brothers. They live south of here." My mother's face was pale.

"Oh, Ami!" she said. "I can't believe you walked all the way here by yourself. What if they'd taken you?"

"They seemed too lazy for all that," I joked, but I still remembered how scared I'd felt when I saw them coming down the river.

"You might be right about that. I think they'd rather run moonshine up and down the river than stolen girls," Marcus said, but his face looked troubled. "They give this place a wide berth since Helen took after them with a shotgun a couple of years ago. And they won't like mine any better. I don't think we'll need to worry about them."

The trip that took me five days to walk took only two going upriver on the boat. By the morning of the second day, I'd worked up the courage to talk to my mother about Jessie and me. We were sitting on one of the long benches that ran along the side of the boat, just watching the water roll by and not saying much while Marcus and Penny tinkered with the motor at the back.

"Mama," I said, not wanting to have this conversation but knowing we needed to. "You know that no matter how this goes with Papa and Ruth, I'm coming back to Lake Point, right?"

"I do, but it makes me so happy to hear you say it that you can tell me again if you want." She smiled. I smiled back and wished I could just leave it at that.

"It makes me happy too. I know we got kind of a bumpy start, but I feel like I'm doing better with understanding why you left now. Any fool can see that you and Marcus belong together, and Penny." I looked toward the back of the boat and then down at my hands in my lap. "Well, y'all have done a real good job with her."

"Oh, Ami," she said, and scooted closer to put her arm around my shoulders. "It means a lot to me to hear you say that. I know none of this is easy. But I don't know if I can take too much credit for how Penny has turned out. Look how good you turned out in spite of who raised you. You're just good girls, both of you." She shook her head, and I could see she was trying not to cry.

"I'm glad you think so," I said, "but you might not after what I need to tell you." She looked up at me, surprised.

"Now what foolishness is this?" she asked. "There's not a thing in the world you could tell me that would make me any less proud of you!"

"Even if I took it into my head to love someone in a way you thought was *unnatural*?" I asked, forcing myself to look at her and not down at my nervous fingers. Her eyes darkened, but she didn't look away.

"Ami—" she started, but I held up a hand to stop her.

"Please, Mama, just let me get this out, okay? If I'm gonna come back with you and be a real family, I don't want to start out hidin' things because it's easier." She nodded, and I made myself say it. "It's Jessie." I expected her to look surprised, but she didn't. She just looked sad.

"You knew?" I asked.

"Lake Point is a small place, honey," she said with a little smile. "I didn't really know, but I suspected. But, Ami—"

"Please don't, Mama," I said.

"Don't what? Tell you how young you are? This is all so new to you; how can you really know what love is?"

"How did *you* know? You weren't much older than me when you met Marcus! And you wanna hear something really funny? You sound like Jessie." She did look surprised then. "She's so worried about not rushin' me and makin' sure I really know what I want. She says my feelings could change because that's how people are."

"Well, she's right about that," she said. "You just haven't met the right boy, honey. When you do, you'll know it." I stood up and started pacing.

"*How* will I know? Will I feel like I just found a piece of myself I didn't even know was missing? Will I feel like I'll die if he smiles at me and I'll die if he doesn't? Will I know because I've never felt so much like myself as I do when I'm with him?" Her face had gone from surprise to shock. "Because that's how I feel with Jessie. And I know, I *know*, people can change, feelings can change, I get it! But that doesn't mean these feelings I have right now aren't real. I love her, and I don't see that goin' away anytime soon. So I hope you can find a way to be okay with that, because I didn't run away from Papa and Ruth just so *you* could be the one to tell me that all I'm good for is making babies."

"Ami! I would never say that!" she said. She stood up and put her hands on my shoulders to stop my pacing. "I'm sorry if I made you feel like that. I guess it's just . . . like I said, some of the old ways I was taught stuck a little harder than others. I'm sorry I ever said that about you and Penny maybe bein' able to have babies. I shouldn't have! All I want is for you to be safe and happy. That's what I thought I was giving you by leaving you at Heavenly Shepherd, so I guess I've just never been any good at this."

"Don't say that," I said. "I was safe and happy most of the time, and I'm safe and happy now. But what would really make me happy is if we all go home together and you get to know Jessie and see that she wants the same things for me as you do." She still looked doubtful, but she took a deep breath and nodded.

"Okay," she said. "I'll try."

"Well, I'm glad that's settled," Penny called out. "I don't think I can squat back here by this motor for much longer!"

We docked at the fishing camp where Jacob had brought me years before, but I barely recognized it. It took us two more days to walk inland to the hi-way, and then there it was, Heavenly Shepherd. I felt so different, it was hard to believe the whole place looked exactly the same. We barely made it across the road and into the yard before Papa and Ruth came out the door.

"Ami!" Ruth cried out. "Oh, thank you, Jesus! I was worried sick about you. How could you scare me like—" She'd been rushing toward me, but Papa reached out his hand to stop her. She looked at him like she wanted to push on past, but she obeyed.

"The prodigal returns," Papa said in his same slow way as always.

"Hello, Daddy," my mother said, and her voice only shook a little. "Mama." Ruth put a hand over her mouth, but I could see that she was crying. Papa looked his daughter up and down, then did the same to Marcus and Penny. I was right beside her, but he didn't look at me at all.

"You got something you want to say to me?" Penny called out. I looked over, surprised, and saw that her hands were clenched into fists by her sides. "Maybe an ugly name you want to call me?"

"Penny," Marcus said, his voice low and warning. I reached over to take her hand, and when she opened her fist, it was shaking. Papa's eyes got wider in his face, then he let out an ugly little laugh and looked back at my mother. Billie and Rachel had come out of the main house to stand behind him by then, and as we stood there, I saw Jacob and David come out of their trailers and freeze, taking in the scene. But when Amber came out, she let the door slam behind her and ran to where we stood.

"Oh, thank God," she said, wrapping me in a hug. "I was afraid I'd killed you, sending you out there like that."

"Yeah, we're gonna have a talk about that," my mama said, but she smiled when Amber hugged her next.

"I always knew you'd be back here someday, draggin' that little ragtag, half-breed family of yours behind you and beggin' to come home. I don't know why you think it'll be any different this time," Papa called out. Mama gasped like she'd been slapped. I saw Billie look at Ruth and shake her head in disgust, but my grandmother didn't seem to notice. She was looking from me to Penny and back again, her hand still covering her mouth like she'd forgotten she held it there. I remembered my short hair, pulled up into a ball of curls at the crown of my head, and I knew she could see that I'd cut it. Penny wore hers the same way, and I wondered if Ruth thought we looked alike. Was she seeing what she could have had, what *we* could have had all these years?

"She didn't come to beg you for anything," I said. "They came because I asked them to. Now are we gonna stand here in the yard all day, or are you gonna invite us in? It's hot out here, and we got a lot to talk about." Papa reacted before he could think about it, and for the first time in my life, I heard him yell.

"Whore of Babylon!" he hollered. His words went through me like a shot, but I didn't fall down dead.

"Don't you *dare* call her that!" my mother screamed, stepping out in front of me. "Don't you dare stand there and think you can talk to my daughter that way!" Papa looked shocked. No one had ever talked to Solomon Miles that way. Not as long as I'd been alive.

"Elisabeth." Ruth finally spoke. "That is your father you're speaking to. Show some respect." My mother laughed a bitter, ugly laugh.

"Respect? Respect, Mama? Like he respected me when he bred me to a stranger like a dog? Respect like he showed me when he spit in my face and turned me and my family out to freeze and starve? I knew we shouldn't have come here," she said, turning to Marcus. "This was a mistake, just like the last time."

"Ungrateful slut!" Papa hollered at her. "I gave you everything a good woman could want—a safe home, a family, plenty to eat. But you chose—"

"That's right, Daddy. I *chose*," she hollered, turning back to face him. "That's the part you really can't stand, ain't it? Sometimes I think you didn't even really care about all that *mixing of the races* garbage. You just couldn't stand the thought that

I disobeyed you. That I could've done a single thing by myself, without your permission or your plans for me. You hated that so much that you turned away the one thing you always claimed to want!" Her voice broke then, and she put her arm around Penny's shoulders and hugged her closer. They were both crying.

"That's not true," Ruth said, but it sounded almost like a question. She was crying too.

"Oh, Mama," my mother said, and she sounded so tired. "You know it is."

"That's enough," Papa said. His voice was back to normal then, sure and controlled. "Ami, you come on in the house now. The rest of you can go back where you came from." I laughed in disbelief. I looked down at the ground, trying to gather the courage to defy my grandfather for the first time in my life. I'd stood in this same spot staring at the ground the day I came home to find Zeke Johnson waiting for me. But what I saw now was my own two feet. Those feet had carried me far from home and back again, and I was not the same scared little girl I'd been that day. I looked up at him and caught his eyes with mine.

"We've been traveling for two days, and we need to rest," I said. "And then we're gonna sit down as a family and talk." They all looked at me then, and I heard Amber chuckle behind me. Papa stood there a few seconds, shaking with rage, then he turned around and went inside.

"Ruth," I started, but she just shook her head and followed him into the house. We all stood there for a minute, not sure what to do, until Rachel finally spoke.

"You always were trouble," she said with a smirk, and then she stepped forward and it was like a spell had been broken. Mama laughed, and suddenly we were surrounded by my aunts and uncles, everyone hugging and crying. They all exclaimed over Penny and how she'd grown from the tiny baby she'd been the only time they'd seen her.

"Y'all favor!" Amber said, looking from me to Penny and back again. "I wouldn't have thought it, but you really do." Penny looked at me, and I could see she felt overwhelmed by so many adults fussing over her.

"Of course we do," I said, taking her hand again. "We're sisters."

After a whirlwind of cleaning and gathering of supplies from their own trailers, Rachel and Billie got us set up in one of the double-wides that had been sitting empty for years. I thought about Jessie packing up and clearing out of her cabin and wished I could be there to help. I wondered how Teenie was doing and if the baby had come yet. I hoped I would have the chance to meet them both when I got back to Lake Point. *Please God,* I prayed, *watch over them and keep them safe.* I wasn't even sure I knew who I was praying to or if I believed it could make a difference anymore, but I figured it couldn't hurt, and at least it felt like doing something.

My aunts and uncles spent two days trying to convince Papa Solomon to sit down and talk to us, but he wouldn't budge. That second night, though, Ruth came over to the trailer where we were staying. I was surprised—I'd never known her to go against Papa's wishes, and I wondered what it would cost her. We all squeezed in around the little kitchen table—Ruth, Mama, Marcus, Penny, and me. My aunts and uncles sat nearby in the den where they could hear what was going on, even Amber. We all sat there for a few minutes without saying anything, and then Ruth sniffed and looked right at me.

"Well, Ami," she said in a quiet voice, "I can't imagine what you think you have to say for yourself, but I don't reckon I'll ever see you again after this, so I came to hear it."

"What?" Penny blurted out. My mother looked at Marcus and held her hand out toward Ruth like *you see?* But I wasn't really surprised. I took a deep breath before I answered.

"If you don't ever see me again," I said softly, "that will be your choice, not mine." I could see that I'd surprised her, and I pressed on. "You lied to me about Mama. And not just about her. Every day of my life, you kept things from me and taught me just the little bits of things that you wanted me to know." Ruth shook her head and tried to interrupt, but I wasn't finished. "You and Papa both, you think if you stay here and shut the world out, you can make whatever kind of truth you want, but it ain't workin'. It never has. Your family is dyin', and you put it all on me to save it, but I can't do that. And I don't even need to! There's people still out there, Ruth, good people. We don't have to stay here like this—"

"That's enough," she cut in. She looked at me and shook her head. "You are just like your mama in spite of my best efforts," she said. "Ungrateful, always thinkin' you need *more*. We don't have to stay here like this? There's good people out there? Look what those good people have led you to already—wearin' them clothes with your arms and legs stickin' out everywhere, your hair cut short, talkin' back to your elders. I'm *ashamed* of you, Ami. I thought I raised you better." She might as well have slapped me. I felt tears well up and spill over, and all the words I could have said got caught in my throat. Penny stood up fast, almost knocking her chair over backward.

"You're awful!" she said, pointing a finger at Ruth.

"Penny!" Mama said.

"No! I'm not gonna sit here and listen to this . . . this . . . *mean old lady* talk to Ami like that!" She looked back at Ruth. "I don't see *you* being brave enough to leave this place all by yourself. I don't see *you* tryin' to make things right with the people you've hurt like Ami is doing. She could have stayed at Lake Point with us and . . . her friends, and forgot all about you, but she wanted to try to talk sense to you and give you a chance to come back with us! I even wanted to meet you because you're my grandmother. But you're just . . . just . . ." Her shoulders slumped and she sat down hard, all the wind gone out of her. Marcus reached out to her, and she scooted her chair closer to his so she could rest her head on his shoulder. I saw Ruth watching them, but I couldn't read her face. Then she got up and left without another word.

In the end, Amber, Jacob, and Billie went with us, and Rachel and David stayed with Papa and Ruth. "I wish y'all would reconsider," Mama said as we all stood in the yard to say goodbye.

"Now, Lissie, we been over this already," David said, hugging her. It turned out that Lissie had always been her nickname growing up. "We can't leave them alone, as old as they're gettin', and somebody has to stay to keep the place up." *For who?* I thought, but there was no point in saying it.

"I'll be back to check in from time to time," Billie said. She hugged Rachel for a long time, and there were tears in both their eyes when they broke apart. "I promise."

"That's a long trip for a woman alone," Rachel replied, but Billie made a show of looking at me and then back at Rachel, and we all laughed. It would be hard on everyone, but we knew that Papa and Ruth wouldn't live forever. Why did they have to be so stubborn? Couldn't they see how much better life could be? There had to be a way to make them see. The whole way back to the boat, I kept thinking about all the supplies on the compound just sitting there going to waste, and then suddenly I wondered if we had anything at Lake Point Papa might be willing to trade for.

There's more than one way to skin a cat, I thought. Ruth taught me that.

Epilogue

We float on our backs, just past the end of the old dock, watching the sun set. It's only Jessie and me this time, and I've got an ankle hooked over her tire tube so we don't drift apart.

"Summer'll be over soon," she says. "This might be the last chance for swimmin'." I nod and make a noise of agreement that's not quite a word.

"You awake over there?" She laughs, splashing a little water toward my face.

"You think that'd be the way to wake me up if I wasn't?" I ask, making a bigger splash back at her. That's all it takes, and it's war. By the time I declare victory, the sun is all the way down, and I'm shivering as we climb back up to the dock.

"Come on now," I say. "I promised Teenie we wouldn't be late. You know she's tryin' to get the baby on a schedule."

"I was thinkin' maybe we could cancel," she says, pulling me close. "We could just stay in . . ." She kisses me slow, and I'm tempted, but I pull away and start walking.

"Now don't you start that," I say. "I'm sure she's already cooked, and I've got one of Amber's pies to bring."

"Another pie? Just how much sugar did that woman sneak out of there?" Jessie asks.

"Had to be fifty pounds." I laugh. "I couldn't figure out why her bags were so heavy, but Amber never was one to pack light."

"I guess we're just lucky it's the baker she's shacked up with and not a moonshiner," Jessie says, "or we'd all be in trouble."

We walk back to the lodge to get cleaned up for dinner, swinging our hands between us the whole way.

Acknowledgments

Thank you to Swoon Reads and all the amazing Swoon readers who read and loved Ami and helped her story to become a real book. Thank you to my insightful and steadfast editor, Holly West, who pushed me to make this book the best that it could be, even in the face of my denial/bargaining/acceptance cycle every time she gave me notes. Thanks to Kat Brzozowski for lending her expertise for line edits, and to everyone else at Macmillan who helped make this book what it is. And bottomless thanks to the authors of the Swoon Squad for your support, transparency, commiseration, celebration, and unfailing awesomeness in all things.

Thank you to the wonderful writer Cary Holladay for teaching me to "begin on the day that is different," for introducing me to the work of Lee Smith, which in turn introduced me to Appalachian ballads, and for graciously referring to me as a writer during all the years that I wouldn't make that claim for myself. Thank you to Lee Smith, my favorite living author, who read and believed in this book and tirelessly encouraged me not to give up on getting it published. I cannot overstate the debt that I owe to both of these incredible writers and their work.

I have somehow managed to find myself surrounded by smart, fabulous, wildly supportive women who help to keep me sane. Thank you to the #1 Ladies Book Club, and to my soccer team, the Ruby Slippers, for celebrating my successes and for sustaining me with your friendship throughout this process. Thanks to Melissa Whitby for being my unfailing ride-or-die in this and all endeavors. Special thanks to Marilyn Koester, Stephanie Chockley, and Chip Chockley for the way you enthusiastically dove into reading and supporting this book, and especially to Chip for taking not one but two rounds of headshots even though there has never been a more thankless task.

Thank you to all my students for inspiring me and keeping me grounded. Thank you to my work wives, Niki Yarbrough and Shonda Keys, for keeping me laughing and feeling appreciated and loved throughout this process, and to Lischa Brooks for being so excited for me that she put my announcement in the parent newsletter.

Thank you to Richard Alley for showing me what it looks like to write because you love it and because you have no choice, and to our kids, Calvin, Josh, Somerset, and Genevieve, for being excited about this book while also acting like *of course* I would write a book and get it published, NBD. And thank you to my parents for being proud and supportive of me, even though I've always made things complicated.